T0194319

Inverted Love

Tom Berry

iUniverse, Inc.
Bloomington

Inverted Love

*This is a work of fiction. All of the characters, names, incidents, organizations, and dialogue
in this novel are either the products of the author's imagination or are used fictitiously.*

iUniverse books may be ordered through booksellers or by contacting:

iUniverse
1663 Liberty Drive
Bloomington, IN 47403
www.iuniverse.com
1-800-Authors (1-800-288-4677)

ISBN: 978-1-4502-9450-8 (sc)
ISBN: 978-1-4502-9451-5 (ebk)

Printed in the United States of America

iUniverse rev. date: 2/28/2011

Chapter 1

Late spring, 2001

It simply can't be true! Mrs. Louise Dudley kept repeating in her mind as she paced around her large, elegant family room, waiting for three of her sons. *As if my own shame was not enough to drive me crazy, and now this!* She detested the thought of another crisis. In her hand was a piece of paper, which she was squeezing as she moved from one large-paned window to another. She looked at the large stone urns full of pink and white tulips that stood along the outdoor patio, but she did not see their beauty. She felt more like crying, hoping desperately that her suspicions about her youngest son, Kevin, were not true. Her conscience was already carrying the burden of her incestuous liaison with her son Phillip and she felt that she could not bear yet another disgusting situation in her family. Still, the poem on the paper in her hand could not be explained in any other way. Her youngest son, her beloved and darling Kevin, was simply "not right"! It was the only way she could express her fears as she waited for a family council with her other sons.

Walking around her large, comfortable home in the Connecticut hills near Stamford, Louise again thought of the evening when she and Phillip had sinned beyond reason. He had been wallowing in his bed from an overdose of drugs, and she had been sitting by his side, holding his hand. Her thoughts had been about her husband, who she knew was having an adulterous affair. Suddenly Phillip's hands had gone around her waist and pulled her onto the bed. She had laughed, but when he slipped his hand under her blouse and caressed her breast, she instantly knew that he was uncontrollable. The sensation had been both repugnant and wonderful. She had tried freeing herself, but his strong arms tore off her top, and he buried his face between her breasts. It was a moment of utter confusion. She had immediately thought of her son as the baby who used to cling to her, but at the same time, she wiggled, trying to free herself. His strength was incredible, and she soon collapsed

1

into his embrace as he continued caressing her breast. It was a magical and frightening feeling. Since her husband, George, had not touched her for some time, the sensuousness was overwhelming. It was then that motherhood went further than God or humanity allows. Whether it was rape or consensual would be on Louise's mind forever. She could not discern. She only knew that it had happened and had haunted her ever since.

Suddenly she stopped in front of a hall mirror and examined her graying hair. While attending Vassar, she had been an outstanding student and had been considered one of the cutest blondes on campus. It was the early 1960s and sexual freedom was blossoming. At graduation she had a place of honor in the distinctive Daisy Chain. Soon after, she had married George Dudley, thereby gaining wealth and social position. The Dudley family was descended from Robert Dudley, the First Earl of Leicester. He was an English courtier and favorite of Queen Elizabeth I of England, who had appointed him captain-general of her armies against the Spanish Armada in 1588. The American branch of the family had had a general in the War of Independence, which allowed them membership in the prestigious Order of Cincinnati. Membership in the Daughters of the American Revolution was naturally bestowed on the family wives. Louise was very proud of the Dudley heritage and had tried to instill that feeling in her children.

Rearing four sons in a quiet Connecticut suburb had been a joy. She had lived a full and happy life for years until her world had suddenly collapsed. She had discovered that her husband, George Dudley, a noted lawyer in New York City, had been unfaithful. Then her firstborn son, her attractive, manly Roger, had revealed his intention of marrying a young woman who, in Louise's opinion, was not worthy of him. Even worse, her second son, the adventurous Phillip, had been caught in a drug raid at the apartment of a fashionable New York hostess. Keeping him out of jail and placing him in a rehabilitation program had been very costly. Then, in her efforts to help him during one of his illnesses, an unintentional physical encounter between mother and son had occurred. The experience haunted her. Her third son, the handsome ladies' man Paul, had also caused much worry because of his treatments for gonorrhea. Now her delightful Kevin was in trouble, and the poem proved it. It seemed as if the present generation of Dudleys were not upholding the family prestige, which, until now, she had so earnestly protected. Yet she had also demeaned the family honor with a sin more horrible than those of her sons. What should she do? The question plagued her.

Louise walked around her garden for a while, trying for peace of mind. She stopped in front of a glass pane in the garden shed. Her white hair was pinned high on her head, but a few strands were slipping down. A flashback in her mind recalled the day she first used bleach on her hair when she was at Vassar. Everyone had always complimented her on the lustrous sheen of her hair. Now it was gray. She began straightening up her hairdo when she suddenly heard the loud, low-pitched voice of a neighbor, Mrs. Sarah Kale, who was calling over the white wooden fence between their yards.

"Good morning."

Mrs. Dudley quickly put the wadded poem into a pocket of her tweed suit. She certainly could not share her torment with anyone outside the family.

Louise turned toward the fence and waved. "How's the llama?" she called out, hoping for diversion.

"Oh, she's fine, but she's still eating my bushes."

"My boys had a dog once that chewed on shoes. I love animals, but he was a nuisance."

"I remember one dog you had that chased the mailman."

"That was Skipper, but he was actually a good dog. He never bit him. I love animals, but I don't think I could handle a llama."

"I'm beginning to wonder if she's not too much for me."

"Sorry," Louise answered and waved as if she must go.

"Are you all right?" Mrs. Kale asked. "You looked so sad."

"No, I'm fine," Louise lied. "Just been thinking about the recent crimes up the street."

"Oh, it's terrible!" Mrs. Kale exclaimed, her fat jaws opening wide. "Why, that kind Mrs. Flint was robbed again."

"Doesn't she have an alarm system?"

"Yes, but they waited for her to come home and went in with her. That's the way the clever ones do it now."

Louise shook her head.

"Come over for some coffee, and I'll tell you all about it."

"Can't now. I'm expecting Roger over."

"Anything wrong?" the neighbor asked as she retied the knot that was holding a bun made of her long, black and silver hair.

"No, just some family things."

"Is he really going to marry that Sharon?"

"I think so, dear. We like her very much."

A smile of disbelief spread over the neighbor's face as she said, "Well, people get what they give."

"What do you mean?" Louise asked, staring.

"Oh, it's just my feelings about things. I believe you get as equally as you give."

Louise was confused and said, "I don't see how that applies to what we were talking about."

Mrs. Kale waved her hand and said, "Oh, don't pay any attention to me. I ramble, you know. Now I guess I'll feed Bertha. What ever made me want a llama, I'll never know." Mrs. Kale turned away and wiped her hands on her long, ever-present denim apron. Suddenly she turned back and yelled, "Oh, Louise, Wal-Mart has a sale on Basis cream today."

Mrs. Dudley thanked her and waved good-bye before entering her kitchen. She was relieved that she had escaped from her neighbor's prying questions. Also, Mrs. Kale's obsession with money and sales seemed her only reason for living. Louise liked Sarah but could not share her dreadful feelings about her relationship with Phillip or about her suspicions pertaining to Kevin.

Unfortunately, Roger arrived for the family council with his fiancée, Sharon Clarke. Louise felt revulsion when they both entered the spacious, well-appointed family room. She had wanted only her sons for the meeting, and even though Sharon was soon to be a member of the Dudley clan, Louise felt that she was not yet entitled to family secrets. Nevertheless, she greeted them, but Sharon, an astute and attractive bleached blonde, realized quickly that her future mother-in-law had not expected her. When Louise announced that she needed a talk with her sons, Sharon suggested that she leave. Roger immediately objected and, after observing the look her son gave her and against her own desires, Louise said that Sharon should stay.

"What is it that's so important?" Roger asked his mother as he and Sharon sat down on a long, U-shaped sofa in front of the large, stone fireplace.

"I'd rather not talk about it until the others arrive. They should be here very soon."

"Then let me divert you with the wonderful idea we've worked out for our bachelor-bachelorette party," Sharon blurted out with great enthusiasm.

"What kind of party is that?" Louise asked.

All smiles, Sharon explained. "Well, I thought it was unfair for Roger to have a bachelor party, so we're combining it and making it a bachelor-bachelorette party. And what a theme we've worked out. It's to be mythological. Everyone has to come as some kind of god or goddess and act like that god would. Isn't that marvelous?"

Louise gave a weak smile. "It's certainly different, dear."

"Roger will be Zeus, of course, but I haven't decided whether I'll be Venus or some scandalously wanton goddess from the Kama Sutra."

Louise could not react. Her mind was on the poem in her pocket, and her future daughter-in-law was speaking about something that seemed so frivolous, Mrs. Dudley was dumbfounded.

"You seem so nervous, mother," Roger interjected.

"Oh, I am," Louise replied and realized that she must leave the room for a few minutes to compose herself. "Excuse me just a second," she stated and walked out into the hall, where she stopped for a few deep breaths.

Her doctor had advised her that such an exercise would help calm her nerves, and the practice had become habitual with her. With each breath, she thought of Roger. He had been her pride and joy. He had been magna cum laude at Harvard Business School and was now secure in a noted law firm. Yet, so far as his mother was concerned, he was marrying a piece of trash. Louise felt that Sharon's bleached hair and dark eye-browed eyes only made her look cheap, even if it was considered stylish by young people. When she finished her three deep breaths, she could still hear the newcomers in the family room.

Roger was talking, "Well, something's up!"

"I don't think she liked the idea for our party. It boils down to the fact that she just doesn't like me." Sharon leaned back on the couch.

"Don't start that again. She just has to get used to you."

"Why don't you tell her that I'm the best fuck you've ever had?"

Roger laughed. "Do you want her to faint?"

"Well, I'm getting a little tired of her attitude."

"She'll change once we're married."

Sharon looked at the ceiling and winced. Roger reached for a decanter on the large, round coffee table and poured them a glass of sherry. Perhaps he found his fiancée's language uncouth as well, but if he did, he certainly didn't show it. Louise knew that he considered Sharon to be a good catch. She was very entertaining, and her family was very wealthy. She seemed just the right choice for a young lawyer wanting success. As far as loving her, he assumed he did. Besides, she had so much more to offer than just love.

In the hall, Louise, having heard Sharon's comments, walked slowly away, hating Sharon even more. The girl was definitely immoral and uncouth. Her family might be wealthy, but they were "nouveau riche," without quality or taste. Louise felt that Roger had let her down. Now he was committing fornication, and it was evident that he had no remorse about his behavior, which she considered sinful. All of her sons seemed incapable of living up to the high standards that they had been taught in their church and their private schools. And now that ridiculous party! Heaven only knows what things they would do. Then again, her own secret tore into her mind. She felt ashamed. How could she judge them so severely if she herself was the worst of all? Louise could only shake her head as she went for some aspirin.

From the kitchen window, Mrs. Dudley saw Phillip drive up in his yellow Mercedes convertible. She wondered how he could afford such a fine automobile. If he really was so affluent, why hadn't he suggested helping with the legal expenses that kept him out of jail? Any time she questioned him about money, he would say that his position as an international trade representative was very lucrative. She and her husband could not understand why his firm used him in foreign business arrangements when he did not speak foreign languages. He had studied French and Spanish in college but certainly had no fluency. They feared he was involved in drug trafficking but could never insist on further explanations when he so carefully and skillfully dodged their questions and insinuations. He was fulfilling his parole obligations, so they assumed that he was not into illegal activities, at least for the present.

Phillip, a tall, gaunt man with a receding hairline, saw his mother in the kitchen window and waved. She was glad that he seemed in a good mood. It was more and more difficult for her to look into his eyes because she feared reproach. She waved, and he came in the back entrance. She was disturbed by his unkempt appearance; he did not have the good looks and savoir faire of his brothers. Trying to keep up their normal routine, she went into his arms for an embrace.

"Are you eating correctly?" she asked, but stepped back quickly when his hand patted her derriere.

He smiled, but to her it seemed like a smirk. It was if he were mocking her because of what had happened between them.

"Of course," he replied, but, as if sensing that he had upset her, he immediately changed the subject. "Does ole Mrs. Kale still have that llama?"

Louise nodded and laughed rather nervously. "I understand it spit on a visitor the other day, and it was quite a mess."

Phillip laughed and sat down on an oak captain's chair at the kitchen table. "Well, the ole gal was always a bit crazy."

"Don't say that. She's always been a good neighbor, and you weren't reared with any bias."

"She just always reminded me of some sort of gypsy fortune-teller. I don't know why. You'll have to admit that most people consider her rather eccentric." Taking a cigarette out of his pocket, Philip changed the subject. "Well, what's this all about?"

"You'll see. I'm waiting for Paul, and then I'll tell you all at once. It's just too distressing."

"Well, you've really aroused my curiosity. Has one of us been a bad boy again?" Phillip laughed and winked.

"It isn't funny, Phillip, and when you have children of your own, you'll understand."

Phillip looked at the ceiling and took a puff from his cigarette. When he exhaled, he said with irony, "Oh, that happy day when my children will gather at my knee!"

Mrs. Dudley winced. "Oh, Phillip, why do you tease me? Don't you want your own family?"

"Mother, we've been through that too many times. Let's not start again." He inhaled again and then remarked as he exhaled, "That can't be the reason you called me here."

"No, it isn't. You'll see. Now let's go into the family room. Roger and Sharon are already here."

"Why did you include that bitch?"

"Phillip, please! You shouldn't talk about her that way. She's going to be your sister-in-law. Besides, I didn't invite her. Roger just brought her."

Phillip hunched his shoulders and followed his mother toward the family room. Walking along, he suddenly reached over and pinched her breast. She turned with a frightened look. He laughed and whispered, "Someday we must talk about it, darling." Then he put his arm around her.

She was trying to wiggle away from him when they entered the door where Roger and Sharon were waiting. Louise was afraid Roger and Sharon had noticed the exchange, for, if so, surely they would think it very peculiar.

The brothers exchanged greetings, and Sharon waved at Phillip as he sat down across from her. Just as they started a conversation, the front door bell rang, and Mrs. Dudley left the room.

When she opened the door, her handsome son Paul stood before her with a bouquet of spring flowers. Her hands went up into the air as if showing her surprise. Paul, statuesque with curly black hair, entered and embraced his mother. "Still my best girl?" he asked as he released her from his grasp.

"Always," she replied, smiling. He always cheered her up. It was part of his charm, which captivated women.

"Come to the family room. Everyone's here."

Paul followed his mother but whispered, "Are they behaving?"

Mrs. Dudley smiled, paused, and put her arm around Paul as he came alongside her. "You behave. You're the mischief-maker!"

He laughed as they entered the room. Again there were greetings and casual comments. Finally Phillip said, "Well, mother, isn't it time for the big surprise?"

Several said yes and all turned their attention to Mrs. Dudley.

Louise took a deep breath. Looking at her sons, she realized that she might start crying if she began talking. She quickly stood up and asked to be excused for a moment. She walked into the hall and began talking deep breaths.

"What's bothering her?" Paul asked, hunching his shoulders.

Everyone looked around. Finally Roger said, "She hasn't told me what it's all about!"

No one had an explanation.

Paul leaned back and said, "Well, I'll tell you my pet grievance of the moment. I'm sick and tired of not being able to talk about anything anymore."

"What do you mean?" Phillip asked, lighting another cigarette.

"You can't talk about anything anymore without upsetting someone. Where's that famous freedom of speech we're always shouting about?"

Sharon gave her bawdy laugh. "Oh, that! It doesn't bother me."

"Nothing would," Paul said to her ironically as she stuck her tongue out at him.

"I mean, what's going on today? You can't mention Mexican illegals without being called a racist! You can't say anything without someone jumping down your throat."

Roger chucked and said to his brother, "Evidently you've had a run-in with someone!"

Paul nodded. "Yeah! And it made me mad as hell. I merely said that the Israelis would be better off not to take land illegally, and an asshole in the office called me an anti-Semite. I could have choked him. How does that opinion make me one of those?"

"Well, learn to keep your mouth shut," Phillip commented and exhaled a line of smoke.

"Yeah," Sharon added and in a teasing tone said, "Keep your mouth shut!"

Paul wrinkled his nose at her and said, "How would a---"

At that moment Louise returned. "Oh, I should have known you'd start talking politics if I left the room."

Roger said, "Just a friendly argument, Mother."

"Yeah," Sharon added and made a face at Paul.

Roger put his hand over Sharon's face and said, "Mother, why have you asked us here today?"

Louise cleared her throat. "My sons, I've told you before that I am disappointed about many things." She waved her hands as if the movement would stop any comments. "But now a new problem has arisen. It concerns Kevin."

"Isn't he still at Williams?" Roger asked.

"Yes, and your father and I are going up for his graduation in a few weeks."

"So, what's the problem?" Phillip asked.

Mrs. Dudley took the wadded paper out of the pocket of her tweed suit. "This!" she replied, as she unfolded the sheet. "I want each of you to read it."

Sharon spoke for the first time. "If you don't want me to see it, I won't mind?"

Mrs. Dudley shook her head. "It's all right."

Roger took the paper and read the short poem. When he finished, he asked, "Where did you find it?"

"Kevin came home last weekend and brought a lot of his things with him. Since he's moving back next week, he had to make two trips. After he left, I tried straightening up his room a bit, and that's when I found this poem."

Roger handed it to Phillip, who quickly read it and laughed. "Mother, are you trying to say that ..."

"Let Paul read it first before we comment."

Paul took the poem from his brother and read it. Before he had finished, his handsome face broke out in a smile. Then, handing it to Sharon, he asked his mother, "But how do you know he wrote it?"

"It was in his notebook."

"But that doesn't mean he wrote it," Roger interjected.

"It's his handwriting."

"He could have copied it from something," Paul suggested.

"No, I have a horrible apprehension that he wrote the poem and that he's got that terrible disease of the mind."

Paul laughed. "Mother, being gay is not considered a disease."

Sharon laughed and blurted out, "My brother's gay and we love him. In fact, he's going to be Ganymede at our party."

Mrs. Dudley stood up and started crying. All three sons gathered around her, but her tears flowed.

Finally, she said, "I don't think I can take any more disillusionment."

"What do you mean, Mother?" Paul asked.

Shaking her head, she looked at Paul and said, "You're a fine one to ask! How do you think I feel when I know that you, my dear son Paul, are being treated for a social disease and not for the first time!" She turned to Phillip and added, "And you, taking drugs like you did, and now you're on parole!"

Roger said, "Mother, don't upset yourself."

"You, too, are a fine one. Just think of ..." Mrs. Dudley stopped when she remembered that Sharon was in the room. The young woman sensed the implication.

Standing up and shaking her long, blonde hair as if she were putting it in order, Sharon stated, "I think I'd better go, Roger. Please let me."

Roger did not argue. He took his car keys out of his pocket and handed them to her. "Come back in an hour."

As Sharon started out of the room, Mrs. Dudley blurted out in a tearful voice, "I'm sorry, dear." Sharon waved as if there were no problem and left.

"Does Dad know?" Paul asked, watching Sharon's derriere slip from side to side as she walked out.

Mrs. Dudley shook her head. "I was waiting for your reactions. Now I know that I was right. He's that way."

Roger and Phillip both started a rebuttal, but their mother waved her hand for silence. She began talking as if she were revealing her most secret thoughts.

"I reared you boys in the church. You could never know how proud I was to walk in on a Sunday morning with my four sons following behind me. It was so wonderful. I thought that I was instilling a sense of morality and faith in you. It didn't affect one of you. You don't attend services, and you have forgotten whatever morals we tried giving you. I remember reading Milton in college, and one line has stuck with me forever. 'The mind is its own place. It can make a Hell of Heaven and a Heaven of Hell.'"

Roger put his arm around Louise and let her cry on his shoulder. He looked at his brothers and raised his eyebrows as if asking what they should do.

Phillip smirked and looked at his mother. "It seems to me that we're all capable of making a Hell out of Heaven."

Louise bit her lip and put her face into her handkerchief.

After a brief silence, Paul asked, "Mother, didn't Kevin bring a student home with him last Easter for their spring break?"

Mrs. Dudley nodded. "Yes, a wonderful young man named Juno Carino. He's from that wealthy Italian family that owns so many factories."

"What do they make?" Phillip asked.

His mother laughed as she wiped her eyes. "Wouldn't you know? Pasta!"

Everyone smiled and Phillip continued. "Did you suspect anything between him and Kevin during the vacation?"

Mrs. Dudley shook her head again. "No, they were so wonderful together. They seemed so happy and had such a good time. It was just a wonderful visit. I was just lost when those two young men left."

Paul laughed. "It sounds rather gay to me!"

"Don't, Paul," Roger scolded. "We don't know yet, and it's not something to make light of."

"But the whole country's talking about sex. President Clinton did some mighty gay things in the oval office. Have you forgotten?"

"Yeah, and he got away with it, too," Roger stated.

"What am I to do?" Louise asked as if one of her sons would have an answer.

Phillip spoke first. "Mother, there's nothing you can do. If it's true, it's just one of those things. Besides, when I went to scout camp years ago, a lot of the kids buggered each other. Young guys do that. It's nothing, really. So, let's wait and see."

The others agreed with his view of the matter. Phillip added, "Tell Dad and show him the poem."

Paul interjected, "I think the poem shows that Kevin, if he wrote it, has had a rather bad time of it. He might need help."

"But what can I do?" Mrs. Dudley asked again.

No one answered.

Finally Roger said, "After you've told Dad, I think you should confront Kevin about it. Once you know for sure, then we can talk about what should be done."

"Perhaps that's true," Louise said, and the others agreed.

"By the way," Paul said to Roger, changing the subject, "what's that party Sharon was talking about?"

Roger laughed. "Oh, she's thought up another goofy party. You'll all get invitations, but you have to dress up like some kind of mythological creature. You know Sharon. Anything for a laugh."

One by one the young men took leave of their mother. She watched them depart and wondered to which realm of Hades they were taking themselves. She was sure that Roger was heading into a disastrous marriage, that Phillip was trafficking in drugs, and that Paul was still living with prostitutes. And now she knew that Kevin had joined his brothers in misery and ruin.

What hell they are making for themselves, she thought, *and we were such a happy family!*

Suddenly her secret came to mind, and she wondered whether her genes had corrupted her sons.

That evening George Dudley returned from Manhattan.

Louise was in the garden when he drove into the parking area in front of the garage. She observed that he was early and concluded that he had not visited his mistress after work. She called him over by a rose trellis.

Louise could tell by his sluggishness that he was feeling very tired. For some time he had been having abdominal pains after his lunch. He and Louise always assumed that they were from an upset stomach, because after he took some antacid powders, the pain would subside. Today, however, the pain had remained, and he looked as miserable as he felt.

"Darling, there's something I must discuss with you."

"Darling, please, not now! I've had a full day of meetings at the office, and my stomach is giving me heck." He explained that he had taken medicine, but it had not helped. When Louise suggested seeing a doctor, he scoffed and started walking toward the house.

She followed, saying, "I really need to talk with you."

"Can we do it during dinner?"

"Yes, but I'd rather not."

George turned and said, "Well, let's go into the family room. I'll have some soda water. Maybe that'll calm me down."

After they were seated and he was slowly drinking the bubbly water, Louise gave him the poem.

He read it and said, "You think Kevin wrote this?"

"I'm sure he did."

"Well, why are you so upset? It's a fact that young people take life and death themes much more seriously than adults."

"But don't you realize that it means that Kevin is ..." she started, but she couldn't finish her thought.

"Queer?"

"They don't say that anymore."

"Gay, you mean."

Louise nodded and turned her eyes away.

"Now listen, dear, it doesn't mean that at all. Maybe he had some kind of experience. That happens among young men, and they outgrow it. I remember cases of that in Vietnam. It just happens. Don't worry about it. Kevin seems fine to me."

"But darling, I couldn't stand it if he were one of those."

George laughed. "But we don't know. Besides, the world is so crazy today, I'm not sure it matters."

"How could you say such a thing? You remember how Mary Thomas suffered when her son died of AIDS."

"Well, I don't think Kevin is going to die of AIDS, so stop it! You're upset over nothing right now. We don't even know if it's true."

"I just have the apprehension that it is."

George grimaced. "Here I am in pain, and you want to talk about such a frivolous subject."

Louise winced. His attitude disturbed her. She would have liked to mention his mistress or anything if it would have inflicted upon him some of the agony she was experiencing. Instead, she told her husband about the discussion with their sons.

He seemed surprised that she had bothered and agreed with them. It wasn't definite that Kevin had written the poem, and it wasn't the end of the world if he was gay.

Louise, dissatisfied with her husband's reaction, excused herself so that she could start their dinner.

Placing the poem on a window ledge above her kitchen sink, Mrs. Dudley read the lines aloud as she peeled potatoes.

> I was a child and he was a boy
> And our trouble was one and the same.
> I sought the answer to the question, "Why?"
> He followed his cross in vain.
>
> Beauty and truth we cherished in life
> And together our friendship grew.
> Companionship faded and turned into love,
> A love that is known by few.
>
> All that we asked was to be left alone.
> Our happiness was full and free.
> But a meaning in life brings on envy and strife,
> And society would not let us be.
>
> Time has a way of healing a wound,
> But our trouble's again the same.
> I seek the answer to the question, "Why?"
> He follows his cross in vain.

Tears began rolling down Louise's cheeks. *My poor Kevin,* she thought. *What joy he must have experienced to suffer so severely. What will it do to him? Was the poem written about Juno, his Italian friend? What happened between them? What will it do to them? Oh, Kevin, how could this curse have come on you? Was it my fault? Was it my sin?*

Louise was still distraught when George entered and said, "Darling, I'm having terrific pains." His hands were on his stomach, and his face was very pale.

Alarmed, Louise asked, "Did you take your medicine?"

"At noon, but this has continued. I don't know if I can take it. It's really awful."

13

Turning off the stove, Louise told her husband to sit down while she went for her purse and called the hospital. She ran out of the room, very perturbed. She was obliged to take care of her husband even though love had ceased between them. Why couldn't his mistress take the responsibility?

She's the one that receives any benefits from him. He won't even sleep with me, and now I have to be his nurse. How absurd it all is!

Everything seemed distorted and painful, but she did what was required. In a few minutes, she returned and informed him that they were going to the emergency ward. When he did not object, she knew something was seriously wrong.

She helped him to her car, and they drove off. Before they reached the medical facility, George was bent over from the pain in the middle of his chest. It seemed strange to Louise that she could feel dispassionate about his suffering.

When they drove into the hospital complex, she followed signs to the emergency entrance. Once there, she ran into the building and told a nurse at the main desk that she needed help for her husband. Within seconds, two attendants followed her out. George could not straighten up, so they carried him along. Louise had never seen her husband cry, but still she could not sympathize.

When she heard his moans outside his curtained unit in the emergency room, however, she felt sad. Not for her husband, but for herself. What more could happen that day!

In a short while a doctor approached Louise, and she stood up. He escorted her down the hall as he talked. George would be staying in the hospital for tests. His symptoms would indicate stomach ulcers, but the severity of his pain could also imply other problems. He would be transferred to another unit in the hospital that evening, and the next morning various tests would be done. Since George was now asleep from the injections they had given him, the doctor suggested that Louise return home and come back the next morning. She agreed.

Driving home, Mrs. Dudley felt weary and exhausted. It had been a nerve-racking day, and she had the sensation that her world was falling apart. She recalled the poem and her family's comments. There had been no consolation. She almost regretted that she had shown them the few poetic lines. What did they care? They weren't close to Kevin. In fact, she concluded, her sons were not close to each other at all.

They only think of themselves. How could it have turned out that way? We loved each other, and we were so happy. There was much fun and laughter in the house. What made this hell of our heaven? Was it my sin? Oh, God, forgive me.

Arriving home from the hospital, Louise called all her sons and told them about their father. First she called Kevin. When he answered, he was breathing very heavily. He explained that he had just returned from the library at the Clark Museum, where he was doing research for his degree in museum management. He had run most of the way back and was still panting. She related what had occurred with her husband, and Kevin asked whether he should come home. She did not think it necessary, especially since his graduation was so close. Her son seemed in such good spirits, Louise decided that she would clear her mind about the poem. Expressing herself with as much tact as she could, she explained that a poem had fallen out of Kevin's notebook when she was straightening up his things, and she didn't understand it.

"What poem?" Kevin asked.

"Something about a boy and forsaken love, as I remember," she replied, trying to sound matter-of-fact.

There was a pause, and then Kevin answered, "Oh, that's a Rupert Brooke poem that we read in a class. You know, he was the English poet who was killed in the first World War."

"Oh, really? Somehow we didn't study his poetry in college. Well, I slipped it back into your notebook. I hope I didn't mess up your notes."

"No, it won't matter," Kevin responded.

"Are your classes over?"

"Yes, it's study time now, and I'm going with Juno up to his family's place in the Adirondacks for a cramming session."

Mrs. Dudley paused. "You mean the boy who was here over the holidays?"

"Yes. You remember Juno Carino."

"Oh, yes," Louise replied, wondering about the poem.

After a pause, Kevin continued. "I'll send you an e-mail with the phone number up there in case you need me."

"Please do, my dear."

Again there was a pause. It was as if neither could think of what they should say. Consequently, they said good-bye, but the tone of their voices sounded forced, as if they were being careful not to reveal something.

Louise put the phone down and sat on her bed. *He's lying,* she thought. *There is something going on. How can I sleep, knowing that my suspicions are true?*

Next she called Paul. A woman's voice answered.

When Mrs. Dudley asked for Paul, a voice whispered rather quickly, "Hey, some dame wants you."

Paul came to the receiver and laughed when he heard his mother's voice. He said that his cleaning woman was in his apartment and had answered the phone. Louise wondered if he really thought she could believe such a lie. What kind of a cleaning woman worked at night? She related the news about her husband, however, and Paul asked whether she needed him that evening. She replied in the negative but suggested that he drop by the hospital the next afternoon or evening if he could. He assured her that he would.

Before he could hang up, a saucy voice yelled in the background, "Hey, buster, you're going with me tomorrow night."

Louise could not hear what Paul shouted as he put his hand over the receiver. When he did speak, he said, "Mother, are you sure you don't want someone with you tonight?"

Mrs. Dudley assured her son that she was fine, and they said good-bye. When she hung up the phone, she thought, *Well, another son, another lie.*

After dialing Phillip's phone number, Louise leaned back on her bed.

She quickly sat up when he answered and said, "Listen, you two-faced, double-crossing bastard, if you call me again tonight, I'm going to tell Harry and have you wiped out." He hung up the phone with a bang.

Louise was disturbed by her son's rudeness and by the implications of the remark. She feared he was in serious trouble. Redialing, she waited for another blast of crudities. The phone rang at least ten times. When Phillip answered, he said, "So, you want Harry to know."

"Phillip!" Louise called into the phone.

A startled, hoarse voice asked, "Mother?"

"Yes, your mother!"

"Excuse me, darling. Did you call earlier?"

"I called just now, and I must say, you really scared me."

"Oh, it's nothing, Mother. A guy I know thinks that I've been seeing his wife, but it's not true."

Louise winced. The explanation did not fit the blast of words that had poured out of her son's mouth. She thought of trying for a better explanation but decided that his lie would only become more entangled.

When she related the news about her husband, Phillip said he could hardly believe his ears. He thought his father was supposed to be doing well, but, as he said, "One never knows!"

Phillip expressed condolences but never suggested that he drive over so that she would not be alone. Nor did he mention any visits with his father the next day. When Louise asked whether he could drop in on his father, he said that he certainly would but couldn't for two days. He was going out of town and simply could not break the engagement. His mother did not ask for details. She just assumed that her son was mixed up in something. He did say that maybe he would call her each day and inquire about his father.

She appreciated his concern and said that she would tell his father that he would visit as soon as he returned.

Phillip replied in a suggestive tone, "Mother, you're such a peach. You know I love you, don't you?"

His comment startled Louise. *Was he referring to their dark secret? Surely not! How could he be so brazen with her?*

She remained calm, but when she hung up the phone, she felt even more depressed. She had been correct. Phillip was again involved in some illegal activity and was breaking his parole. She shook her head but felt helpless.

Roger answered the phone immediately after Louise dialed. He was greatly distressed by the news about his father and offered his services. His mother refused any company for the evening, especially when she heard Sharon's voice in the background.

As if realizing that Louise had heard his fiancée's voice, Roger said, "But mother, I could drop by after I take Sharon home!"

"There's no need," Louise assured her son, knowing full well that Sharon was spending the night with him. "Just go by the hospital tomorrow. Your father will be so happy to see you."

"Of course, Mother. I'll be there right after work. Now call me if you need anything."

Louise thanked Roger and hung up the phone. She leaned back on her bed in thought. *Each son had lied. Why do they feel that they must cover something up with me? Am I to be protected from everything? Was it that way when they were growing up? How did I not see it? Where was I, and what was I doing? I feel as if I have been living in a bubble that has suddenly burst. I thought I knew my sons, but I didn't, and now it's too late. They've all gone their own way, and I am alone. Oh, God, help me!*

That night Louise turned and tossed on her bed until she suddenly realized that there was an ominous darkness closing in on her. She ran toward the bright sky shining over a grassy vale where she had been walking, but she could not reach the summit. A feeling of necessity overcame her. If she did not attain the crest, the darkness would enfold her. She looked back, but nothing was discernable. It was obvious that her attempt was failing. She ran faster, but to no avail. Quickly breathless, she turned and screamed.

Her movement and utterance awakened her, and she sat up in bed, gasping. Lying back on the bed, her eyes filled with tears. What did it mean? What could she do? Was the darkness her sin and suffering? Was she being stalked by an evil force?

"Oh, God," she cried aloud. "What can I do?"

Agitated and nervous, Louise remembered the vibrator that her husband used sometimes in order to sustain his erection. She cringed at the thought, but she slipped out of bed and opened the drawer of his nightstand. She plugged in the cord and lay back on her bed.

When she started the instrument, it quivered strongly. She felt for the control and calmed down the vibrations. Feeling disgust for committing such an act, she slowly lowered her hand to her vagina. The first movements there made her body tremble, and her legs quickly drew up as she moved on her side. Quickly removing the vibrator from her enclosed legs, she relaxed for a minute before placing it back. Soon she was embroiled in rapturous sensations, which quickly culminated in her fulfillment. Then she released her hold on the apparatus and languished at ease.

Suddenly she realized that she was thinking of Phillip, not of her husband. The darkness in her dream was now evident.

She sat up in bed and cried aloud, "Oh, God, I'm yearning for my son!"

Chapter 2

After a restless night, Mrs. Dudley dressed quickly for her stay visit to the hospital. She had planned on going early. When she arrived, however, the doctors had given instructions that George should not have visitors.

Louise immediately sensed a serious situation and demanded that the primary physician talk with her. Two hours later, after many agonizing thoughts about her dream, she was greeted by a Dr. Shultz. Louise stood up and held out a hand, which the doctor took most carefully into both of his hands as he asked her to be seated.

Louise was greatly distressed. "Is he so bad, doctor?" she asked.

Dr. Shultz informed her that an operation was scheduled for one o'clock. He was sure that her husband's condition could be corrected, but for the present he should be allowed as much sleep as possible. He recommended that she return about three o'clock in the afternoon. At that time, the surgery should be completed, and he would give her a full account of the operation and the predicted recovery period.

Louise asked the usual question. "Is there a danger that he might not survive?"

The doctor assured her that everything was being taken care of, but he did suggest that she inform her children.

Louise thought of the troubles she had incurred when last communicating with her sons. Yet they would hold it against her if their father suddenly passed away.

Again, four phone calls were necessary, but she could not contact any of her sons.

She called Kevin first, but he did not answer.

At that moment, Kevin was waiting with his suitcase in front of his dormitory. Around him was the beauty of pink cherry blossoms that blended into the palette of colors around Williams College on that beautiful late-spring morning. He was ecstatic, carried away by the fresh air and splendor around him while he waited for an adventure with his friend. Kevin's feelings were heightened by the incredible impossibility of the forthcoming episode. He and Juno were renewing a wonderful and incredible relationship. That it was considered immoral and dangerous by society only added excitement. Plato had called such an affair the greatest of loves. No matter how others might look at it, Kevin was enraptured.

Juno Carino's silver Corvette convertible drove up in front of Kevin's dormitory. When Kevin saw the car, he ran toward it. His enthusiasm was reflected in his boyish smile, which showed great joy.

Juno waved. His muscular body looked terrific in a light-brown cashmere sweater. His dark, curly hair glistened in the early-morning light. When Kevin approached, Juno opened the trunk of his car. They shook hands while looking into each other's eyes.

Juno's coy smile indicated a bit of devilishness, and he whispered, "I'll fuck you twice tonight!"

Kevin laughed. "Wait till you see what I'll do to you."

Juno smiled and winked.

They looked at each other for a few moments until Juno said, "Let's go!" He slammed the car trunk and they both got into the convertible by slipping over the doors.

Driving out of Williamstown toward the Adirondacks, Kevin began telling Juno about his mother's call. "She found a poem I wrote after you dropped me last month."

"You didn't mention my name?" Juno asked, concerned.

"No. I told her it was by an English poet we had in class."

Juno laughed and hit Kevin on the knee. "So, you were sorry we sort of parted?"

"You bastard! You know I was!"

"It wasn't my fault, you know."

"And it wasn't mine either!"

They looked at each other. Juno finally said, "Let's forget it. All's forgiven, isn't it?"

Kevin nodded, and they drove off into the cool, spring air. After a few hours of vistas and conversation, they arrived at Glen Falls, where Juno stopped for provisions. His family's summer place did not have a live-in attendant, so he and Kevin planned on preparing their own meals. They entered a grocery store and bought whatever appealed.

When they were ready, Juno suggested that they put the top up on the convertible, but Kevin refused and insisted they put on jackets instead. Soon they were driving through the cool air into the Adirondacks, heading for Shroon Lake.

Tall pine trees lined the road that led up to the Carinos' large log cabin. The beauty of the surroundings and the cool breezes was stimulating.

"First we must build a big, roaring fire," Juno commented as they stopped in front of the log porch.

Kevin could see the lake in the distance and marveled at the view.

"We'll take a hike later; right now let's get everything in," Juno said, interrupting Kevin's exclamations on the beauty of the area.

They carried their provisions into the two-storied hall that contained a large stone fireplace. A balcony around the hall led to various bedrooms. Kevin thought it was like a movie setting.

In a short time, Juno had a furiously raging fire crackling in the fireplace. He motioned for Kevin to sit down with him on a white polar-bear rug before the fire.

They sat silently, listening to the wails and howls as the heat rose up into the cold recesses of the chimney.

Juno suddenly put his arm around Kevin. "I love the time when the fire is reviving the house. Hear those noises? That's the moans of the chimney giving birth to life."

Kevin turned to his friend. "Juno, you have a poet's soul."

Juno leaned Kevin back on the rug. Their arms entangled, and they remained close for some time, continuing kisses and embraces.

Suddenly Kevin whispered, "Isn't it incredible how much hatred there is in the world against two people as in love as we are?"

Juno whispered back, "It's ignorance. The Greeks knew human nature better than anyone. Remember the Greek army that was made up of lovers? They were heroes and appreciated by the nation. If we had been there, I'd have defended you till death."

They embraced.

Juno said, "It's my church that's caused so much hell for us. We don't know the true nature of Christ, and it's silly that priests must be celibate. Gosh, I've been propositioned by many priests. There's such hypocrisy in my church ..."

"There's hypocrisy in everything anymore."

They were silent for a few moments, but when they finally sat up, Juno noticed tears in his companion's eyes.

Kevin explained without being asked. "I thought I had lost you. It hurt so much. I thought we had something wonderful, and then it was gone. Now it's back, and I realize that I can't ever lose you again."

Juno smiled. "You won't, so don't worry." Again they embraced. "Shall I take you upstairs and prove how much I love you?"

Kevin smiled. The twinkle in his light-blue eyes aroused Juno's passion, and he kissed each eye before going to the lips. Again they were entangled in tight embraces. Finally Juno rose up and tried lifting Kevin into his arms. The latter broke away and stood up.

"Let's wait until later," Kevin suggested, smiling at his friend.

A coy smile flashed across Juno's face. "Very well! Let's eat and then waste our energy in bed. Okay?"

Kevin embraced him. They embraced for a few minutes, holding each other tightly so that their erections rubbed against each other.

"I'm not sure I can wait," Juno stated.

Kevin laughed and walked over by the fireplace. "Me either!"

Juno started toward Kevin, but the phone rang before he could grab him. Interrupted, he went to the phone by the entranceway to the kitchen.

"Hello? Yes, he's here. Just a minute." He looked at Kevin and said, "It's for you."

"It must be my mother. I gave her this number."

Kevin went to the phone and heard the news about his father. He explained that he could not possibly leave until the next morning, but would be home as soon as possible. When he hung up, his face showed his distress. Just when everything was so perfect, he was being summoned home because of his father's illness.

Juno listened sympathetically and then stated that he'd drive Kevin home the next day. The two young men embraced, saddened by the news that their happy sojourn was to be disrupted.

"At least we'll be together," Kevin commented, and they went into the kitchen for dinner.

Mrs. Dudley hesitated to use her telephone during the afternoon because she was awaiting the call from their surgeon about George's operation. When the doctor called and informed her that her husband was in the recovery room, she felt great relief. It was short-lived, however. When the surgeons examined the interior of George's stomach, they had found evidence of serious problems. Tests done during the process revealed advanced cancer. Whether George would survive was questionable. He was under heavy sedation and probably would not awaken until the next day. The doctor advised against any visits until morning.

Mrs. Dudley thanked him and hung up. She sat back on the lounge chair and stared at the windows of the family room.

Suddenly she said aloud, "My God, is this the end?"

She realized that nothing would be the same anymore. She shivered, sensing fear. It was then that she needed her sons.

First she called Kevin at the number in the mountains. When she hung up, she knew from his voice that he had reluctantly agreed to come home. He said that he was cramming for examinations, but she felt that there was more than he was telling her. She found it strange that he had gone off into the mountains for a study period. And it was with that young man who had visited them. Kevin was hiding something, but Louise felt that one crisis was enough. She then called Roger about his father.

When Roger answered, he apologized for not having returned her call. There had been an avalanche of briefs at his office, and he had been busy all day. He hadn't even had time for lunch. He had called the hospital, but they had told him that his father could not have any visitors. At the moment he was relaxing with a martini in his hand and had been planning on calling her.

Louise didn't care about his explanation; she was simply glad that she had reached him. She was merely inquiring whether he could join her at the hospital the next day. He replied that he would come in the afternoon, and she thanked him most gratefully.

"Do you want me to come over?" he asked, making a face of disapproval at Sharon, who was busy invading his shorts.

"No, dear. There's no need. I'll be all right," Louise lied.

"I can, Mother, if you need me."

When Mrs. Dudley heard Sharon say, "Oh, shit!" in the background, she knew that Roger was not being sincere. She again assured him that she was perfectly all right and said good-bye.

Roger hung up the phone, and Sharon said, "My Gawd, one can't even have a good screw anymore without that woman interfering. Besides," she added in a suggestive tone, "she's got her dear, sweet Phillip!"

"What do you mean by that?"

"Didn't you notice that little tug of war they were having when they entered the room yesterday? There was something just a little odd about it, wasn't there?"

"What on earth do you mean?"

With a sly smile on her face, Sharon said, "Oh, there's nothing like mother love, is there?"

"Don't be so crass," Roger snarled, pulling Sharon's hand out of his pants. "We'll fuck later. I want to finish my drink."

Sharon, already undressed to her slip, stuck out her tongue and coyly said, "Couldn't we whip off one load now and another after dinner?"

"Do you think I'm some kind of bull? Listen, woman, I've worked all day. I can't tell you how many briefs I worked out."

"Oh, you lawyers are a sorry bunch. Who ever heard of putting a brief before a good fuck?"

Roger grimaced. "Were you just born crude or did you major in it at college?"

"Listen, we Vassar girls know what's good and what isn't. And you, Big Balls, had better start being good or your little sweetie is going to find a different candy store."

"Now it's threats, eh?"

"Oh, shut up." Sharon stood up and went to the bar that separated the living room from the kitchen area of Roger's apartment. "I guess I'll have to satisfy myself with another drink."

"Why don't you stick the liquor bottle up your pussy? Maybe that'll calm you down!"

Sharon turned and raised a finger at Roger. "So, who's being crude now? Surely not that up-and-coming big lawyer husband of mine?"

"I'm not sure I'll marry you," Roger commented.

"You will, all right, or my daddy will shred you in his machine."

"Well, don't expect me to screw you twice a day."

"One will do," she replied in a sardonic tone, swaying her derriere as she walked back toward him, adding, "Usually!"

"Come here, you vixen," he snarled, and she quickly fell on his lap.

They began smooching in a wild manner, like cannibals biting at freshly killed meat. Soon Sharon was on her knees again with her hands in his shorts.

When she pulled his elongating penis out of his pants, he said, "One suck only, you bitch."

In seconds Sharon was down on him. After a few strokes, he tried taking her head off his organ, but she fought him. Finally he leaned back and let her play. No one had her technique. He could not understand how she could make it so pleasurable, but he was soon moaning with delight. When he came, she made slurping sounds as if she had swallowed something delicious.

As she stood up, she said "Now we can have dinner!"

She started toward the kitchen, but the phone rang. Since she was up, she walked over and answered.

When Louise said hello, Sharon yelled rather disrespectfully, "It's your mother!"

Mrs. Dudley merely inquired whether Roger knew where Phillip was, since he was not answering his phone. He assured her that he didn't.

When Louise hung up the phone after her second conversation with Roger, tears filled her eyes. That disgusting woman was still with him. He valued her more than his own parents. Louise shook her head, but the negative feeling that accompanied her action did not relieve the pain. She stared at the floor for a few moments and then dialed Paul.

"Is that you, Mother?" Paul asked. "I was just getting ready to call you."

Louise thought it was a lie, but she said, "Thank you, dear. I hope I'm not bothering you."

"No, Mother. I've just returned from work, and a friend is preparing dinner for me."

"That's nice, dear," Louise replied, wondering what kind of woman he had picked up for the evening. Before she could think, she asked, "You are taking your medicine, aren't you?"

Paul laughed. "Darling, the doctor says that I'm cured. Yes, it's over!"

"Then you will be careful in the future."

"Of course, you sweetheart." He laughed again. "Now listen. I have great news. The most wonderful girl in the world is in my kitchen this evening. I want you to meet her."

Louise was silent, so Paul continued. "You'll love her," he stated with enthusiasm. "She's even more religious than you!"

"What's her name?"

"Delores Wilson. She's tops, mom, I know you'll agree."

"This is so sudden, Paul. How long have you known her?"

"I think long enough to know that she's perfect and just the girl for me." Paul winked at Delores and continued, "Listen, I did call the hospital today, and they told me that Dad could not have visitors."

"Thank you for doing that, dear. I'm calling to find out if you'll be able to join us tomorrow?"

Paul said yes and added, "May I bring Delores with me? I want Dad to meet her, too."

After a slight pause, Louise suggested that he bring her home with him after the meeting at the hospital. His father was too ill for company that would cause him strain.

When Paul said that he would take her advice and pick up Delores on his way home from the hospital, Louise was relieved and said good-bye.

When Paul hung up the receiver, Delores came out of the kitchen smiling and shook a finger at him. Her long, brunette hair was tied back, accentuating her oval face.

"I heard that remark," she said softly. Her eyebrows were raised over her large, dark eyes as if she were about to scold him. He laughed and grabbed at her, but she slipped away. "Just for that, you'll have to say grace at the table this evening."

Paul laughed again. "I haven't done that since I was a kid."

"Well, if you are as interested in me as you say you are, you'd better get used to it."

Paul stood up and walked toward her. When she retreated into the kitchen, he followed and took her into his arms. She allowed an embrace, but when he tried for a kiss, she turned her head.

"Let's not get carried away," she stated in a sanctimonious voice and broke out of his embrace.

"You know," he said, sitting down at the kitchen table, "you're an enigma for me. I can't quite figure you out. I know you like me, and yet you won't let me get close."

Delores turned away from the stove where she was stirring a pan of pudding. "Listen, Paul, I told you that I was warned against you. Please don't make everything I heard a reality!"

"That I like you? Is that so bad?"

"No, that's fine. I like you, too. But I'm not willing to be just another one of your so-called conquests."

"Oh, am I such a ladies' man?"

"You have the worst reputation in the company."

"Ah, Delores, you can't believe all that crap."

"Please don't use that word. I don't care for vulgarities."

Paul looked at her and asked himself, *How am I going to lay this one?* "Darling, there's nothing wrong with that word, it's …"

"I said I don't like it. So please don't use it."

Paul shrugged his shoulders. "That's fine with me. Crap is out!"

Delores turned again and gave him an ironic smirk. "Aren't you clever!" she commented, her tone showing her disapproval.

After a pause, Paul asked, "You will go home with me tomorrow, won't you?"

"Why should I?"

"I want you to meet my mother."

Delores turned again. "Listen, Paul, I don't think our relationship has reached that point. Couples do that when they're serious."

"But I *am* serious."

"But I'm not!"

Taken by surprise that a woman wouldn't be interested in him, Paul asked, "And why not?"

"I like you, of course. You're handsome and you're successful in the company, but you aren't ready to settle down. I know it, and you know it; so don't deny it."

"I could settle down with you."

Delores gave a forced laugh. "That'll be the day!"

"What do you mean? Don't you feel for me at all?"

"Yes, I do, but we are so different. You don't believe in God, and I do, very strongly."

Paul made his rebuttal: he had been reared in the church and was a firm believer.

She scoffed again, and he dropped the subject by beginning a conversation about their office work force. He told her that she was the only secretary in their firm whom he trusted. Also, that her work was excellent and that the head office was impressed with her.

Delores stopped whipping some potatoes and looked at him. All his compliments seemed deliberate, and she wondered about his ulterior motive. When she accused him of trying a new approach, he walked over and tried embracing her again. Throwing his arm off her waist, she said, "In case you haven't noticed, I'm busy. Now please go sit down. We'll eat in a few minutes."

Paul went back into his living room and stretched out on a sofa.

He wondered what it was that fascinated him about that woman. He would not have tolerated such rebuffs from others, yet there was something about Delores that had gotten under his skin. Fucking her was a challenge and a necessity. A failure was out of the question. Yet something was wrong. Why was she so standoffish? No other secretary had refused him. That is, after a period of time. Perhaps that was the problem. He was rushing things. He had suggested that she meet his mother before any serious talk had taken place. Yes, that was it. He was rushing it. This woman could be conquered, but it would take time. He'd even have to attend church services with her, if necessary, but he was determined to lay her no matter what.

He called into the kitchen. "What excuse should I give my mother tomorrow for your not coming?"

"Oh, I'll go," she called back. "If you really think I should."

He stood up when she walked into the room carrying a platter of steak and potatoes. "I think it would be great," he replied and walked over to embrace her.

"Let's eat," she said, slipping away from him. "By the way, what time are you planning on visiting the hospital?"

"I forgot to ask mother." He went to the phone and dialed. Louise answered, and they agreed on four o'clock.

When Mrs. Dudley hung up the phone, she dialed her son Phillip again. She had been trying all evening, but his message system wasn't turned on. This time, however, he answered in a low, anxious voice.

"Yes?"

"Phillip, it's your mother. Why are you speaking so softly?"

He continued in a whisper. "I can't talk now. I'll call you back in a bit."

When he dropped the receiver, Louise stared at the phone a few moments before hanging it up. Again, something was wrong. Phillip's voice reflected a sense of fear. She was sure he had broken his parole and was dealing in drugs again. She winced. The thought of his addiction was very depressing. She had heard many times that once one is heavily into drugs, the desire for them never leaves. What a future for her son, her dear Phillip! While he had never shown the promise of his brothers, he had finished college and had started a career in shipping. Yet something had led him astray, and he was now a dope addict. He had also led her into a sinful relationship. She winced again.

Suddenly the phone rang. When she answered, a rough voice said, "Mrs. Dudley, your son Phillip has missed a payment. It will be very bad for him if he doesn't come through."

The voice didn't sound like a parole officer, but she assumed that it was Phillip's director. His use of the word *payment* instead of *meeting* seemed odd, but she reacted before she could think. "Did he miss his parole appointment with you?"

A husky laugh resounded on the phone before it was hung up.

Oh dear, she thought, *what have I done? What has he done? What's going to happen to him? What can I do? Should I call his parole officer or would that only complicate things for him? Oh, dear God, help me in this distressing situation.*

The phone rang, and Louise seated herself on the chair before answering. "Phillip?"

"Yes, Mother." His tone was normal.

"What's wrong?"

"Nothing's wrong, dear. I was expecting a call when you rang, that's all."

"But Phillip, a very strange voice phoned me after you hung up."

"Who was it?" he asked, his voice again rather excited.

"I don't know. They said something about your missing something, and I thought it was your parole officer."

Phillip laughed. "No, Mother, I haven't missed a meeting. That was a guy I owed some money, but he just received it. That was the call I was waiting for. Everything's all right."

Louise didn't believe her son, but questions about the matter seemed pointless. He would only lie. Instead, she told him about his father and asked if he could join the family the next day at four o'clock.

Phillip, to her great satisfaction, replied that he would. He also informed her that he would be meeting his parole officer earlier the next day and would then be free from any legal entanglements.

She was most grateful and informed him before hanging up that his brothers would be there.

Phillip expressed surprise that Kevin was also coming and asked, "Mother, is Dad in danger?"

She assured him that his father would be all right. The meeting with his sons was just for the sake of bolstering his spirits.

Phillip seemed to accept her explanation and, to Louise's astonishment, he added, "See you tomorrow, Mother. I can't wait to hold you in my arms." He laughed, but she hung up without saying good night.

While Louise was disturbed by Phillip's remark, she at least had the satisfaction that she had reached all her sons. She stood up and started toward the stairs in the hall. Before she reached them, the outdoor light in the front of the house came on, reflecting through the glass panels around the door, and the doorbell rang. She went over to the door and looked through a glass panel.

Mrs. Kale, dressed in a baggy, green sweater, waved. Her head was covered with a long scarf, and she was holding a pole that resembled a biblical staff.

"Sorry to bother you so late," the visitor remarked when Louise opened the door. "I saw your light, and I wanted to check up on George. Is he all right?"

Louise said yes, and told her what the doctors had said. She also informed Mrs. Kale about the forthcoming meeting the next day with her sons.

"Then it must be serious if the doctor told you to call your sons."

Louise hesitated. "Well, yes, it's serious, but I think the doctor wanted them more for the sake of cheering their father up. Don't you think?"

A peculiar smile, so typical for Mrs. Kale, flashed across her face. After a brief hesitation, she said, "Why, yes! I'll bet that's it." Then she added, "By the way, how are the boys?"

Louise felt too tired for a pointless conversation about her sons, so she asked Mrs. Kale if she could talk with her later. She suggested that they get together after the hospital visit the next day.

Mrs. Kale agreed and apologized for coming but mentioned a sale on vitamins as she left. Louise took a Valium and retired. It had been a day, and she dreaded the morrow. She also prayed that the darkness that had infiltrated her dreams would not return.

The next day, Kevin and Juno arrived in the early afternoon. Their enthusiasm cheered up Mrs. Dudley. They were all talk about events at college and their brief stay in the Adirondacks. Their behavior seemed so natural that for a long time Louise did not think about the poem or her suspicions. The handsome boys were so youthful and so full of energy; she was carried away by their anecdotes and teasing jokes. Only when they brought in their overnight bags and took them to Kevin's room did Louise wonder how she could separate them. If she offered Juno a guest room, wouldn't that make it obvious that she was thinking about the poem? After some thought, she decided that she had better leave things as they were.

Juno drove Kevin and his mother to the hospital in his sports car. She asked the boys to wait until she checked on her husband before they entered. They agreed and went to the cafeteria for a soda.

When Louise entered George's room, Roger and Paul did not hear her. They were on separate sides of his bed in a heated argument about world affairs. "I don't care what inventions you mention," Paul declared, raising his voice, "I still say the country is going down the tube!"

"Listen, you idiot," Roger snarled in rebuttal, "every ten years our technology astounds the world. In the sixties we developed satellite broadcasting; in the seventies the Concorde flew; in the eighties—cell phones and CD players; in the nineties—DVDs. That's hardly a record of failure."

"Yeah!" Paul snarled back and then laughed. "And all those things are made in China and everywhere but here. We're heading for catastrophe!"

George, who had been looking up at his sons, suddenly saw his wife. He weakly waved an arm and tried pointing at Louise. Roger and Paul turned and saw their mother. They both went toward her, but Paul added to his outburst, "And we're going broke!"

Louise, smiling as they embraced her, said, "Still saving the world, I see."

They all laughed and walked over to George. He told them that he was feeling somewhat better and asked about a Cardinals game. Roger began giving details, but Louise interrupted him.

"No, you're not going to get off on baseball. We have company."

The men stopped and watched as Louise went to the door and ushered in the college students. When Kevin introduced his friend to his brothers, he noticed that Paul had an affected smile. At that instant he remembered how Paul had molested him when they were children, so Kevin found it odd that Paul would be sneering at anything between him and Juno. Yet, the smile was very obvious.

Pretending not to notice, Kevin led Juno over to his father.

Mr. Dudley apologized for not shaking hands and weakly explained that he could not lift his arm.

"Oh, don't bother," Juno said kindly.

"Dad," Kevin said, pointing at his friend, "he's on our lacrosse team."

"Great!" Mr. Dudley commented and closed his eyes for a second. When he opened them, he said, "Forgive me. I doze off so easily."

No apologies were needed. The son and his friend made pleasant banter for a few minutes, and George even smiled a few times. When they stepped away from the ailing man, it was obvious that they had cheered him up. The smile did not leave his face, and his eyes sparkled with tears.

Louise was delighted at the effect the young men had on her husband and put her arms around both of them. She was commenting on her joy at having them all there when Phillip, disheveled and pale, entered the room. His appearance was distracting. It was the moment Louise had been dreading.

She quickly went to the latecomer and put her arms around him, whispering, "Phillip, are you not well?"

"Sure, Mother," he grinned with a coy smile. "I don't need your motherly comfort now."

His strange remark and its tone caught the attention of the other family members. Roger wondered about Sharon's comment. George looked at his son and shook his head. Phillip leaned over him and softly said a few words, which the others could not fully comprehend. When his father gasped, he stepped back from the bed and stood away from the others, almost in a corner. The awkwardness of his sudden appearance and conduct had brought on a silence, which Roger and Paul quickly broke by continuing their discussion of baseball.

To distract attention and make an effort to see whether Juno was an all-American type, Paul asked him a pointed question about the forthcoming baseball season. To his great surprise, Juno answered with many details about his favorite team, the Giants. Soon the two were in full discussion about the great American sport. Kevin was amazed at the depth of his friend's knowledge of the game, but Juno told him later that he was adept merely because his own father was such a baseball fan. Paul, however, was impressed and accepted Juno as a regular guy.

Sports and current events monopolized the conversation among the family members for a while. Mrs. Dudley was pleased that the visit was so pleasant. Her only distress came from watching Phillip. There was no doubt that he was very nervous. He scratched himself continually while looking at the floor and ceiling. At one point he even turned and faced the wall for a few seconds.

Finally, just as Paul was making a point about his favorite baseball team, Phillip sidled over beside his father and asked out loud, "Can you give it to me?"

"What?" Roger and Paul asked.

Mr. Dudley tried speaking, but his voice was very weak. His efforts at raising an arm and making some motion were in vain.

Louise rushed to her husband's aid. She leaned over him, and he whispered softly but audibly, "Help Phillip!"

Mrs. Dudley turned to her son and asked, "What did you ask of him?"

As though he didn't care that his brothers and a stranger were in the room, Phillip replied in a most dejected tone. "I must have ten thousand dollars."

Louise caught her breath and stared at Phillip. Her other sons began asking questions all at the same time.

"Why?"

"What's wrong?"

"Are you in trouble again?"

Mrs. Dudley, her face wrinkled from her emotional pain, said, "Not here! Not now!"

Phillip, his expression also showing his desperation, shouted, "Do you want them to kill me?"

Louise tried putting her arms around her son, but he grabbed her and shouted into her face, "Give it to me or I'll tell them what we did!"

Louise broke into tears and closed her face in a handkerchief. Roger and Paul, who seemed amazed and confused at what Phillip had said, pulled him aside and began questioning him.

Kevin looked at Juno and nodded his head toward the door. They slipped into the hall, where Kevin told his friend about his brother's parole. As they were talking, a nurse came and informed them that visiting hours were over.

Kevin motioned for Juno to wait outside while he entered the hospital room. He opened the door as Phillip was literally screaming, "But they'll kill me!"

Roger and Paul were talking at the same time, and Mrs. Dudley was interjecting comments. They had not noticed that Mr. Dudley was gasping for air as he tried to raise up and stop the argument.

"Look at Dad!" Kevin shouted.

They all turned and quickly went over to the ailing man's side.

"Let the nurse see him," Louise implored, her voice full of anxiety.

The family members tried comforting Mr. Dudley, but he was in a very agitated mood and was gasping for air.

When the nurse came, she started an oxygen machine and placed a mask over the patient. She then ordered everyone out of the room. Protests were in vain. The nurse, a very strong-looking woman, had a voice that commanded authority. The family left Mr. Dudley and went into the hall. There the arguments started again.

"See what you've done to your father?" Paul exclaimed, holding Phillip's arm.

The others also blamed him for the obvious setback of the patient.

Within seconds Phillip fell to the floor on his knees, crying. "Oh my God, what can I do? Now I've even killed my father!"

The apathy and hopelessness in his voice caused an immediate response from his family. Roger and Paul lifted their brother and tried comforting him. Mrs. Dudley insisted that they all come with her to the house, where they could discuss everything in detail.

They all agreed and consulted with a doctor. After he informed them that Mr. Dudley needed rest and that he would call when he felt that they could visit again, they all walked slowly to their automobiles. Each dreaded the meeting they would have at home, but circumstances demanded it.

Mrs. Dudley was greatly depressed. Phillip had alerted her sons. They would be asking questions she could not answer. Would he?

Chapter 3

While Phillip had been in a pitiable condition in the hospital room, he quickly gained control of himself on the way to the parking lot.

Once on the road, Louise said to her son, "You've hurt me very much. How can I explain your remark to your brothers?"

Phillip's looked downward. He was embarrassed. "I'm sorry, Mother, but I'm under such stress I don't know what I'm doing."

"Your father told me to give you the money, but I would like to know why you need it so desperately."

Phillip, usually a bit cunning, was so dreary and depressed that he made a confession, which he later regretted. His mother's accusations and suspicions had been correct. He was dealing in drugs.

Louise gasped when he admitted it and commented about his parole.

Phillip explained that he was not in trouble with the federal authorities; his problems related to his smuggling activities.

When Mrs. Dudley asked how he could smuggle anything when he never traveled, Phillip smirked. "How naive you are, dear," he said and told her how he worked in a ring of drug dealers. He was sort of a middleman. Young girls would be recruited in eastern Europe and flown to South America. There they would have cocaine-filled breast-pads sewed into their breasts. Once in the states, he would meet them at the airport and take them to an illegal clinic where the cocaine would be retrieved.

Mrs. Dudley cringed when her son related such astounding information.

"Oh, Phillip, how could you be involved in something so despicable?"

"Mother, I'm sorry, but circumstances forced me into such a life."

"What could possibly have led you to such decadence?"

Phillip shook his head. His eyes became moist. He pulled the car over to a curb and stopped the engine. Looking down at the wheel, he sorrowfully whispered, "Mother, I would never have hurt you if I could have avoided it. I'm just so weary."

Louise was silent for a few moments. "But why did you fall into such a mess? We gave you an education. We tried to be fair to all of our sons."

"You were, Mother. I don't blame you. I blame myself for feeling inferior. I never had Roger or Paul's looks or personality. They were always such realists. Their values were always so straightforward. I always felt left out. I didn't have what was necessary for success. Look at Kevin, he's so bright and cute. He's like you, mother—so aesthetically imaginative. I never was like that. I'm just a mess."

Louise took a handkerchief out of her purse and wiped some tears from her eyes. "Oh, Phillip, I didn't realize you were so unhappy. Your father and I just assumed that you had gotten in with the wrong crowd. We didn't suspect that you were suffering so badly."

"I tried keeping my feelings from you. You were always so fair and honest. I'm just ashamed that I have let you down so."

Again Louise paused for a few moments. "You've let yourself down, and now I'm involved in your troubles."

Phillip turned and looked at her. "Mother, I shouldn't have done that to you, but it was wonderful."

"Phillip, don't say that. I'm traumatized by what I did. We should have never become so entangled."

"But we did, and it was wonderful."

"Please, Phillip," Louise replied, her eyes filling with tears. "Let's not talk about it and try to forget it ever happened."

"I can't forget. I know now that I love you."

Louise cried. "Oh Phillip, please don't talk that way. What are we saying to each other? It should have never happened."

"But it did."

"But we must forget it."

"We can't, and you know it."

Louise shook her head and cried.

Phillip reached over and petted her shoulder. "Mother, we've reached a point in our lives not traversed by most of the world, but that doesn't mean that it shouldn't be. We can't let it ruin our love for each other. It might never happen again, and it might …"

In tears and shaking her head, Louise interrupted him. "No, it mustn't." She turned and looked out the window. After a few moments of silence, she said, "Now tell me more about your predicament."

Phillip explained his precarious position. Two weeks earlier, two girls had flown in together. Usually they were alone. When Phillip met them at the airport, they expressed in broken English their desire for a rest before going to the clinic. He understood that they were tired after such a flight and took them to his apartment. When they arrived there, two men beat him up and kidnapped the girls. It had been a set up by a rival faction. The members of his gang did not believe him, however, and demanded money. He knew they would kill him if he didn't pay them, or else they might take vengeance on his family.

Louise looked at her son in disbelief. She whispered, "Oh, Phillip, you poor darling. Of course I'll give you the money, but will that stop them?"

"Yes, Mother, it will."

"Then will you quit helping them in that dastardly business?"

After a brief silence, Phillip answered, "Oh, yes, Mother. I'm sick of it. Really disgusted with it."

"Then your father and I will be glad to help you."

Phillip thanked her and started the car. Louise suggested that they not discuss the matter with Phillip's brothers when they arrived at home. "But they will want to know!" he exclaimed.

"Yes, but we'll just say that you and I have decided on a solution to your problem, which isn't as bad as you assumed. I'll just say that your father and I are making you a loan."

"Would you really do that, Mother?"

"Of course. You'll see."

"And what will you say about my remark?"

"I don't know. I just hope they don't ask anything about it."

Phillip was relieved. His mother was protecting him from the criticisms of his brothers, and he was most thankful for that. He had lied to her, but again the falsehood had covered his problems. He would have the payoff and could still be a member of his gang. They considered him a valuable player because he was on parole; therefore, in their opinion, the police did not suspect him. He needed them for his supply of cocaine. He was hooked, and he knew it. For that reason, he felt that he had no choice but to lie to his mother and stay with the mob.

Roger and Paul were waiting for them at the house. After they were settled in the family room, they immediately started questioning Phillip. When their mother informed them that she was making a loan to him over a matter that she did not wish discussed, Roger and Paul insisted on knowing more details.

"It's not as bad as Phillip has made it sound," Louise said, as she tried explaining her position regarding the matter.

While Roger and Paul were not satisfied with the explanation, their mother diverted their attention by saying, "It's just a loan, which your father and I would do for any of our sons."

Roger and Paul would have liked further discussion, but they realized that their mother preferred to avoid any unpleasantness. She changed the subject of the conversation to Paul's new girlfriend. Since Paul was planning on bringing her over that evening, she suggested that Roger bring Sharon so that the whole family could meet this ideal young lady whom Paul had found. The event was agreed upon and Roger and Paul left for their respective friends.

Mrs. Dudley and Phillip went into the den, where she wrote him a check from a savings account. Phillip then said that he would go because he did not want his brothers discussing his problem in front of their girlfriends.

Louise understood and accompanied him to the front door. As they were finishing their conversation, the door opened. Kevin and Juno had returned.

It was an awkward encounter, especially after Phillip laughed and said in a wistful tone, "My, what pretty boys!"

Juno was offended by the remark and stepped aside. Blushing, Kevin pretended that he hadn't heard, and quickly asked Phillip, "I thought you were in trouble?"

"No, it was a misunderstanding," Louise quickly stated and said good-bye to Phillip, who went out the door looking at the two young men with a smirk that had implications of a dubious nature.

Louise immediately started talking, as if she, too, had not noticed anything in Phillip's behavior. She asked whether they had eaten and also told them about the upcoming visit of Roger and Paul with their girlfriends.

Kevin made a face and asked, "Could we stay in my room? We'd like to study."

"Sure," Mrs. Dudley answered, "but you must come down and meet Paul's new friend. You already know Sharon."

Kevin nodded and made a face. Louise pointed a finger at him as if to say that he must be more charitable. He laughed and led Juno up the stairs to his room.

Louise overheard her son tell his friend about Roger's girlfriend. "She's a bitch if there ever was one."

Mrs. Dudley was perturbed that Phillip had been so inconsiderate. She had just done him a great favor, and he had behaved in such a rude manner. She asked herself, *Why do brothers demean each other?* She had reared them in a home full of love and companionship, but now they were acting as if they were strangers. Kevin was hostile toward his brother's fiancée. Phillip, free of his worries, was acting in a most derogatory manner. Louise shook her head. Everything seemed off-kilter.

Suddenly Kevin came down the stairs and asked, "Mother, what did Phillip mean when he said that he would tell something you did?"

Louise smiled, "Darling, I don't know what he meant. He was so excited. I don't think he knew either."

"He seemed so vindictive."

"It's his nerves. You can understand how miserable he must be with the parole business."

"I guess," Kevin replied, but his face showed his confusion. He was sure there was more to the remark than his mother was saying, but he returned upstairs to unpack.

When Roger and Sharon arrived, Mrs. Dudley was having some sherry in the family room. They all greeted each other as Sharon, dressed in a very expensive St. John pantsuit, plopped onto the triangular sofa in front of the fireplace.

Roger went to the bar and started making drinks as he asked, "Mother, what did Phillip mean when he said he'd tell on you."

Louise laughed. "I'm not sure. I think it was his nerves."

"Has Phillip broken his parole?"

"No, he hasn't. But don't worry about him. I think I've taken care of his problem."

Roger answered in a haughty voice, "Ten thousand should take care of a problem!"

Sharon interrupted the drift of the conversation by saying, "Mrs. Dudley, my mother would like to meet with you about the arrangements for our wedding."

"That would be lovely, dear," Louise replied and listened as Sharon related various plans.

The wedding would be in their home because it had a large entranceway and staircase. Sharon had always dreamed of throwing her bridal bouquet to one of her friends from Vassar.

Louise smiled.

Then the reception would be at the exclusive Fairmont Country Club. It wouldn't be a long affair because she and Roger were taking a late-evening plane to Paris.

"Is your mother also helping you with that party you are planning?" Louise asked.

"Well, in a way, but I'm actually doing most of that. She thinks the whole idea is rather bizarre, but I'm not inviting my parents, so her opinion doesn't matter."

Mrs. Dudley was surprised at Sharon's nonchalant attitude toward her parents but made no comment. Instead, she asked, "Your mother did receive my guest list, didn't she?"

"Oh, yes."

Roger interjected, "But mother, why did you invite that ole poop next door? She might bring her llama. She's so eccentric."

"How could I not invite Sarah? She watched you grow up and loves our family."

Sharon asked, "Is that the hag that's always leaning over the fence?"

Roger nodded, but Louise quickly said, "She's really very nice, Sharon. It's true that she is a bit eccentric, but she's a lonely person, and I feel sorry for her."

"Wasted effort," Roger commented.

Sharon continued giving details and descriptions concerning her "bachelor-bachelorette mythological party" and her wedding. Both would be grand occasions because her father wanted only the best for his only daughter. Louise was taken aback by some of the things Sharon mentioned. The expense would be tremendous.

Suddenly Paul opened the front door and led in Delores, his new girlfriend. When they entered the family room, Mrs. Dudley rose and greeted them. Roger waved, and Sharon turned and nodded her head. Paul introduced Delores as the most charming girl he had ever known.

Sharon looked at the ceiling, and Roger laughed, saying, "Don't listen to him, Delores. He's said that before."

"Oh, I know," she commented, taking a seat across from Sharon. "I was warned about him at the office."

"What would you like to drink?" Roger asked.

Delores shook her head. "I don't drink. My religion doesn't allow it."

Sharon sat back. Her face showed amazement. "What religion is that?" she asked.

"The Christian religion."

"Well, I'm a Christian," Sharon stated, "but I drink."

Paul tried changing the subject. "Delores is considered one of the most efficient secretaries in our firm."

Sharon asked, "Where did you go to school?"

"The Christian Academy."

"Where's that?" Sharon asked, a look of bewilderment on her face.

"Nashville."

After a few seconds of silence, Paul said, "Delores is determined to make a new man out of me."

Louise quickly responded, saying that she was delighted that Paul had found someone who could influence him in a positive manner.

Delores said that she wasn't sure Paul would take her advice, but she was happy that he cared enough for her to respect her convictions.

In an especially low tone, Sharon asked Roger for another drink. "Make it a double. I think I'll need it."

At that moment, Kevin came into the room and in his usual cheerful manner called out, "Hello, everybody."

The family returned his greeting, and Paul introduced Delores.

"Well, at last he's found a pretty one," Kevin joked.

"Thank you," Delores commented, looking a little embarrassed.

"Don't listen to him," Paul interjected. "He says that to all the pretty girls and boys."

There was an awkward pause.

"Where's your friend?" Roger asked.

Kevin explained that they were studying for their senior examinations, which were in a week. The trip from the cabin had taken time that they needed for their research. Consequently, they would leave the next day if Mr. Dudley was better.

"Why not bring your friend down for a few minutes?" Roger asked. Others joined him in the request.

"Juno's too busy. I'd rather not disturb him."

Roger and Paul looked at each other, and the latter winked.

Louise saw the reaction and was furious that Kevin's brothers would treat him so unkindly. She finally said, "Kevin's right. Those examinations are very important, so let's not bother them."

After telling Delores that he had enjoyed meeting her, Kevin said a general good-bye and waved as he went out of the room.

Sharon turned to Mrs. Dudley and asked, "What's this I hear about him? You think he's gay?"

"Oh, no!" Louise blurted out in an unrestrained voice, which was so unusual for her. "Kevin's just a lively young boy. It's a pleasure to watch him with his friend. They're such fine companions, so respectful of each other."

Roger and Paul again looked at each other, and a quiver of a smile showed on the latter's face.

Louise noticed and again spoke in a voice unnatural for her. "How brothers can act so disrespectfully of each other, I don't know."

"Mrs. Dudley," Sharon interjected. "I didn't mean anything derogatory. Heavens, my brother's gay, and I think it's cool."

Louise frowned and looked askance.

Sharon continued. "Really, Mrs. Dudley, whether it's true or not about Kevin, it really doesn't matter. Heck, my brother Jerry is so much fun. I wouldn't want him any other way."

Louise frowned again, and Roger asked Delores her opinion about gay people.

"Oh, I think it's an abomination. The Bible strictly forbids it."

"Oh, give me a break," Sharon uttered, twisting her face into an ugly expression. "If you knew my brother, you wouldn't condemn him for anything he did."

Delores responded in an apologetic tone. "Oh, please, I didn't mean to offend you."

"Well, what else could that diatribe of yours do to me?" Sharon said in rebuttal.

Roger interrupted their exchange by asking, "Who needs another drink?"

Delores turned to Paul and softly said, "I think I should go."

Paul started to object, but when he saw the forlorn look on her face, he decided that he'd better take her away. He made a weak excuse about some things he and his girlfriend had been planning. Louise tried keeping them for a while longer, but Paul was insistent. As the couple left, Delores told them all that she had enjoyed meeting them.

As soon as Mrs. Dudley escorted them from the room, Sharon said, "That hypocrite. She no more enjoyed meeting us than we enjoyed her. What a bigot she is!"

Roger laughed. "Well, she's certainly not the sort that Paul usually brings around. Wonder if he's screwed her?"

"Ha!" Sharon snorted. "You'd have to find a biblical reason to get into those panties."

Roger laughed. "No problem getting into yours."

Sharon smiled coyly and said, "Shall we do it here in front of Mother?"

"You really are a crass bitch, darling."

"Thanks. And you can be a prize nerd at times."

"Guess that's why we get along."

"Gosh," Sharon gasped. "I just thought. If Paul is still going with the Virgin Mary when we have the party, we'll have to invite her, too."

"I'm afraid so."

"God, what would she come as, an ill-accoutered archangel?"

"I'd suggest we find her a Beelzebub costume."

Sharon laughed. "Yes, that'll do it. Now sit down here and let me feel your big cock," she whispered, winking and wiping her lips with her tongue.

"Mother's coming."

Sharon moaned. "Oh, must Mrs. Perfect continually interrupt?"

Louise walked into the room and expressed her delight that Paul had taken interest in such a refined young beauty. Sharon objected, saying that she was sure Paul would quickly drop Delores because she was so uptight about everything. Roger agreed with Sharon, but Louise remained firm in her belief that Delores might be just what her son needed.

"Well, I just hope she grows up a bit before she joins our family," Sharon stated and, turning to Roger added, "Do we have to invite her to our wedding, too?"

Roger shook his head, but Mrs. Dudley interjected, "Let's wait and see what develops. You might be glad you invited her."

Sharon smirked. "I don't want to sound discourteous, but that one and I will never get along."

"Time changes everything," Louise commented, but apologized for using such an old adage.

When Roger and Sharon left, Mrs. Dudley sat for a while thinking of all the things she had to do. Much of it depended on the health of her husband. She suddenly realized that her sons had not spoken of their father during the whole evening. *Maybe we were always apart, and I didn't realize it,* she thought. *We were all too wrapped up in ourselves; strange that I didn't see it. I thought we were such a loving family, but actually we were all just individuals living together, taking what we could and leaving the rest for the others.* She shook her head. What a realization!

On the top landing of the stairway, Louise knocked on Kevin's door. Her son opened it. He and his friend were in pajamas. Juno was at the desk, and Kevin's books were spread over the bed. She asked whether they wanted any refreshments. Both young men told her they didn't need anything, so she wished them a good night.

As she walked away from the door, she wondered about Sharon's brother. Surely Kevin was not involved with his friend in that way. She regretted that she had shown the poem to her other sons. They had not been interested in helping their brother; they had only used the information to demean him. He could be innocent, but Louise knew she had made him guilty in their eyes. Later in the night, she started downstairs for a drink of orange juice. Passing Kevin's door, she heard giggling. She stopped and listened. She now felt that her fears were confirmed. Some kind of emotional and physical relationship existed between her son and his friend.

Kevin and Juno had studied until midnight. Occasionally they would find themselves looking at each other. Juno would wink and Kevin would stick his tongue out at him; or Kevin would send a kiss, and Juno would rub his lips with his tongue. Finally, after such an exchange, the two young men stopped their studies. Kevin put his books on the floor, and Juno joined him on the bed. "I've dreamed of having you here with me ever since I met you," Kevin whispered, and they went into a tight embrace and a prolonged kiss.

"Should we do it here?" Juno whispered.

"Why not?"

"You don't think your mother will hear?

"No. Her bedroom's at the other end of the hall."

Juno began kissing Kevin's neck, face, and ears. The latter chuckled softly at various times, but soon Juno was on top of him in a tight embrace. They kissed for some time before their passion led them into activities forbidden by the God who they believed had created them. They were so in love that there was no reasoning or questioning. They were loved, and they loved. It was as simple as that.

The next morning Mrs. Dudley called the hospital and checked on her husband. He had rested well, and the doctor had left word that she could visit him in the afternoon. She asked the nurse whether George was still listed as "serious" and found out that he had been upgraded. A feeling of despair overcame Louise as she thanked the nurse. If he survived, it meant that he would come home for her to nurse. Immediately she realized that she had hoped for his death. She felt ashamed but admitted to herself that it was true. She no longer loved him and did not want him anymore.

When Kevin and Juno woke the next morning, their bodies were entangled at a diagonal on the bed. They pulled themselves apart and slowly rose.

Juno, before going to the bathroom, said, "Kevin, your brothers suspect you, don't they?"

"I'm afraid it's because of that damned poem. Mother must have shown it to them. I can just imagine the conversation that it brought on."

"Phillip was the worst. His sneer made me want to punch him."

"I understand, but it wouldn't be worth it. He's a dried-up shell of a man from his drug habit—pathetic, really. I hardly know him, as he's older than I am. Paul's closer to my age—about four years older."

"Well, the less I see of them the better."

"I'm sorry we had to run into them. In the future we'll avoid them like the plague."

Juno entered the bathroom and brushed his teeth. Kevin did the same. Then they fell into each other's arms for a prolonged embrace.

They were starting to be aroused when Kevin said, "We'd better stop. There's always tonight."

Juno agreed and backed away. They looked at each other and fell into another embrace, which they started again when they entered the shower. With the water bubbling and splashing over their heads, they were able to speak the endearments that flowed from their hearts. After their passion was fulfilled, they clung to each other as the soapy water ran over them. When they left the shower, each dried the other's back. They were together, and it seemed the only important thing in the world.

Kevin and Juno were radiant at breakfast. Louise watched her son keenly, wondering if his new life showed in his behavior. She saw no difference and couldn't help but think she might have been mistaken. Still, she was sure she had heard sounds that could only be from passionate encounters. The young men joked and teased continually. They seemed so happy and so full of life. How could there be anything inappropriate in them?

Mrs. Dudley responded to their merriment to the point that she finally said, "Oh, what will I do when you two wonderful boys leave? I'll be so lonesome."

Juno and Kevin both expressed their regret that they must depart, but George's improvement would allow them still a couple of days up in the mountains before their examinations.

Louise, though she appeared understanding, asked whether they couldn't study at home. She promised that she wouldn't interrupt them.

They thanked her but said that they had plans for some hiking in the mountains along with their studies. She bowed to their plans and watched them depart with sorrowful regret.

Roger and Paul called in the morning and asked about their father. Louise was gladdened by their interest, but she could not understand why Phillip had not done the same. As she prepared for her hospital visit, she wondered about his predicament. Just when she was ready, her back door bell rang and she knew it was her neighbor.

When she opened the door, Sarah exclaimed in her low, rough voice, "So much activity over here! I do envy you."

Louise explained that she was just leaving for the hospital, and Sarah assured her that she would only stay a minute. Louise sat down with her guest, who continued her comments.

"I saw all of your sons at home yesterday. Was there any trouble?"

Louise shook her head.

"Oh, I was so afraid that maybe George was worse, and you had brought them all home for a serious matter."

Louise assured her that it was just simple family affairs and informed her that George was much better.

"Thank God," Sarah gasped. "I was so worried, and I could tell that you were, too. I'm never wrong in that category."

Louise thanked her and picked up her purse as if she were leaving.

"I won't keep you another second," Sarah insisted, standing up, but as she started toward the door, she asked, "Who was the young man with Kevin? My, what handsome young men they are."

Louise went into some detail about Kevin's examination period.

"Well, they looked so cute in that fancy car. Oh, I wish I had my son back instead of that menagerie of animals."

Louise laughed and waved good-bye.

Oh, dear, what a case that one is, Louise thought as she left for her drive to the hospital.

Once there, she discovered that all was not as well with George as she had assumed. After waiting some time, she finally arranged a meeting with his primary doctor. She informed him that there were two events in a few weeks, and she wanted his opinion on whether George would be able to attend them. Their son Kevin was graduating from Williams College in late June, and they had planned a trip there for the ceremony. Then their oldest son's marriage was during the same month.

The doctor thought for a few seconds and then shook his head. "I'm sorry to be pessimistic, but I doubt that Mr. Dudley will be able. He is in a very precarious stage at the present. He could easily develop internal bleeding. I am hoping that he can go home in a few days, but he will need a nurse's care for several weeks. He's had a serious operation, and his heart is weak, so precautions are quite necessary."

Louise stood erect and, hiding her anxiety, asked, "Is it cancer, doctor?"

The doctor looked straight into her eyes. "We do not know yet if his ulcers were cancerous."

Louise's face showed her fear,

He tried comforting her. "Now, remember, it is not possible to know for sure at this stage. We must wait for the results of the tests. I gave my opinion because I felt that you would want the truth. Please remember that cancer is not a death sentence anymore. There are so many things that can be done. While his condition is severe, there's always hope."

Louise thanked the doctor for giving her his honest opinion and then went to her husband.

George was sitting up when she entered the room. His face was not as flushed, and he greeted her kindly. She felt relieved and sat down beside him. While he could hardly talk, he seemed eager for news about his sons, especially Phillip. Louise went into detail about the money and her concerns and her insights.

George appeared amused at Sharon's reception of Delores; Louise knew that George hoped Paul wouldn't bring someone into the family who would cause disruption and exasperation.

"Well, if anyone will do that, it'll be Sharon herself," Louise commented.

"Yes, she's quite a gal," George whispered in broken gasps.

"That's putting it mildly. Her ungraciousness and disdainfulness shock me at times. I can be honest with you, Dad. I would not be upset if that marriage didn't take place."

George was silent for a few seconds. Then suddenly he could speak fairly clearly, though softly, "In many ways it's quite a fine marriage. Her father is truly loaded. There's nothing wrong with having money around, my dear."

"Yes, that's nice, but when it's made a strumpet out of you, it can't be worth it."

"Oh, darling, Sharon isn't that bad. She's contemptuous all right, but you're going too far. True, she's a spoiled brat, but she's not a Jezebel."

"You didn't hear a conversation I overheard between her and Paul. Honestly, you would have thought that some slut from a bordello was talking."

George laughed weakly. "I can see that we're going to have quite a family life in the future. Sharon will certainly change our ways."

Louise grimaced. "No, I think we need to change hers."

"Oh, dear," George sighed and whispered. "The troubles are starting already."

Mrs. Dudley realized she had brought up a subject that could have been put off until George was feeling better. She quickly comforted him by saying that she would do everything that she could for Roger and Sharon.

George thanked her and said that he knew that she would be fair. "That's one of your strong qualities, my dear. I'm sure that your reserved nature will overcome any unpleasant situation,"

Mrs. Dudley spent the afternoon with her husband. When George wasn't sleeping, Louise would talk about various topics, apart from the troubles of their sons. Activities at their church and their country club predominated. Finally, in the late afternoon, a doctor came and told the patient that he should have as much rest as possible. He did, however, feel that George could go home in about two days. Then he would have to return for regular radiation treatments. The Dudleys were very pleased with the news.

Before leaving for home, Louise told her husband that she might be late the next afternoon because she was spending the day with Roger and Sharon.

"Concerning the wedding?"

"Yes, and I dread it."

George smiled. "Remember your reserved nature."

"I'll need it," Louise commented and looked at the ceiling.

George laughed as she departed.

That night Louise drank two gin martinis before retiring and fell asleep very quickly. After a couple of hours, however, she awoke from a frightening dream. Her heart was beating fast, and she was breathing with difficulty.

"What's wrong with me?" she asked aloud.

Then she relaxed and thought about her dream. She could only remember that the darkness of her former dreams had appeared again. Phillip's comment before the family came to mind. She felt that she was to be forever condemned for what she had done with her son. Finally she concluded that her family was moving away from her. It was disintegrating. Each member of the family was thinking only of himself. They were all lying and deceiving her. Even her husband was unfaithful.

"Was it my fault?" she asked aloud. "Was my pride so great that I deserved punishment? What happened? We were so happy. We had everything anyone could want. My sons were handsome and educated, my husband was successful and content, our family was wealthy and secure. What went wrong?"

Sleep was long in returning.

Chapter 4

After the visit with the family, Roger and Sharon decided on spending the night at his apartment, instead of at hers, because it was not as far from the Dudley home. The next morning they were taking Louise with them out to the Hamptons for a meeting about the wedding. They dreaded the occasion as much as Mrs. Dudley.

Undressing, Roger related the incident at the hospital when Phillip made such a strange comment to his mother.

Sharon, brushing her hair, said, "Well, I told you that there was something between mother and son!"

"Oh, don't be insipid! It can't be anything like that!"

"Ha! Wouldn't that be priceless? Louise and Phillip in bed! Ha!"

"Shut up, you bitch. That's preposterous, and you know it.'

"Well, if my mother and your mother have another snag about our ceremony, we're just going to the justice of the peace and getting it over with," Sharon stated as she started taking her clothes off and throwing them on various things in Roger's bedroom.

Her dress flew over on a chair, her bra was thrown up on a chandelier, and her panties were tossed into a wastebasket. Roger watched and shook his head as she undressed.

"Thank God we'll have a maid," he commented when she flopped on the bed stark naked.

"Oh, shut up and get that big cock of yours over here," Sharon snarled and then laughed as she rolled over onto her stomach.

Roger went into the bathroom and brushed his teeth while Sharon continued her diatribe about Delores. "I'll bet that silly woman's a virgin. Can you imagine? At her age?"

"She's not so old."

"Well, she's old enough to have had a good screw."

Roger called from the bathroom, "And what age were you when you lost that divine gift from the gods?"

"Wouldn't you like to know?"

"Well, I'm sure I didn't rob you of it!"

Sharon laughed and teased in a babyish voice, "Yes, you did, Daddy. I was Snow White when you tore those panties off of me."

"Honey," Roger said in rebuttal, "those panties hadn't been white since you left kindergarten!"

Sharon laughed. "Well, it wasn't my fault that Uncle Herbert thought I was so cute."

"Oh, he's the one."

"Yes. I was only fourteen. He had me on his lap and did things that a decent man just shouldn't do."

"You must have fought like hell."

After a short pause, Sharon answered again in her babyish tone, "Yeah, I did. I kept putting his hand where it felt better. It was a terrible fight." Then she laughed.

Roger came out of the bathroom smiling. "After that you probably corrupted half the kindergarten."

"I was in junior high at that time, you idiot. Who ever heard of a fourteen-year-old in kindergarten?"

"You never know, in that dysfunctional family of yours. Look at your brother. You must have had trouble keeping him out of your closet."

"No, mother's clothes fit him better and she, idiot that she is, thought he looked so cute in drag. She didn't realize she was making him gay."

"He's what they call a swish, isn't he?"

"Call him what you like. You've one in your family, too."

"Kevin's got more man in him than your brother."

"Well, man or not, he's one of the boys."

"All right, so we're even. One in your family and one in mine!"

"Do you think it's really genetic? If it is, I don't want children."

"Are you crazy? I'm going to knock you up so many times, you won't care if the litter is gay or mongoloid."

Sharon laughed as Roger slipped onto the bed and put a leg over her torso. She turned toward him and grabbed his penis. They began kissing and rubbing their bodies. After a few minutes, Roger slipped down and began sucking one of her breasts.

"Ohhh," she sighed and then added, "Don't forget the other one."

He changed breasts. Again she sighed. After a while she used her babyish voice again and said, "Has Daddy got something for baby to play with?" She slipped down and began sucking his erection.

The foreplay continued for some time.

Finally Roger said, "If you expect me to screw you, you'd better quit milking the cow!"

Sharon laughed and pulled herself up on his body. She took his penis and plunged it into her vagina. It was her favorite position, and she passionately rocked and rolled herself into several orgasms. When she finally uttered her last pleasurable gasp, she rolled off him and spread out on the bed.

Roger softly said, "Well, you wore me out with that one!"

"Oh, shut up and sleep, stud!"

Since the next morning was Saturday, the couple slept until nine o'clock. When Roger noticed the time, he shook Sharon a little and informed her that they were leaving in half an hour. She objected vehemently and called him every derisive name in her vocabulary, which was extensive. When he came out of the bathroom partially dressed, however, she realized that she must arise, so she did.

Mrs. Dudley was ready when they drove up the circular drive in front of her house. She came out quickly, greeted them, and climbed into the Infiniti Coupe.

As if sensing that Roger and Sharon were tired, Louise talked little, saying that she was enjoying the scenery. The daffodils were in bloom in gardens along the way, and the pink cherry blossoms and white dogwoods made a colorful panorama. Spring was in the air, and nature was decorating the landscapes beautifully.

Occasionally Louise would comment on a particularly splendid scene, and Sharon would open her eyes and say, "Umm."

After an hour and a half, Roger drove up to the Clarke's estate. "Such a lovely place," Louise commented, and Sharon again made some kind of sound in response.

"Dad had the gates widened after Mother scratched her Cadillac the second time."

Roger snickered. "I can just hear her blaming the gates, not her driving."

Sharon nodded with her lips pursed, showing her sarcasm.

When they pulled up in front of the large Georgian mansion, Roger slipped out and opened the door for his mother.

"He wouldn't do that for me," Sharon commented as she climbed out of the car.

"Mothers first," Roger teased, and Sharon stuck out her tongue.

When Sharon opened the front door, Mrs. Clarke's voice called out from the library, "In here, my dears."

Sharon led her guests past large Japanese statues of samurai into a room filled with glass-paned bookshelves from floor to ceiling. The leather book covers glistened, but Louise could not believe that the family had ever read any of the literature so elegantly arranged on the shelves.

Mrs. Clarke, tall, thin and dressed in an Yves St. Laurent pantsuit, greeted her guests with charming phrases. She was very excited because she had just found out that her favorite orchestra would be available for the wedding reception.

Sharon exclaimed, "Oh, no, Mother. Not that mess at the club."

"Darling girl, you know how your mother loves to waltz, and they play so divinely."

"Roger, tell her that the waltz went out with Attila the Hun!"

"Naughty girl!" Mrs. Clarke corrected, waving a finger at her daughter. "Don't start putting Roger between you and your parents. It's too early for that." Having made this observation, she chuckled lightly. "Don't you agree, Mrs. Dudley?"

There was no answer, but Mrs. Dudley did say, "Why don't you call me Louise, since we're going to be relations?"

"What a lovely idea. And you may call me Inez."

Mrs. Dudley smiled and started thanking her hostess, but the latter interrupted and called a servant who was walking through the parlor. She ordered tea and "something utterly marvelous" and then continued her revelations about her plans for the wedding. With the three hundred people the Dudleys were inviting and her seven hundred, there would, of course, be a thousand. She had hired the exclusive Mercers Company in New York City for the catering, and they had recommended a business she didn't know named "Special Occasions" for various functions pertaining to the wedding. "They showed me a picture of their large, striped tent. Oh, it's just so utterly charming, I can hardly wait."

Sharon grunted and said to Roger, "Come with me. I want to show you something."

Mrs. Clarke was aghast that her daughter wasn't staying for more of the details about her own wedding, but Sharon assured her mother that she trusted her implicitly because "you have such good taste."

Sharon knew that a compliment always pleased her mother and would allow her an escape from the drivel that she was hearing. She took Roger by the arm and led him back into the main hall. Mrs. Clarke continued to amaze Mrs. Dudley with the details of the wedding planning.

Inez would occasionally say, "Yes, I can tell by your eyes that you're surprised by that, but Harold insists that we give a wedding that will make shock waves even out here in the Hamptons." A laugh usually followed such a confession, but Louise only smiled condescendingly.

As Sharon and Roger ascended the large, curved staircase, she told him that she was planning on throwing her wedding bouquet to her sorority sister Helene and had told her where to stand below the staircase.

"Isn't that cheating?" he asked.

Sharon stuck out her tongue and went on up the stairs. They went down a large hall past part of the Clarke's portrait collection in the West wing and entered Sharon's room, which had a very feminine color scheme of pinks, violets and light yellow. The modern version of cream-colored French provincial furniture added lightness. Through the large-paned windows one could see a fine rose garden, which was in bloom. Roger had been there before, but he commented on the oncoming beauty of the flowers. Sharon paid no attention and flopped on the bed.

"Come here, stud, and give me a juicy kiss so I won't rape you."

Roger remained at the window. "No, you're not getting me excited this morning. You wore me out last night."

"Listen, you fine-faced fart," she snarled in a cynical tone, "when I want a kiss, I want it. Now get over here and deliver."

Roger walked over to the bed. "Listen, my Messalina, you're not going to order me around, get it?" he spoke resolutely, but then in a kinder tone said, "If you want a kiss, you must ask for it kindly."

Again using the babylike voice that she found so amusing, Sharon uttered, "Daddy, dear, would you please plant one of those great, big, juicy kisses on Mama's twat!"

Roger laughed and leaned over and kissed her. She threw her arms around him, however, and pulled him down on the bed. They were squirming on the bed when Sharon's father, Harold, came in. He laughed.

"What's this? Hot pants can't wait till the wedding?" He laughed heartily, holding his large, overweight stomach. "You'll have to watch her, Roger," he commented as he sat down in a yellow-chintz bedroom chair. "She'll get those pants off ya." He laughed again.

Sharon slipped off the bed and stood by her father. She kissed his forehead and said, "Daddy, are you going to let Mother do all of that crap she's planning? It's my wedding, but she seems to think it's hers. I'm getting sick of it."

"Now honey lamb, you just let Mama have a good time. You've got to remember that she didn't have such a grand affair and has looked forward to yours for years. Let 'er have her fun."

"Oh, don't give me that ole crap again about how you had to struggle in the beginning," Sharon stated as she walked to a full-length mirror in a French frame and fussed with her hair. "It wasn't my fault."

"No, but you should show more respect for having life so easy," her father replied and turned to Roger. "You'll have a heck of a time with this one, I tell you."

Roger laughed and said, "I already know it."

Sharon made a face at both of them as she picked up a hairbrush. At that moment, Cindy, the black maid, entered and told Sharon that her mother wanted her.

"Oh!" Sharon complained. "Now what!"

She threw down the brush and marched out of the room. Roger and Harold followed.

By the time the two men reached the bottom of the stairs, Sharon was coming out of the salon. Smirking, she said, "Oh, it was nothing. Roger, come with me."

Her father laughed and said, "Better do what she says. We don't want any cats yelling around here."

Sharon paid no attention and marched Roger to a patio. The spring air was lilting, and Roger commented on the beauty of the surroundings.

"What are you, some kind of nature freak?" Sharon asked, looking at him as if he were crazy. "Listen, there's a few things I want to get straight before I walk down that staircase to be your virgin bride."

"No one will assume that!" Roger teased.

"Oh, shut up. Sit down and listen to me." She pointed to a white, wrought iron love seat. He obeyed, and she joined him. "Now, listen. You do agree that there's to be no children. I don't want any brats running around."

Roger nodded. He had earlier agreed with her plan, feeling that she would change her mind with time, and he need not worry.

"Also, you do understand that I want to be true to you, but there might be mitigating circumstances that would entice me into being unfaithful?"

Roger smiled. "Don't worry. I'll keep that pussy of yours so busy, you'll never look at another man."

Sharon laughed and said, "Sounds good to me!" She fell over on him and kissed him.

Then a high-toned voice called down from an upstairs window, "Hey, don't be so intense. It'll frighten the squirrels."

Sharon sat up and said, "Jerry, I didn't know you were home. Come down. We'll bitch a little. You can tell us about your latest conquests."

Roger had only met Sharon's brother one time and found him obnoxious. He did not like the way Jerry made it obvious that he was gay, and his affected voice sounded extremely put on. Since Jerry was to be his brother-in-law, however, he had tried being friendly. Jerry had responded by teasing him and making suggestions that they have a rendezvous. Sharon thought such antics were very funny and would sometimes encourage her brother. Once she even said, "Roger, let him, it might be fun."

When Jerry came out on the patio holding a tennis racket, he was dressed for shipboard in white pants, shirt, and shoes. His captain's hat had a multicolored strip around the base of the top, and his bleached hair stuck out from under the front of the cap. His overall appearance was that of a debonair young man. His eyes were a bit too close for perfect facial features, however, and that bothered him greatly. He was still pleasant-looking, but his walking gait was more of a swish than a walk, and, for that reason mainly, he appeared gay to the knowledgeable eye.

He greeted his sister and future brother-in-law with a teasing phrase, imitating a hoarse nightclub habitué. "Hello, my dears. May I have him next, Sis?"

Sharon laughed, but Roger was tired of such jokes and said, "Drop the act, Jerry."

"Oh, he's in a cruel mood, my dear. Watch out."

Sharon gave Roger a light slap on the face, "Don't you insult my brother. I'll have him beat you up."

Jerry laughed, but Roger asked, "With what, an eyebrow pencil?"

Sharon slipped away from Roger and said, "And another thing, you'll treat my family members respectfully."

"Oh, he was joking," Jerry piped in. "Couldn't you tell?"

Sharon sat back on the wrought iron love seat and said, "What are you doing home?"

"Wore myself out and had to come back for a few days' rest," he replied and sat down in a white armchair.

"You, tired?" Sharon smirked. "Well, tell us about it. Did you run into more than you could handle?"

Jerry made a face and laughed. "Sis, dear, you know that will never happen. Remember the Colossus of Rhodes?"

Sharon laughed. "Yeah, how could I forget! Roger, you wouldn't believe what happened. We were on Mabel's boat off the island of Rhodes when a fisherman built like Hercules came by in a boat. Jerry flipped and fell purposely into the water. Course the native dove in and saved him, but Jerry has claimed ever since that he had him in the little cabin on his boat."

"But it's true," Jerry interjected. "I did have him, and I'll never forget it. It's so wonderful to have had the famous Colossus. You know he fell into the water centuries ago, and I'm sure he became a fisherman, because that man was just incredible."

What a dysfunctional family! Roger thought. *Do I really want to marry into this pack of decadents?*

"Well, darling," Sharon said, "what do you think of that tale?"

Roger responded quickly. "I think you both want to put me on just to see how much bullshit I'll take."

Jerry exploded. His high voice almost screeched. "But I did have him. No matter whether you believe it or not, I had the Colossus of Rhodes."

Roger smirked. "I don't care if you had Buddha or Zeus. I think it's rather sick to be proud of doing something like that."

Sharon sat up and looked at Roger in disbelief.

Jerry also showed amazement. Then he said, "Well, so you are a prude, and I bet you find me objectionable."

Roger worded his reply carefully, as if realizing he'd made a mistake. "No, I don't object to your goings-on. I just don't care for them at lunchtime." Then he laughed.

Both Sharon and Jerry joined him. He had been joking, Sharon, and probably Jerry, assumed, and they all kissed and made up. Roger did not care for the two kisses that Jerry planted on his cheeks, but he played the game.

Sharon continued her inquiry. "Well, tell us what gorgeous guy grabbed your grubby butt? Or did he break your heart again?"

Jerry acted offended. "You don't realize the hurt one can experience from such an affair."

"Oh, it was an affair."

"Yes, of three hours' duration."

All three of them laughed.

"I met him at Fudogs and he was gorgeous, as you say."

"How much did he want?" Sharon asked

"He went home with me without even suggesting any payment."

Sharon continued in a matter-of-fact tone, "Did he spend the night?" Jerry nodded. "Well, that's what he was after, a bed for the night. No, it was more than that. He surrendered completely."

"And then slept till morning," she countered.

Jerry sat forward on his chair. "You really are a bitch today, aren't you? Well, it just so happens that he's going to call me again."

"When he needs a bed," Sharon replied.

Roger interrupted them, saying, "If you two bitches are going to be so intense all day, I'm going home."

"Oh, calm down, asshole," Sharon quipped. "You might be a well-known up-and-coming lawyer, but you don't have the sense to see that we're just talking."

"Yeah," Jerry agreed. "You'll have to get used to us. We tell each other everything. Like I know the size of your cock."

Roger stared at Sharon with a look of disbelief. "You wouldn't," he uttered.

"What's wrong with my brother knowing the size of the Eiffel Tower?"

Roger only shook his head as the brother and sister laughed at him. "Is there anything about me you don't know?" Roger asked Jerry.

"Well, frankly, I can't think of anything. Seems you can stay on her long enough for an orgasm, and that's quite an accomplishment."

Roger was dumbstruck. He looked out at the beautiful garden and wondered whether these two decadents ever saw the beauty around them. His reverie was chased away by Sharon's laughter.

"Jerry," she said, "I do believe you've got him by the balls."

"Oh, if only I could," he responded and winked at Roger.

"Let's stop this banter," Roger suggested and stood up.

"Yeah," Jerry agreed. "Let's go listen to my new Elton John recording. It's cool!"

Sharon refused and told her brother that she and Roger must check in with their mothers about the wedding. "You will be at the practice, won't you?"

"Sure, Sis, if you'll throw me the bouquet after the ceremony."

Sharon laughed, but Roger walked away, shaking his head. She whispered to her brother, "Don't pay any attention to him. We'll make him into one of us yet—you'll see."

"I believe it, dear," Jerry agreed and put his arm around his sister as they walked into the house.

Mrs. Clarke was flabbergasted when Jerry walked into the salon with Sharon and Roger. She did not know that he was home and asked whether he was in trouble. Louise found it odd that the hostess would ask such a personal question in front of a stranger.

"Yes, Mother," Jerry answered in a put-on tone, "aliens from outer space are after me, and I knew they'd never find me out here. Who would even think of living way out here?" He made a face and sat down.

Mrs. Clarke was amused at his comment and happily introduced her son to Louise, who had never met him. Jerry did stand up and make a pretense of cordiality, but he quickly flopped back in his chair and informed his mother that he had come home for a few days' rest. She said, "Well, I'm glad you did, because we'll need some help for the wedding."

"I said 'rest,' dear, not work," he replied and looked at the ceiling as if he had more than he could bear.

Inez turned to Louise. "Aren't children the most ungrateful things these days? Why, when I was young, I was only too happy to help my mother."

"Give me a break!" Jerry snapped and walked out of the room.

"Pay no attention to him," Inez whispered to Louise. "He says these things, but he's really such a nice boy."

Roger's and Louise's eyes met, but they said nothing.

Lunch was served in the sunroom. Cindy had prepared a buffet table of crab salad and various luncheon meats. When Sharon and Jerry teased Cindy about some petty thing, she would joke back with them, and sometimes her comments were a little crude. Louise was amazed that the family would allow such language during a luncheon, but no one minded. In fact, they were amused.

After eating, Roger and Mrs. Dudley prepared to leave. They were going by the hospital to visit with George. Sharon was spending the weekend with her family, so Louise had a chance to talk with her son on the drive back to Connecticut. For a while, she said nothing, but finally she revealed her feelings. "Roger, are you really comfortable with that family?"

Roger laughed. "Mother, I knew that you'd be rather taken aback by them, modern as you are. They are something, all right, but actually, they're a typical American family."

"How can you say that? What's typical about them?"

"They do represent the 'nouveau riche,' but the American middle class has achieved that status today. They act the way they do because they have no restraints. They give token attention to their church, and they do as they please. They can afford it, and they're the result of such a life."

"But Roger, you were reared in a home where there were what you call restraints. We believed in God and worshipped in our church. We never acted like they do. Such language at a luncheon with strangers!"

"We're not strangers, Mother. We're going to be part of that family."

Louise shook her head. "How can you, with your fine education and distinctive personality, be a member of that family?"

"You have the wrong impression of me, Mother. Yes, you gave me a fine education, and I'm in an outstanding law firm. I've got it made, as they say. But I'm also a part of the American culture, and the Clarkes are the way it's developing."

Louise shook her head again. After a few moments, she asked, "Roger, I'll never ask again, but tell me, is Sharon really the sort of wife an outstanding lawyer needs?"

"Yes, she is. Oh, I know she can be crass, but that's the way young women talk today. She's a Vassar grad, and in society, that stands for something."

"Well, when I was at Vassar, we never talked like that. We thought we left school with considerable sophistication."

"But Sharon *is* very sophisticated."

Louise shook her head. "My goodness, if that's the new sophistication, I really am medieval."

Roger laughed. "No, Mother. You just went to Vassar at a different time. Everything's changed now. That's life. Every generation looks at things differently."

"So you'll allow your children to curse and be vulgar and call it sophistication?"

"Not in public, Mother. Sharon doesn't talk that way in public. When she's at my office, she's the ideal sophisticate. I'm envied by many of my colleagues."

"I can hardly imagine it."

"She and Jerry talk that way when they're at home. You'll see in the future that they conduct themselves quite well in public."

Louise was silent. "Thank you, Roger. I'll never bring the subject up again."

"By the way, Mother, I still don't understand what Phillip said to you at the hospital. Are you keeping some secret that he knows about? I can't imagine what it could be, but the tone of his voice and the way he threatened you made it sound as if he knew something you didn't want known. Am I right?"

Louise cringed slightly but said, "I don't know what it could be. Actually, I've wondered what he meant, too." She lied and felt terrible about it. She had always been honest with her sons and now she was forced to be untruthful. It seemed so wrong.

They drove in silence most of the way to the hospital in Stamford. Occasionally Louise would ask questions about the wedding, and Roger would explain his interpretation of the many activities planned at the Clarke estate.

"Seems like plans change quite often," he concluded.

"I don't wonder. They all seem ..." Louise did not finish her sentence. She preferred avoiding any more criticism and was very pleased when they arrived at the hospital.

The head nurse stopped Roger and his mother and explained that Mr. Dudley was being x-rayed. They asked whether something was wrong and were told that it was merely a routine checkup. The nurse could not see anything on the doctor's chart that would indicate a worsening condition.

Consequently, Roger said that he would not stay, since he and Sharon would be visiting the next day.

Louise went into her husband's room and waited. She sat thinking of the Clarkes for some time but finally fell asleep.

After a while, hospital orderlies rolled Mr. Dudley into the room on a bed. When they left, Louise sat down by the bed. She had much on her mind. As she revealed the events of the morning at the Clarkes', Mr. Dudley would laugh or wince, depending on how the information struck him. Finally he said, "My dear, they do sound berserk."

"Oh, darling, I can't tell you how many mixed emotions I have about that marriage."

"Don't worry, dear, they'll work out their problems."

"There aren't any problems about the wedding. That will stumble through, I'm sure. I'm concerned about the future. What kind of a home life will Sharon give Roger? He's our most stalwart son. I've expected more from him than any of the others."

"Well, he couldn't have a more promising career, and Sharon's going to inherit a fortune."

"Oh, it's money again! That's not the answer. You know that. How many miserable people have lots of money!"

Mr. Dudley turned his head so that he faced his wife. "My dear, we can't live their lives. Of course things will be different for them."

"But I want Roger to have a fine, noble family worthy of the Dudley name. I tried to instill that in our sons, but look at this marriage. Sharon couldn't care less if our name was ..." She hesitated and then added, "Oh, I don't know what!"

"You've got to accept the fact that Sharon is from a family that has come into wealth in our age. They have no traditions or inherited dignity. They're caught up in the fast life of our world today. The past means nothing to them."

Louise shook her head. "I had such high hopes for Roger."

"I'm proud of him, and I think Sharon will be a good helpmate, really."

"Oh, if only I could believe that!" They were silent for a while. Then Louise explained that she was going to church with Paul and his new girlfriend Delores the next morning. Mr. Dudley was amused at her descriptions of Paul's new flame and how Sharon had reacted to her. Finally he said, "Well, we are certainly going to have some contrasting daughters-in-law, aren't we?"

Louise nodded and said, "Speaking of contrasts, I forgot to mention that I met Sharon's brother, Jerry, today." She described his appearance and actions in great detail.

Finally Mr. Dudley said, "Well, my dear, aren't your suspicions about Kevin in the same vein?"

Tears came to Louise's eyes. "Oh, if I thought our wonderful little boy would turn into something as affected as that creature, I'd die of a broken heart."

"Well, he won't, I'm sure. He's—"

Louise interrupted. "I didn't tell you. But last night I heard sounds from Kevin's bedroom that could only imply some sort of activity."

"Gay, you mean."

Louise nodded and turned her face away, trying to hide her tears.

Mr. Dudley smiled. "Listen, sweetheart, young boys do that sort of thing. There are all sorts of names for such monkeylike activities. Most men outgrow it. Louise remained silent, looking away. "Well, girls play 'doctor' with each other, don't they?"

"Oh, let's drop this sordid subject, please," she whispered and put her head down on the bed. Mr. Dudley raised an arm and petted her.

"You poor dear," he said. "The world just isn't the way you would have it. Isn't that the problem, darling?"

Louise nodded.

That evening at home Louise retired early, but she continually thought of her husband's mistress and her confusion about Phillip. Everything seemed wrong. That night, sleep was a stranger.

Chapter 5

While Paul was driving Louise to his girlfriend's apartment, he asked, "What did Phillip mean when he said he would tell on you? Tell what?"

Mrs. Dudley was surprised at his asking about the incident. She had hoped that it was forgotten. "Nothing, really, I'm sure. He was so upset, I think he could have said just about anything."

"Don't cover for him, Mother. If he's threatening you in some way, let us know."

"Heavens, darling! Phillip would never do that. Besides, why would he threaten me?"

"Well, if I know Phillip, he'd do anything for money."

"It was merely a loan, remember that."

Delores was waiting on the front stoop of the building when the Dudleys arrived. While her blue suit was plain and inexpensive, she still looked very beautiful. She was holding a white, leather-covered Bible, and she waved when they drove up. After greeting and joining them, she directed them to the Church of the True Trinity.

Louise asked why the edifice was called "True Trinity" and Delores explained that their interpretation of the Bible allowed them wisdom above the usual run of churches. "For instance," she said, as if reciting a memorized passage, "the 'filial' argument between the Eastern Orthodox Churches and the Roman Catholic Church is absurd if one reads the Bible correctly. We do."

Louise avoided further questions on the subject. It was obvious that Delores would not accept any criticism, and she wanted good relations with Paul's new friend. Instead of pursuing the subject, she asked, "Were you reared in this area?"

"Oh, no," Delores replied, with a pleasant smile. "My parents live in Louisville, and I must say that I was really sorry when our company transferred me to this area."

Paul interjected, "Delores, as I mentioned, is highly valued in our firm. She is a legal secretary of outstanding merit."

"That's quite an accomplishment," Louise commented.

"Oh, Paul likes to exaggerate."

Paul protested. "Not true. You know you're the highest-paid secretary in our firm. Why, Mother, she can scan the most difficult briefs and find problems that save the firm considerable money."

"You must be as intelligent as you are pretty."

Delores smiled at Louise. "You're very kind. I also appreciate your coming to visit my church. It means a lot to me."

"Well, our family has always attended church. Paul was reared in the Christian faith, but I fear that he, as well as my other sons, rarely attends services anymore."

"That must be worrisome for you. I shall pray for Paul."

Louise was so surprised at Delores's comment that she impulsively turned around for another glance at the very attractive young lady sitting in the backseat. Her beauty somehow did not fit her character. Louise felt that any girl that appealing would usually be more involved with herself than with spiritual matters. So it seemed strange that Paul was so captivated by her.

They arrived at the church and drove into the parking lot. When they left the car, a couple exiting from another vehicle waved at Delores. They came over and greeted her with, "Sister Delores, God bless you."

Delores answered them with a blessing and then introduced Mrs. Dudley and Paul, who also received a blessing from the couple. The Dudleys were rather uncomfortable with what was for them a very unnatural situation. Their own church was more reserved. The familiarity implied in their being blessed by strangers seemed strange to them. Still, Mrs. Dudley thanked them graciously.

The threesome encountered many couples on the way into the church. As they were being seated, Paul whispered to his mother, "One more blessing and I'll sprout wings."

Louise looked at him and very slightly shook her head. It was no time for jokes, but she was also amused that everyone they met was sanctifying Paul.

The ceremony in the Church of the True Trinity was one of the most unpleasant experiences of Paul's life. He could not believe that people would rant and rave in a religious ritual. Louise was also taken aback by the boisterousness of the program.

When the minister entered the church, he shouted, "Let us dance and sing to the Lord!"

The congregation exploded. People stood up and either danced a solo where they were standing or else went into the aisles and joined in with others. If they weren't dancing, they were singing at the top of their voices. Delores had a pleasant voice and could be heard above those around them. Mrs. Dudley and Paul just sat in amazement. Occasionally a woman or man would dance or jump in front of them and ask them to join in, but they kindly refused. One large, rotund woman grabbed Paul's hand and almost spilled her large breasts out of her dress in her efforts at pulling him from his seat. He finally slipped his arm from her grasp. Louise knew that he would never marry Delores after that ceremony, but she didn't know what his motives were. Now he was determined more than ever to seduce the beauty that had involved him in what he considered sheer madness. He would show her what life was really all about and what a blessing it could be.

When the dancing and singing finally ended, the minister asked whether anyone had any guests. Delores proudly stood up and presented the Dudleys, mother and son. They were obliged, much as they regretted it, to stand and acknowledge the applause of the overly excited audience. When they sat down, Delores leaned over and thanked them for coming. They could only smile in response.

The minister's sermon took one hour. It was a literal interpretation of various passages from the Book of Revelations. The minister did not mention the fact that revelations were a genre in the second century when St. John wrote the book on the Island of Patmos. He also failed to discuss the interesting story of how St. John's revelations had made their way into the Bible.

Why had his tract made it into the holy book when so many authors were writing in the same genre? The minister probably did not even know those historical facts. He was too busy choosing verses that supported the illogical point he was forcing upon his congregation. Paul was bored stiff, and Louise was astonished that so many people would listen to the drivel the man was spouting. She looked at Delores several times but saw no doubts or confusion in her expression. The girl was actually following what the minister was preaching, and she was accepting his message for fact. It was at that point that Mrs. Dudley realized that she did not want Delores as a daughter-in-law, no matter how attractive she was. Louise also thought of her own impiety and was sure the congregation would have stoned her had they known her violation of Christian law.

After the ceremony the Dudleys were again accosted and blessed by many in the congregation. Delores was evidently very popular in the church, and her acquaintances were interested in meeting the gentleman friend whom she had brought into the congregation. By the time the three of them had reached their car, their souls had been blessed far too many times.

When asked how she had enjoyed the service, Mrs. Dudley kindly answered that she was not familiar with such a program but had found it very interesting. She also invited Delores to her church for a service, and the latter readily accepted. Paul did not respond with such civility. He expressed his amazement that people could "carry on" like that in a holy edifice and said he thought the minister would make a great emcee in a nightclub. Delores quickly shamed Paul for demeaning the minister, so he lied and told her that he was just joking. She accepted his apology and confessed that she had felt especially moved that morning because Paul and his mother had attended the service with her.

At dinner Louise decided to find out some information about Delores's background. Politely she brought up the subject of the girl's family and education. Delores was so elated from the church ceremony that she blurted out an expression of her pleasure in being with such a distinguished family as the Dudleys. Paul almost laughed, but he controlled himself. Delores expressed her love for her parents but admitted that her own family was just working class. Her father was a television repairman, and her mother was a seamstress. Her brother was in a Bible college, and her sister was married with five children. She was the only one of the children who had "gone on" to school, and she had finished the two-year legal secretary course at the Louisville Business College.

Paul finally interrupted the conversation between the two ladies by saying, "Mother, are you writing a biography?"

Louise laughed and apologized to Delores for asking so many questions. Delores assured her that she did not mind. "I'm sure a mother is curious when a son introduces a new girlfriend."

"Are you my new girlfriend?" Paul teased.

Delores blushed, and the flash of pink on her skin heightened her beauty. Paul said, "Mother, look at that face. Isn't that perfection?"

Louise looked at Delores and said, "You are a very beautiful girl. Surely you know that."

Delores blushed red, and Paul laughed. He was delighted with her appearance, but the religious ceremony he had just attended made him wonder whether he was really interested in someone so engrossed in religion.

When they arrived at the hospital and opened the door to Mr. Dudley's room, a smartly dressed lady in a green St. John suit was leaning over his bed and kissing him. She quickly stood up, showed that she was quite startled, and began straightening her hair and pulling down her jacket. Louise was just as surprised. Mr. Dudley uttered something, but it was evident that he, too, was dumbfounded.

Louise and the others entered the room as Mr. Dudley blurted out weakly and rather awkwardly, "My dear, allow me to introduce Mrs. Partridge. She's a friend of Harold's at the office."

The situation was very embarrassing for everyone.

Mrs. Partridge nodded and said, "I am glad to meet you."

Louise nodded, but looked at her husband, who was becoming a little more composed and said softly, "She has brought me well wishes from everyone at the office."

The situation was still too uncomfortable. Mrs. Partridge abruptly said, "I must go now. Glad to have met all of you, and I'm glad you are feeling better, Mr. Dudley."

George thanked her as she tried slipping past the newcomers, but it was inconvenient, and she brushed against Louise as she departed. At the door, she waved and quickly left.

Mr. Dudley laughed. Then, in a voice that was forced and weak, he said, "Well, it could look as if Mrs. Partridge and I were involved, couldn't it?"

Louise didn't answer. She was so taken aback and hurt that she could not find words.

George continued, "Well, she's just like that: kisses everyone in the office."

Sensing the pain his mother was experiencing, Paul stepped forward and introduced Delores.

George whispered, "Wow! Isn't she a knockout! I'd like her myself."

Delores blushed as Paul laughed, but Louise showed no emotion. She was sickened by what she thought she had seen. When George asked her, "How are you, dear?" she merely nodded.

As if sensing her feelings, he continued talking. He had good news. The doctors would release him in two days, and he could return home. He was delighted, and Louise nodded, but she felt like crying. She knew that her husband had a mistress, and now she believed that she had met the woman. Paul continued teasing and joking as a means of changing the atmosphere. Yet after a while, the young couple left so that Paul could take his friend home and return for his mother at the end of visiting hours. It was then that Louise asked for explanations.

"George, there is something between you and that woman, isn't there?"

He looked away. It appeared he could think of no lie or explanation. Finally he turned toward her and nodded. Speaking in a soft voice, he said, "Yes, my dear, and I am so ashamed. I would never hurt you."

Louise turned away, took a handkerchief from her purse, and wiped her eyes. Again everything seemed so wrong. Her life was not at all what she had assumed. She was not the typical suburban housewife that she had believed; her children were not the model human beings she had always presumed; and now it was true that her husband was not the faithful companion she had supposed. To whom could she turn? She was alone.

George made a few comments that were deliberate efforts at comforting her, but Louise did not really hear them. When she finally stopped crying, she looked at him and said, "Do you want a divorce?"

"No!" he exclaimed, louder than usual, but his voice showed his weakness. "My dear, I never loved that woman as I love you. It just happened at the office."

"When?"

"About a year ago."

Louise's eyes filled with tears again. She wiped them away and said, "I can hardly believe it."

"I can assure you that it's over. She came here to tell me that she would not expect anything from me. She's really not a bad sort."

Louise walked away from the bed, repeating the phrase, "Really not a bad sort!"

George, who looked increasingly tired, seemed to have said more than his strength would allow, but he continued. "You know what I mean. It happened, and it's over. Forgive me, my dear."

Louise nodded. "I only wish that Paul had not seen it. Now the children will know. We must think of what to tell them."

George paused, gasped for air, and then said, "Let's have the nurse bring something to drink, and then we'll talk about it, okay?" Louise agreed and sat down by his bed, wondering how Paul was explaining the situation to his new girlfriend.

Driving back to Delores's apartment, the young couple did not speak about the incident at the hospital. Paul avoided the subject, and Delores's modesty would not allow her to question him about it. Instead she asked Paul whether he had enjoyed the ceremony at her church.

He confessed that he found it rather bizarre. "All of that dancing and jumping around seems so silly to someone like me who is used to a more sedate ceremony."

"But the Bible says for us to dance and sing in praise of our Lord."

"But surely it doesn't mean one should go nuts like some of them did."

"Oh, Paul, they were just showing their enthusiasm."

"Well, they showed more than that."

Delores was silent for a few moments. "I'm very sorry you didn't like the service."

"Oh, it was all right. Please don't feel bad. I guess it takes some getting used to."

Delores turned toward him with a smile. "Then you will come again?"

"If that's what you wish, of course," Paul lied. He knew that he had no intention of ever going near that place again.

When they reached the apartment building, Paul asked if he could come in. She hesitated but soon invited him for a cup of tea. They walked up two flights of stairs, avoiding some toys left by a neighbor's children, and entered the one-bedroom apartment. The living area was decorated in a very feminine style. The lacy nylon curtains that covered the two windows were tied back with large pink bows. Hand-crocheted doilies were on the worn spots of the sofa, and a round, multicolored, pastel rug was in the center of the room. There was a feeling of daintiness. Paul congratulated her, and his remark pleased her immensely.

Drawing back a curtain with colors that matched the rug, Delores revealed her small kitchen nook. She put some water on the stove for tea and returned to her guest. "You've made me very happy."

"Why?" Paul asked, sure that she was thinking of the church service again.

She was. "By your going to church with me."

He took her by the shoulders and pulled her closer. She tried breaking away, but he said, "I'd do anything for you, don't you realize it? I really care for you."

She quit resisting and looked into his eyes. "Paul, I'm actually delighted that you've taken an interest in me. I think you're a fine gentleman, and I would like to know you better."

He suddenly pulled her to him, enclosed her in his arms, and kissed her. She broke away and stared at him with fright in her expression. "Paul, don't destroy the image I have of you, please."

"I won't, my darling, but surely you know that I love you."

Delores looked downward, her face expressing her pleasure. "Paul, I have dreamed all my life for someone like you to say that to me. And now it has happened. I feel so exhilarated, I could fly away."

Paul could hardly believe what he heard. "Surely other men have been in love with you?"

"Men have made passes and spoken token phrases, but they were only interested in seducing me. I never ever had a man whom I could trust until now. I love you, too, Paul. I have to admit it."

Seizing the moment, Paul walked over to her and again took her into his arms. Looking into her light-blue eyes, he whispered, "I've never held such beauty before. I adore you."

Delores relaxed in his arms, and he kissed her. Her mouth opened, and their tongues pressed together. She started trembling. He held her more tightly, and she gasped for air.

"Oh, Paul, I can't breathe," she whispered, adding, "And I don't want to." She kissed him again and again. Then she began rubbing herself against him, closer and closer, over and over. Suddenly she realized that she was actually pressing against his erection, and she quickly broke away. "Oh, Paul, what have I done?"

"Nothing, darling. We have finally found each other, and it's wonderful."

"No, I was ..."

"Come here, my dear," he softly said, and she went into his arms again.

Whether it was from the excitement of the morning ceremony or from her feelings of awakening love, Delores surrendered herself to his embraces. For some time they enfolded each other in one another's arms as if they were blending into one form. Delores began crying from ecstasy. She had never had such an experience. Slowly, without her even noticing, he unbuttoned her blouse and slipped a hand under her bra and caressed one of her breasts. She cried out, "No!" but tightened her grasp around his body. Paul knew she was terribly excited and picked her up in his arms. Carrying her into her bedroom, he kissed her repeatedly.

When he laid her on the bed, she started crying again but pulled him down on her. "Oh, Paul, you do plan to marry me, don't you?"

"Of course I do, my dearest. In the eyes of God, we are married."

His remark allowed him to continue fondling her. She surrendered to his embraces. Soon he had her undressed and in bed. He quickly slipped off his clothes and joined her. Again they enclosed themselves in a tight embrace. He kissed her breasts until she sighed heavily. When his finger went into her vagina, she curled up in a fetal position. He calmed her by kissing and caressing. Finally he allowed his extended penis to touch her body. She shook.

"Oh, Paul, should we do this?"

"Yes, my darling. We are one."

Penetration was difficult and mainly unsuccessful. He could only ingress a couple of inches. Yet he continued slowly. When he was near orgasm, he suddenly entered her completely and groaned as he reached satisfaction. When he finished, he rolled off her and closed his eyes. He was almost asleep when he heard sobbing. He opened his eyes. Delores was sitting on the edge of the bed in tears. *Oh, hell,* he thought, *now I've got to convince her that she's not going to hell.* It was a routine he had used before, but it bored him. He sat up by her and put his arm around her shoulders.

She leaned against him, saying, "Oh, Paul. I have sinned. I never thought I would."

Paul let her cry a little and then started his act. He had never calmed a woman of such religious intensity, but he charged into battle with the kindest of phrases. A poet could not have been more elegant in a profession of love. Delores practically inhaled his words. She stopped sniffling and rested her head on his shoulder.

Paul, like any man after intercourse, was eager for a release from her hold. When he started moving away, however, she grabbed him and started crying again. He sat back by her and wove another thread of lies. She was his angel, his love, his future bride. His promises followed one after the other. He had never lied quite so excellently, and it worked. Delores believed him and released him from her web. He quickly dressed and kissed her good-bye several times. When he left, she seemed very content and happy. "Not the tears that fill the years—after—after," as the poet Rupert Brooke wrote about the broken heart.

Paul reached the hospital just before visiting hours ended. He talked with his father, who was impressed by the beautiful girl Paul had brought with him earlier. Mr. Dudley whispered that he thought Delores would be an excellent mate for his son. He added that the young lady's demeanor and modesty were really pleasant and that she had qualities similar to Paul's mother. Mrs. Dudley did not say anything, but Paul, to humor his father, said that he would bring her again for a visit. Mr. Dudley liked the idea.

Driving home, Louise was quiet, thinking of Mrs. Partridge. Paul hesitated, but finally asked, "What is the relationship between Dad and that woman?"

Louise began crying. Finally she said, "As if I didn't have enough on my mind, I had to find that out."

Paul, understandably, seemed surprised that his father had admitted his collusion with the visitor. His mother quit crying and said that George maintained that the affair was over. She said that it was best to accept his word about the matter until his health improved.

"Then what do you plan?" Paul asked.

"I don't know. I simply don't know."

"You wouldn't leave Dad, would you, Mother?"

Louise could only shake her head. She was too confused and distraught. After a while, to change the subject, she asked whether Paul was sincere in his relations with Delores. "Oh, sure," Paul quickly blurted out. "She's a fine woman."

"Would you be willing to join her church?"

Paul looked at his mother with a smirk on his face. "God forbid that I'd have to go though life in that place."

"But Delores seems so adamant about her church."

"Well, she can just stay that way, as far as I'm concerned."

Louise nodded and smiled. "Well, I can see already that you've lost interest. What was it, the ceremony?"

"Oh, I guess. Let's not talk about it."

Louise was silent for a few moments. "I do feel sorry for her. I think she likes you very much."

"Too much."

"Oh, be kind. She might be just the sort you need. Besides, she would probably come into our church for your sake. Many people join their spouse's religion. After all, it's one God."

Paul didn't answer. He knew that he was finished with Delores. She was lousy in bed, and the thought of another bout of calming a fallen woman was more than he could take. He kept his feelings from his mother, however.

"Won't you see her again?" Louise asked.

"Well, I'll see her at the office, of course, but I'm not sure about dating. She needs to find a minister and 'sing and dance for the Lord!'"

Louise could not help but laugh. She, too, had been taken aback by the wild, emotional display at the church. Still, she felt sorry for Delores and suggested that Paul think seriously about her. "I don't want her to be hurt," Louise commented, and, after thinking of her own predicament, she began crying again.

Paul was silent, apparently unable to think of nothing that would comfort his mother, and he was tired of talking about Delores. When they arrived at the family home, he refused a light supper. His mother figured he did not want to continue the conversation about the church ceremony and his so-called girlfriend. She knew that, in his opinion, that matter was closed.

"Who's taking you to see Dad tomorrow?" Paul asked when Louise was leaving the car.

"Phillip. I think. It's wonderful that you boys seem to be taking turns in going with me. I know your father appreciates it."

"Well, let me know if Phillip doesn't show."

"Oh, Paul, be kind. Your brother has gone through a very difficult period."

"Well, he's brought it on himself."

"My dear, handsome Paul, please remember that Phillip doesn't have your abilities or your good looks. Life's been more difficult for him. He's just not a winner like you are."

Paul smiled and leaned over to kiss his mother on the cheek. They parted with a wave. Louise drove off, but an unpleasant memory suddenly came to her. Paul once tried bestiality. He had tried sodomy with the family collie, and Phillip had caught him in the act. Not only did he tell on his brother but also teased him for some time. Could Paul resent Phillip because of that incident so long ago?

Chapter 6

Late the next morning, while Louise was waiting for Phillip, she heard a car screech its tires on the curved driveway in front of the house. As she was walking toward the front entranceway, she noticed Phillip running past one of the windows around the door. That seemed strange, so she opened the portal and looked out. His car was in front of the house, but he had evidently run around the side. While considering the possibilities of such an action, a police car pulled up the driveway and stopped behind Phillip's car.

Louise was dumbfounded, but at that second, Phillip came up from behind her and said, "Let me talk with them, Mother."

"What's happening?" she asked.

"Never mind. I'll explain later," he answered and stepped across the threshold.

Two policemen and a man in civilian clothes came to him. They said that they had been following him and believed that he was hiding illegal drugs. Phillip denied it. He admitted that he was on parole but insisted he was clean.

When the man in civilian clothes asked if they could look around, Phillip asked nonchalantly, "Don't you need a warrant for that?"

Mrs. Dudley stepped forward and said, "No, they don't. They can look anywhere they please."

Phillip's face showed his displeasure and surprise, but he raised his hands and said, "Well, if it's all right with her, do as you please."

The civilian introduced himself as Mr. Wilson, a federal investigator. Louise shook his hand and said that she was sure there was some mistake. He asked if Phillip had been home long, and she told him the truth. She did, however, include the fact that her son had gone around the house, which she found very strange.

One policeman and Mr. Wilson immediately walked toward the side of the house, while the other policeman stayed beside Phillip's car. Louise and her son walked into the house. When they were some distance from the entranceway, Phillip whispered, "Why did you do it?"

"Phillip, I would help you any way I could, but I will not lie about drugs. If you've done something you shouldn't have, then you've broken your word to me, and you've harmed yourself. I love you, but I won't help you break the law."

Phillip looked at his mother with a smirk on his face. "Don't forget that I've got something on you, too, Mother love!"

Louise cringed. She did not know how to respond. It was not the time for that dreaded subject. Fortunately Phillip walked away.

Wringing his hands, Phillip went into the family room. Through the windows he watched the men who had walked around the house. He kept looking in the direction of the garden gate but could not find what he was looking for. Louise was sure he had hidden something, but the men did not seem to be finding it.

Finally they came to the back door. Mrs. Dudley opened it, and they asked whether Phillip had returned home with a package wrapped in blue paper.

Louise denied seeing any such article, and Phillip assured the men that he was innocent.

"After all, I'm on parole. I wouldn't be involved in anything illegal now."

Mr. Wilson replied, "Perhaps we were misinformed. It's a common practice in the underworld." He then thanked Mrs. Dudley for her cooperation, which he said had helped convince him of her son's innocence. She thanked him and walked with him and the policeman to the front door. When they drove away, Louise returned to the family room. Phillip was in the garden, hurriedly going from one place to another as if he were looking for something.

Mrs. Dudley walked out on the patio and asked quite loudly, "Phillip, what are you looking for?"

Suddenly, from over the fence, Sarah's voice called out, "Hello, Louise. I borrowed your wheelbarrow."

Phillip ran to the garden gate as the neighbor wheeled the cart back into the Dudleys' garden.

Sarah, all smiles, said, "I noticed that you had put some weeds into it, and I was weeding, so I just put mine with them. Hope you don't mind."

"Of course not," Louise replied.

"I'll empty it," Phillip quickly said, his voice showing desperation, and he quickly pushed it out to the tool shed.

Louise walked over by her neighbor. "Sarah, you'd done us a great service. You saw Phillip put something under the weeds and you realized he needed help." Tears filled Mrs. Dudley's eyes. "Oh, Sarah, how can I thank you?"

"Louise, dear, I just put a few dead weeds on top."

"No, you know what I mean," Louise responded, wiping the tears from her eyes. "You helped Phillip hide something. How did you know that he needed help?"

Sarah smiled and looked back at the shed, checking whether Phillip could hear her. "It's none of my business, but I did hear Phillip drive up, and I saw him quickly put a package under the weeds. So, when I saw the police car, I borrowed the wheelbarrow."

Louise shook her head. "Sarah, you took a terrible chance. I fear that Phillip has …"

"Don't tell me," the neighbor interrupted. 'It's none of my business. Phillip is in enough trouble, I wouldn't want him to have more."

Louise frowned and looked down. Her eyes filled with tears. "Oh, Sarah, how kind of you."

"Everybody considers me an eccentric, but I don't care. You see, I know what a load is, and Phillip has a heavy one. If I helped him, I'm glad, but I don't want to know about it."

"How can I ever thank you?"

Sarah, thankful that she need not answer the question, exclaimed, "Oh, look, here's Phillip now."

Louise and Sarah watched Phillip push the empty wheelbarrow back by the garden gate. When he dropped it, he looked at Sarah and started to speak, however, she quickly excused herself, claiming that she was very busy. After saying that she'd drop by the next morning, Sarah returned home.

Mrs. Dudley looked at her son as he walked toward her. "So, you did hide something."

"Mother, please don't ask. It won't happen again, I promise."

Louise turned and went into the house. He had betrayed her trust and her neighbor had helped save him. It was all so complex. When he entered, she turned and said, "Once again you've broken your word. You are dealing in drugs."

Phillip, his face showing weariness and sorrow, replied, "Mother, this evening I shall return the money I borrowed."

"Is it from drugs?"

"No, it's from a payoff."

"What does that mean?"

"It means that I'll be out of debt and that I can go straight."

Louise shook her head. She did not know what to believe. She could only ask, "Phillip, my dear son, what are you doing with your life? Wouldn't it have been better to tell the truth?"

Phillip laughed sardonically. "The truth? Do you know what would have happened if I had told the truth? I'd be in jail for years! Is that what you want?" He laughed. "The truth would hardly have made me free. So forget that old idiom. The truth has no place in our modern world. One has to learn when to use it and when not. Besides, you wouldn't want the truth out, would you?" His smirk had returned, and he winked at his mother suggestively. "So no more sermons, please!"

Louise's face showed despair. "Oh, Phillip, how can you hurt me?"

"I don't want to, Mother, but you've got to let me work this out."

"But what will become of you?"

"Mother, I'm going to be all right, you'll see. I'm going now, but I'll be back in a short while and take you to the hospital."

Mrs. Dudley watched as her son departed. He looked older, and his hairline had receded more than she remembered. It was obvious that he had not been taking care of himself. Despairing, she walked around the house. Her mind went from the problems of her sons to the kindness of Sarah. Louise was sure that her neighbor had saved the family from more scandal. It seemed a blessing and a curse. Phillip had succeeded in carrying out his nefarious escape, but that only allowed him to continue in his disreputable and illegal activities. Louise made herself some coffee and waited.

In a short while Phillip returned through the back way and, with a smile on his face, placed ten thousand dollars on the kitchen table. Louise looked at her son. How could he be smiling? Yes, he had returned the money, but as a result of whose anguish? How could he be glad of his gain when it was based on someone else's agony? How could he have strayed so far from the teachings of his church? Then she remembered that she, too, had not upheld the holy commandments. She realized that she had been fooling herself all these years thinking that her family was honest and truthful. What had all those years of church going done for them? Had the church failed or had she? Louise was so confused by the complexity of the situation, she almost cried. Her family was disintegrating, and she could see no salvation.

Suddenly they were interrupted by the phone. It was Sharon. She wanted Phillip's address so that she could send him an invitation to the "bachelor-bachelorette" party. When Louise asked her son for his address, he hesitated, but then told her to tell his future sister-in-law that he would call her.

When Louise relayed the message and hung up the phone, she asked, "Phillip, it's odd that your own parents don't have your address."

Again he hesitated. "Well, I'm moving this week. Then I'll give it to you."

Later that afternoon Louise answered the doorbell and found Mrs. Partridge at the threshold. She was beautifully dressed and smiled kindly.

"My dear," Mrs. Partridge said, as if they were friends and her presence was not unusual, "Would you mind talking with me?"

Louise's immediate impulse was impolite. Slamming the door in someone's face was simply not proper, but she gritted her teeth in making her decision. "Yes, you may come in."

The visitor entered and followed Louise into the family room. Mrs. Partridge made comments about the lovely home, but Louise did not respond. She did indicate a couch where the intruder could be seated, but she remained quiet.

After sitting down, Mrs. Partridge said, "I know that I have created a most awkward situation by coming here, but I felt that we simply must talk."

Louise looked over the attractive woman before her and finally remarked, "I really don't know why we must talk, because I really have nothing to say."

"Maybe not, but I do."

Louise looked at the visitor, showing her puzzlement.

"You see, George and I had made plans, which I think he would still like to carry out."

Louise looked with disdain at her guest. "What sort of plans?"

"My dear, I ..."

"Please don't call me that," Louise interrupted, having taken just about enough of her rival's kindness. "It's just not fitting."

"I am merely trying to make a sad situation more endurable."

"A rather sordid situation, wouldn't you say?"

"I'm sorry you feel that way, but George and I are very much in love."

Louise's face wrinkled. "How can you say that to me? George has assured me that his relationship with you is finished."

"He lied for your sake. You see, you must give him a divorce because I am pregnant."

Louise fell back on the couch and cried, "Oh, no!"

"Yes, it has been confirmed. Even though I am older, it has happened."

Louise began crying. It meant the dissolution of her marriage, the termination of her comfortable life, the end of her family's closeness. Nothing would ever be the same. It had all been taken away by the devious woman sitting before her.

For a few moments neither lady spoke. Finally Louise said, "I think you should go. When I am at the hospital, I'll talk to George about the matter."

Mrs. Partridge hesitated. Louise stood and motioned that she would lead the guest to the door. As if accepting the situation, Mrs. Partridge left the house and drove away.

Louise returned to the family study, sat down, and cried. To whom could she possibly turn? Her sons had drifted away from her, and her husband had strayed. What could she do? And how could she face the man she loved, whose love she had lost?

Rising from the couch, Louise walked toward the stairway in the hall. Seeing the passageway, she suddenly thought of Orpheus and his descent into hell. Yet she quickly remembered that his mission was to save his love, while her task was to surrender hers. She started up the steps as flashes from the past filled her mind: her beautiful wedding dress, the birth of their first son, pleasant trips to the seashore. Suddenly she started crying again and sat down on a step. Taking a handkerchief from the sleeve of her blouse, she wiped her eyes. Then she realized that she did have a friend with whom she could discuss her many problems. For years she had been reserved in her relations with Sarah, but now she saw her in a completely different way. Thinking back, Louise realized that Sarah had actually been a very helpful neighbor. She had certainly passed on news of the community, but it had always been things worth knowing. Then today she had helped Phillip most cleverly and so thoughtfully. Louise concluded that she had never really known her neighbor and decided to chat with her.

Going into the garden, Louise looked over the fence and saw her neighbor's green sweater as she threw feed over the llama's stall. Louise called her and asked whether she had a few minutes she could spare.

"Yes," Sarah shouted back with evident pleasure in her voice. "Just let me finish here. I won't be a minute!"

"I can come over," Louise suggested.

"Better not," Sarah yelled back. "Lilly's not behaving today. She spit on the garbage man. It was awful."

Louise removed her hand from the garden gate. The thought of being covered with a stinking, green eruption from the llama's stomach was repulsive. Sarah soon came, leaving her staff resting against the fence. Louise invited her in for a cup of coffee.

"Oh, just as I suspected, something's up!" Sarah said with a smile.

Louise laughed, and once they had sat down on the captain's chairs at the kitchen table, she said, "I really don't know which problem is the worst."

Sarah smiled, but her face showed discomfort when she said, "I always hesitate to give advice. I've made so many mistakes, I don't feel confident. Is it about Phillip?"

"No," Louise replied and then added. "Well, yes. It's about many things. You see, I'm being absolutely pulled apart. My family seems to be disintegrating, and I don't know what to do."

Sarah listened as Louise opened her heart and mind. She revealed her concerns about her sons. Then, embarrassed by what she was confessing, she expressed the humiliation she felt about her husband's deceit. Tears filled her eyes.

Sarah listened closely without asking questions. When Louise succumbed to tears, the neighbor stood up and patted the hostess on the shoulder. "Lady, you are blaming yourself for things that are not your fault."

"How does one know?"

"Because I know how you have tried. I've been on that road, and I know it well. I, too, failed with my son." Louise looked up, surprised. "Yes, I shall confess it because I think you need to see that others make mistakes, too. You see, I wanted my David to be a prince of a man. In other words, a real man, a he-man! I drove him so hard I drove him away. He ran off to Montana and bought a small ranch. It was his way of trying to be the he-man that I wanted, but I know I forced him to do it. He did not want that life. He did it for me, and I know he's not happy."

"Oh, Sarah, I had no idea."

"Yes, Louise, just like you, I tried so hard for him, but somehow I failed. You have done the same, but at least you haven't driven them away. There's still hope."

"Surely there is for you, too."

Sarah shook her head. "No, I know that I've lost him. Even more, maybe I fouled up his life by wanting him to be what I wanted, not what he wanted."

"Oh, Sarah," Louise kindly uttered. "How could we have known?"

I brought up my sons in our religion. I thought they were following in Christ's footsteps."

"Louise, there's the problem. You see Christ was a Jew like me. His philosophy was for us Jews, not you gentiles. He wanted to change our ways, but his philosophy was so narrow. He left out human nature, which we Jews understand very well."

"What do you mean that Christ did not consider human nature?"

"You can't be Christlike in this world. It's not made for it. For example, honesty must be used moderately. Society demands a white lie. To be Christlike is to be like Dostoevsky's 'Idiot.' It doesn't work in this world. It's a beautiful philosophy, but not practical."

"Oh, Sarah," Louise commented with a pained expression, "you'll destroy my faith."

Sarah was quiet for a moment. "Perhaps I've said too much. I don't want to disturb you. You have enough on your mind without my sharing such thoughts."

Louise was confused. She wanted a rebuttal for Sarah's comments, but she could not think of one. Finally she said, "But Christ was for all mankind!"

"Then why didn't he also go to the Chinese or the Indians? Strange that God should leave out a couple billion people."

"Oh, Sarah, I can't answer such thinking. You confuse me."

"Don't let me upset you. We'll discuss such things another time. Besides, I know you did the best for your children."

"I thought we were doing the right things for them. Everything seemed right, but now everything is sort of topsy-turvy. I don't know what to do. I even believe it's my fault."

"Why?"

Louise cringed, realizing she might have revealed her secret worry. "Oh, I didn't mean anything particular."

Sarah smiled. "You're hiding something, but that's all right. I only wish I could give you words of comfort. I simply don't have them to give. I hope you understand."

"Then you've accepted your situation?"

"Do I have a choice? Since my husband died, I'm alone, and that's it!"

"Oh Sarah, I have misjudged you in the past. I must admit that I don't understand exactly what you were saying about Christ, but I do know that you've been so kind through all of your problems. I never suspected that you were so unhappy with your life."

Sarah shook her head. "I'm not, now. Of course I give the impression of being a bit touched in the head, but my animals are my life now, and I have found contentment in them."

"Guess I'll have to get a llama," Louise said with a smile. Sarah laughed. After a short pause, Louise suddenly asked, "Sarah, would you go with me to see where Phillip lives? I think I worry about him the most."

"Sure, but why do you want to go there?"

"He has assured me that he is no longer in the drug business, but I'd really like to see if it's true."

"Do you know where he lives?"

"I have the address where his parole officer visits him, but I'm sure that's not where he lives. I'd like to find out if I'm right. We could go this evening after I visit George in the hospital.

Sarah's eyes widened, and she jovially said, "I love an adventure! Let's do it!"

That evening the hospital surgeon informed Louise that George was heavily sedated because of some irregular heart rhythms, He suggested that she wait until the next morning before coming for a visit. She was glad for the release of tension and was glad that Sarah would join her for the "adventure!"

As they drove through the hills and into the city, Louise expressed her fears for the future. When George came home from the hospital, he would require much care. Also, she would have to drive him to a clinic for radiation and chemotherapy. It would be time-consuming and unpleasant. She would have been glad to help him under normal conditions, but she was sure a divorce was forthcoming. It seemed unfair that she should have such a burden when he would belong to another woman. It was very stressful. Sarah agreed and said that George had acted disreputably.

When they arrived at Phillip's apartment building, there were lights in his windows and shadows of figures were moving about. It seemed evident that a party was taking place. The two ladies entered the building and went to the right wing on the first floor. Jarring cacophony resounded through the door. Sarah looked at Louise with an expression that suggested a question.

Louise shook her head. "I don't know what's going on. Do you think we should go in?"

Sarah knocked on the door. In seconds it opened a slit. A short Latina lady with large breasts peaked through the aperture. Phillip was quickly behind her and spread the door wide. The look on his face showed utter disbelief, and the young woman began speaking in broken English, "Who they come?"

Phillip avoided the question and said, "Come in, my dears. What on earth are you doing here at this time of the evening?"

Louise and Sarah entered what might be described as a noisy, sleazy bar. A black man in drag was dancing in front of a group of people seated mainly on the floor. He wore a white wig and a tight-fitting white evening dress. His heavy makeup was expertly applied, giving a startling appearance.

Whites, blacks, Latinos, Asians, and Indians crowded the place, and the company seemed to continue into the other rooms. The noise was almost deafening. Phillip pushed two women off a small couch and told the newly arrived that they could sit there. Louise and Sarah were both taken aback by the scene before them, but they did what they were told and sat down. Another young Latina girl slipped through the boisterous group on the floor and asked the newcomers whether they wanted some wine. Both shook their heads and continued staring at the sight before them. Neither Louise nor Sarah had ever seen anything like it. The dancer made gyrations of the most vulgar kind and laughed as if he were having a grand time. The people on the floor were hugging, kissing, and petting excessively. A couple in the corner was practically nude and close to having intercourse. Bottles of beer and containers of fast food seemed to be everywhere.

Louise and Sarah finally looked at each other. Both were perplexed.

Phillip saw their consternation and laughed. He slipped through the crowd and told them to follow him. They stood up and walked carefully behind him, avoiding bottles, hands, and legs. He led them through another room, where the music was just as loud, and a man and woman, practically nude, were doing a sordid dance. Finally the ladies reached the kitchen, which was filled with bottles and various types of fast foods.

Once there, Phillip said, "Mother and Sarah, I'd like for you to meet my parole officer, Mr. Robert Harris."

A short, balding, middle-aged man, standing by a sink, stuck out his hand and smiled kindly. Louise was so confused that she hesitated, but she finally accepted his offer and shook hands with him. Sarah did the same. It seemed incredible that a government officer was participating in such a melee.

Mr. Harris said, "Quite a party, isn't it?"

Louise nodded, and Sarah commented, "I feel like I'm viewing a scene from Dante."

"What's that?" Mr. Harris asked.

"I'm not sure what level of hell it is," Sarah continued, "but I've never seen anything like it."

"Relax," Phillip intervened. "It's just a party of friends. I wanted Mr. Harris to see that I'm clean and not associating with drug dealers."

Louise looked at her son in disbelief. Could such a party prove that? And how could the parole officer know whether there were drugs among the wild, heterogeneous group crowding the apartment.

Sarah asked Phillip, "Do you know all of these people?"

"Many of them, of course, but a lot of them brought friends. That's very common today. I was delighted. The more the merrier, I always say. Besides, it's a great day for me. You see, we're celebrating the end of my parole."

Louise looked at Mr. Harris. "Is this true?"

"Yes," he replied frankly. "Your son has fulfilled all his civic obligations and is a free man. I'm sure he's learned his lesson and will not engage in illegal activities ever again."

"I'll say I won't," Phillip agreed. "I'm a new man," he boastfully stated and then asked the ladies, "Will you have a drink with us to celebrate the occasion?"

"I guess we should," Sarah answered, "after such good news."

Louise made a faint smile and accepted some red wine in a small glass that did not look very clean.

Suddenly a stout, short-haired woman dressed in blue jeans walked by and said to Louise, "How long you two been together?"

Sarah and Phillip laughed, but Louise replied, "Oh, we've known each other many years."

"You're lucky you found someone that will stick."

Sarah laughed again, and Louise turned to her son with an expression of confusion on her face. Phillip was greatly amused by the incident and couldn't cease laughing.

After the woman walked by, Sarah whispered to Louise, "She thinks we're lesbians."

"Oh my God!" Louise uttered and put her glass down on a table.

Phillip, who had heard Sarah's comment, staggered over to Louise and put his arm around her. "Why Mommy, why should that upset you? Remember what we did? What's worse?" He then laughed in a strange tone and winked.

At that point Louise suggested to Sarah that they depart. They hastily offered excuses, and Phillip helped them start toward the front door. As they walked past the dancing couple, they noticed that the dancers were even less dressed than before. In the front room, the man in drag had changed wigs. He now wore a blonde wig with Shirley Temple curls. He had inflated his breasts to an enormous size, and his little-girl dress was above his knees. He was singing vulgar lyrics to Shirley's 1936 hit, "Animal Crackers." As Louise and Sarah passed by, they heard, "Animal crackers in my soup, make me have a great big poop!"

At that point the drag-man turned around and presented his derriere to the audience on the floor. Everyone laughed. Louise and Sarah went quickly into the hall. Phillip followed and asked if they needed help going home. They assured him that they didn't and left.

"He's still on drugs," Louise commented once she and Sarah were driving homeward. "That place had addicts, I'm sure of it."

Sarah was silent for a few seconds before she commented, "We've seen another world. The life we have led doesn't make much sense in the present, does it?"

"No, it doesn't."

Sarah sighed. "I believe these young people don't realize what's coming."

"What do you mean?"

"Our country is being divided by incredible movements of people. We're slowly separating from each other. Each religion wants things its way. It will lead to religious wars like in the medieval times."

"Oh Sarah, I pray not!"

"I do believe that religious wars are coming. Everyone's right! Everything must be their way, and they have no respect for others. You see it in the way the ignorant load up secret hoards of guns and explosives. Heaven knows how much is out there waiting to explode."

"Oh, that would be so terrible!"

"Well, we'll see, but I do believe such madness is coming."

Louise was silent for a moment. "I remember a line in Tennyson's poem 'Morte D'Arthur' that says it all. It went something like this. 'The old giveth way to the new, and God fulfills himself in many ways.'"

"Do you think God's involved with what I've just said and with what we've just seen at that party?"

Louise could not answer. A tear rolled down her right cheek. She was at a loss for words.

After a prolonged silence, she asked, "Sarah, what can the fate of a country be where the young people act like that?"

Sarah laughed. "Those young people couldn't care less. All they want is what they call fun. They seem mesmerized by everything that is debased. It's all so pathetic. I guess I'd better stick with animals. I know what they're about."

"We were in an animal pit this evening."

Sarah laughed. "Yes, the human animal. By the way, what did Phillip mean when he grabbed you and said that you and he had done something worse?"

Louise could not answer immediately. She had hoped that the comment would be forgotten. Finally, she replied softly, "I'm not sure what he meant. Perhaps it had to do with the money I loaned him."

Sarah shook her head. "No, it was more serious than that. There was something unnatural in his comment."

"What do you mean?"

"I don't know. Maybe you could tell me?" Sarah looked at Louise, but she was silent.

"Did it have something to do with that secret you wouldn't tell me?"

Louise did not answer; instead she changed the subject. "I fear everything now. The events of this day have robbed me of my security. Ahead I only see old age, divorce, and the dilution of my family. I used to feel such confidence. Now I don't know why I lived or what it was all about."

That night Louise feared that she would have ghastly dreams, so she took one of George's sleeping pills. She avoided remembering any incidents in her slumber, but the next morning she felt woozy. Still, she had avoided any unpleasantness in her dreams.

Chapter 7

Sharon had rented the exclusive Woodside Country Club for her bachelor-bachelorette party. The building contained an inside swimming pool surrounded by elaborate, white metal tables and palm trees; a beautifully appointed dance hall connected to the pool area and beyond it a large, ornate dining room. All three areas were rented for the party and Sharon spent considerable time and money on details. The invitations alone were a work of art. When the receiver opened the envelope, which was shaped like a large, golden head of Zeus, he was informed that attendance required special dress for the occasion. Each person was to appear in a costume befitting a god or goddess from ancient Greek or Roman mythology. A name tag was necessary so that no one would be confused about identities. Sharon thought of everything.

The club's administrator was pleased with Sharon's plans for decorations except for one point. Her desire to have all the tables and chairs removed from the dining room caused consternation. He did not appreciate having a mattress company deliver its product for a festive Roman feast on the floor. Even though Sharon would pay for the storage of the tables and chairs, the concept seemed too exotic for a prestigious country club. Sharon, however, knew several members of the board, which included her own father. In no time at all, the director of the club approved the changing of the dining room into a Roman banquet hall. He even agreed that the waiters could be dressed in tunics. He didn't know, however, that Sharon was hiring athletes from a nearly gym club as helping plebeians. They were to have nothing on under their tops. Sharon of course, always got her way.

Dr. Pat Hale, a noted dietitian, was approached about the Roman feast that would be served. However, she was not pleased with the additions that Sharon wanted with the dinner—for instance, sausages in the shape of penises. The consultant thought that such food might be amusing for a moment, but the deliberate distortion of a true Roman meal seemed like sacrilege. That did not bother Sharon. She even added tartar sauce before the dietician withdrew her services.

On the night of the party, Sharon, as Venus, stopped by her brother's room to check his costume. She was aghast when she saw him. Jerry, who had promised that he would dress as Ganymede, the boy lover of Zeus, was wearing a strange helmet, and his tag said, "Sacred Band of Thebes."

Sharon shouted, "How dare you change your god!"

Jerry gave a high-pitched laugh. "I was going to be your boyfriend's boy, but when I read about the Sacred Band of Thebes, I had to join."

"Well, who in the hell were they?"

Jerry waved a hand. "Oh, Venus, don't you remember? They were 130 pairs of male lovers who were killed at the famous Battle of Chaeronia."

"But I wanted you as Ganymede so I could tease Roger. As Zeus, he'd have to sleep with you."

"You mean you'd let him?" Jerry asked, opening his eyes wide as if surprised.

"No, you idiot! You leave him alone. I just wanted to make a grand joke out of it."

"Well, he can sleep with all 130 of the Thebans."

"Oh, you shit. You would spoil my joke. Besides, who ever heard of a band of Theban faggots?"

"Phillip of Macedon respected them so well that he gave them a special burial after the battle."

"Why did they lose? Did they trip over their powder puffs?"

"Don't be facetious. They were great heroes, and I'm one of them."

"You don't fit the hero part, you poop. The party's off to a bad start already, thanks to you. Come on, let's go."

When Sharon and Jerry went downstairs, their parents laughed at their apparel. Harold asked Sharon in a teasing tone, "What's that thing around your waist?"

She stuck her tongue out at him. "That's a cestus: Venus's girdle. It enhanced her love making."

He laughed. "Well, I'd say it would hinder love making."

Sharon made a face and walked toward the door.

When Harold looked at his son and read the tag on his helmet, he asked, "What was the Sacred Band of Thebes?"

Jerry smirked. "It was a Greek Dixieland band."

Harold seemed confused, apparently not realizing at first that his son was teasing. Then he laughed again and watched his children leave for the country club.

A few guests had already arrived when Sharon and Jerry reached the club. Zeus was there with his thunderbolts, crown, and long beard. Sharon laughed loudly as she likened Roger to a traveling ragbag. He retorted that she hardly stood out as the beauty of the goddesses.

"What's wrong with me?" she demanded.

"Nothing that a good screw wouldn't take care of," he replied, knowing that a vulgar remark would make her happy again.

"Later, you prig," she snarled and threw her arms around him for a kiss.

They were interrupted by Priapus, known among the gods for his enormous penis. When they saw him, Sharon and Roger broke apart and started laughing. He had concocted a huge cock out of crepe paper and wire. It protruded outward from his body when he pulled a string. It naturally made his tunic stand out in a rather vulgar manner. Whenever he took a step, the projectile waved and flopped. The hostess was delighted.

Harriet Delodge, a chum of Sharon's at Vassar, walked into the pool arena dressed as Demeter, the Greek goddess associated with vegetation. A small ear of corn, which is often associated with her, was arranged in her hairdo, standing high on her head and making her walk stiffly.

When she approached Sharon and Roger, the hostess laughed and asked, "What's wrong, Harriet, got a cob up your ass, too?"

Demeter frowned and held her stiff composure. "If you had this on your head, you'd walk like you had diarrhea, too."

They all laughed.

Paul Dudley arrived with his date, Linda Morrison. He was dressed as Neptune, carrying a long, three-pronged fork, and she sort of resembled his mermaid. He introduced his new girlfriend, who immediately disliked Sharon because she asked, "Paul, what happened to that beautiful girl you had at the house. What was her name? Delores?"

Linda stiffened and said, "My name is Linda, not Delores."

"Oh, I know that, honey," Sharon replied kindly, showing that she was tipsy. "You're all right, too. I was just curious."

Linda smiled haughtily.

Roger suddenly noticed that Linda's artificial crown was slipping and volunteered to correct it. While he adjusted the decoration, Sharon whispered to Paul, "What happened to Miss Righteousness?"

He gave his winning smile and answered, "She won't have to worry about virgin birth anymore."

Sharon screamed with delight. "You didn't! "

Paul nodded with a cunning smile.

Linda asked, "What's the joke?"

"Not you, dear," Sharon replied.

"Amazing!" Linda replied surreptitiously as she walked away with Paul, adding, "What nerve!"

Paul's comment was also audible. "Oh, you'll get used to Sharon. She's always a bit crass."

Sharon stuck her tongue out at them, but they were already engaged with another couple and didn't notice.

When other gods and goddesses entered the enclosed pool area, the host and hostess either waved joyously or ran over and hugged people with whom they were especially close. Soon the large glassed-in sunroom was filled with the hierarchy of the Greek and Roman myths. The friends of the soon-to-be married couple had followed the dictates of their invitations and had designed either humorous or stately costumes befitting the god or goddess they were representing. For some time the cocktail period was a scene of howls and laughter as the various deities tried guessing each other's identity. Hiding their name tags, they would approach each other, either with unseemly gestures or raucous remarks. Sharon set the mood by grabbing Priapus by the penis and pulling him around the pool. While the god waved his arms in protest, he submitted to the indignity because Sharon was pulling the wires that connected the artificial organ to his body. The event caused a sensation.

After Sharon released the penis near the bandstand, she went to the microphone and announced that it was time for a game. It was entitled, "Tell Zeus What You Want!" She called Roger, the Zeus of the evening, to the platform and explained that each god and goddess had to ask something of Zeus that could be fulfilled in the room. "For instance," she explained, "I want Priapus's cock!" Again there was laughter.

"All right, Larry Close, posing over there as Ganymede. Get your ass up here and ask Roger—I mean, Zeus—for something."

Ganymede, sitting at a nearby table, stuck his tongue out at Sharon and yelled, "I want Zeus!"

Sharon distorted her face and snarled back, "Yeah, you would! Well, you can't have him. You have to ask him for something else!"

Larry, a thin, narrow-shouldered friend from childhood, stood up and yelled, "I want Zeus to carry me off like he's supposed to!" Several people applauded.

Sharon raised a fist at her friend, but Roger carried out his task. He walked over to the table and grabbed the god by the waist and picked him up.

"Whoopeee!" Ganymede screamed. "Raped at last!"

"What am I to do with him?" Roger asked in a loud, godlike voice.

Various calls came from the audience.

"Rape him!"

"Beat him up!"

"Throw him in the pool!"

The latter was the most repeated, so Roger carried Larry, in spite of his kicking and screaming, over to the pool and dropped him into the water. The partygoers cried out their delight.

When Larry surfaced, he shouted, "Unfair! Unfair! I demand to be raped!"

Meanwhile a muscular waiter came running with a large beach towel. Sharon had taken all precautions. She was sure someone would end up in the pool and had arranged for towels to be ready. The handsome waiter pulled Ganymede out of the water. When he held the towel up for the god, Larry jumped into his arms, yelling, "He'll do! To hell with Zeus!"

Again the assembled laughed.

Suddenly Sharon noticed that Phillip had entered with a woman on his arm. His costume was undecipherable, and she looked like a tart from a cheap bar. The hostess screamed over the microphone, "Phillip, who in the hell are you?"

Phillip, wearing a short tunic and carrying a strange-looking basket full of twigs, yelled back across the pool. "I'm Pan, you ham! Can't you tell?"

Enjoying the attention and the bit of teasing, Sharon yelled back, "Well, shoot an arrow over here and liven up your brother."

"Tell him to bend over!" Phillip retorted and many laughed.

Sharon left the bandstand and went around the pool to Phillip. He introduced his friend as Sadie Smith, and Sharon, raising her eyebrows and lowering her voice, asked, "Who are you supposed to be?"

The startled woman, who was definitely middle-aged but had tried disguising it by applying her makeup rather thickly, turned to Phillip. She had never been accosted in such a manner. If Sharon had said something in a barroom brawl, the newcomer might have been able to answer, but she was not sophisticated enough for the hostess's type of repartee.

Phillip quickly aided her and said, "She's Pan's helper. Let's just call her Panny."

Sharon laughed and screamed, "Panny's here!" Then she bent over, laughing even more.

Phillip snapped at the hostess, "You're drunk, bitch!" and led his date away.

Sharon was soon back at the bandstand. "All right, everybody," she yelled, "It's time for someone else to tell Zeus what they want!"

Several hands went up among the mighty ones seated around the pool. Sharon called out to Cynthia Fox, a Vassar classmate who had been a close friend until she took one of the hostess's boyfriends. "Who are you, Cynthia?

I can't see your name tag. All I see is that stupid helmet you're wearing. Are you a Valkyrie?"

Cynthia loudly exclaimed, "You've failed your mythology course, dearie. I'm Minerva, goddess of war."

"Well, tell us what you want from Zeus."

"A kiss!" the goddess yelled back in a strong voice.

"Oh no, you don't!" Sharon squealed. "Now you're after my Roger."

The audience wouldn't stand for the refusal. A few started whistling, and others screamed various comments. Soon everyone was demanding that Roger kiss Cynthia.

Suddenly Sharon noticed that Kevin and Juno had entered dressed as shepherds. She quickly told the orchestra leader to play "Strangers in the Night." The music started, and Sharon began laughing.

Kevin and Juno quickly seated themselves at a table far from the bandstand and avoided being associated with the song. Sharon's caprice had been in vain. The audience had not quieted down, and Cynthia was already on her way toward the orchestra. Venus was forced into letting her former rival kiss Zeus. Everyone cheered.

After a few more of the demigods had played the game with Zeus, waiters began opening the louvered doors that separated the pool area from the dining room. The deities exclaimed their approval as they saw the floor covered with mattresses and short tables covered with fruits and sweets spread down the middle of the room. Everyone was ecstatic, and they quickly began converging into the Roman banquet hall. Falling over each other became a popular sport until everyone was spread out over the mattress floor coverings. Immediately the muscular servants began pouring wine into goblets on short-legged tables, while others offered large trays of barbecued meats and vegetables. It was a feast that any ancient Roman would have been proud to offer his guests.

At one end of the room Sharon and Roger were sprawled on a mattress made just a little higher than the rest in the room. From their perch, they ruled the hierarchy. Sharon would yell out abuse and epithets occasionally, but for the most part, everyone ate and frolicked together most peacefully and joyfully. The Emperor Nero would surely have approved of the frivolous folly.

When Sharon had eaten her fill, she rolled over on top of Roger. Several yells resounded, "Look at Venus and Zeus!" "What's she up to now?" "Can't you wait, Sharon?"

Sharon stood and called out, "Dancing in the dance hall!" Several couples left immediately, but most stayed and continued eating. Soon after the hostess's announcement, the denouement of the evening occurred, but it was not at all as planned. Police sirens were suddenly heard outside the building and in seconds, policemen were running into the pool area, the dining room, and the dance hall. It was a drug raid.

Most of the guests thought the explosion of blue uniforms was one of Sharon's bizarre ideas and laughed when the police officers asked for their identification. Since the partygoers were dressed in mythological costumes, many had not brought their driver's licenses with them. Others were too intoxicated for clarity and joked with the police. Only one person knew immediately who was responsible for the onslaught of federal authorities— Sharon. She surmised immediately that Phillip was under observation and had been followed to the club. Furious, she tried to find him, but he was lost in the confusion. She finally caught sight of Roger and informed him of her suspicions. He agreed, and together they looked for his brother. Meanwhile, the hullabaloo continued.

The authorities had considerable trouble convincing some of the guests that a drug bust was taking place. In desperation, the officer in charge of the entire operation asked Sharon to announce over the microphone that cooperation was needed. The hostess was livid that her party had been invaded and spoke harshly. Afraid that Phillip had brought some drugs, however, she informed her guests through the microphone that the police were not her idea but were actually carrying out an assignment. Once the company realized that the situation was not part of the program, all joking ceased. If guests had their driver's licenses, they willingly presented them; otherwise they went to their cars accompanied by police.

Several incidents occurred that were not part of any drug raid. Larry Close as Ganymede was caught being sodomized by one of the muscular waiters in some bushes outside the pool area. The federal officer who came upon the two copulating merely told them that a drug raid was in progress and that they should go to the clubhouse. Larry expected an arrest, but nothing was done. It was assumed that drugs were the major issue of the evening, not the activity of a pervert.

In a linen closet off the dining room, Harry Gould was fucking a cleaning lady. They were also informed of the raid and quickly dressed. When the police informed Sharon about the indecent activities taking place at her party, she said, "Show me a picture or shut up!"

The federal officer in charge of the operation was not pleased with her reaction and told her that she was lucky that her guests were not charged with misdemeanors.

Sharon, contemptuous and disrespectful, shouted, "Well, how dare you break into such a wonderful celebration. You haven't found anything, and you won't."

She had regained her derisive tone because she was sure that Phillip had slipped away without being noticed. Her brave front was quickly shattered, however, when she noticed Phillip and his trollop at the far end of the dining hall. They were talking with several federal officers, and that gave Sharon quite a scare. She looked at Roger and motioned with her head toward the other end of the large room. He turned and saw his brother being questioned. Quickly excusing himself, he started walking away, but Sharon joined him, followed by the federal officers.

Phillip was quite calm when they reached him, but his girlfriend of sorts was upset that she was involved in such an affair.

Sharon gave her a sarcastic look and said, "Honey, I'll bet this is nothing new for you, so shut up!"

A look of anger flashed over Sadie's face, but Sharon's menacing tone kept the woman-of-the-night from blurting out more abuse.

The police and the federal officers had found no illegal drugs among the partygoers, so they sought success in a lengthy questioning of Phillip. They knew he had just been released from parole and they had information indicating that he had resumed activities in the drug market. He denied everything suggested by the authorities. Finally Sharon demanded that the investigating force leave. She was so adamant and disdainful that the officer in charge of the operation agreed. He sent word around the club that the bust was over and that it was time for the departure of the entire police and federal force.

Once the menace, as Sharon called them, had left, she mounted the bandstand and announced that dancing would continue. The mood or spell had been broken, however, and couples began making excuses for their departures. The host and hostess tried to keep the festivities going, but soon so many had left that their efforts were pointless. While Sharon felt that the event had been a success up to the time of the raid, she was greatly disappointed that the raid had ended the party.

When Phillip and Sadie approached Roger and Sharon to give their thanks and good-byes, the hostess would not look at them. Roger was a gentleman and accepted their compliments. As they walked away, Sharon said under her breath, "I'll never forgive him for this."

"We're not sure it was his fault," Roger protested.

"Oh, who else could it be? Didn't they question him the most? Besides, he had no business bringing that trollop with him. God, what a bitch! Where did she find her, in a ditch somewhere?"

Roger laughed, but Sharon did not think it was funny.

Paul and his date left without thanking the hosts, but Kevin and Juno came to their table. Sharon looked at their muscular legs and licked her lips.

Then she made comments about wishing she had been a shepherdess with them in a field somewhere.

Kevin laughed, familiar with Sharon's suggestive humor, but Juno was rather startled at her frankness and seductive manner. When they walked away, he asked, "Is she really such a strumpet?"

Kevin whispered, "I'm afraid so. I think she'd try to make the Pope if the circumstances were right."

Juno laughed, and they went to his car.

Arriving at home, they surprised Mrs. Dudley because they were early. When they told her about the events at the party, she listened calmly until the news about the raid was revealed. She, too, immediately thought of Phillip, but she was greatly relieved when they informed her that he was evidently innocent. She then informed the boys that Mr. Dudley was quite ill again. His latest treatments had affected his nerves and he was suffering from diarrhea. They suggested taking her to the hospital, but she had been informed that it would be better if she came the next day.

"Besides," she added, "you two are leaving in the morning, and I want you to get a good night's rest."

Kevin and Juno were soon inside the shower together, embracing and kissing. When they broke apart, Juno whispered as the water poured over them, "Next summer at the lake, we'll swim nude."

"Can you, there?"

"We have a private section and a pier. You'll love it."

They went into another embrace. When Kevin turned off the faucet, they both had erections. Kevin started down on his knees, but Juno pulled him up and said, "Let's get in bed and sixty-nine."

Kevin agreed.

As they dried themselves, Kevin softly said, "That's the first time you've mentioned next summer. I can't tell you how happy you've made me."

Juno dropped his towel and took Kevin into his arms. "Yes, we'll spend next summer together and then ..."

They looked into each other's eyes. What had been so wonderful was suddenly clouded with apprehension. They had taken the future for granted, but the time for decisions was approaching. They would no longer be schoolmates. How could they continue the joy of living that they had found together? It was too serious a topic, and both were eager for a rendezvous. The subject was dropped, and they rushed under the blanket on the bed. Their kisses were prolonged and hard, their embraces long and tight, and their sexual encounters sensual and satisfying. They loved as if they were bound forever and eternally happy. At that time they could not have imagined anything that could ever tear them apart. Their companionship was that rare love known by few.

The next morning Mrs. Dudley had a large breakfast prepared when the young men came down with their suitcases. She regretted their departure but knew it was necessary. They would both graduate from Williams College the following week. Whether Louise could attend the ceremony depended on George's condition. He was seriously ill. Also, there was that other woman. Would she dare visit George if she heard that the wife was away? Still, Louise had not given up hope and was planning the trip.

Kevin and Juno entered the kitchen in a jovial mood. Louise found their teasing and puns delightful and she looked at them with pleasure. Kevin was so boyish and cute with his blue eyes shining and his blond hair falling over his forehead. Juno was so youthful, yet quite masculine in appearance. After they made a couple of charming comments, Louise embraced both boys as they ate hotcakes and scrambled eggs. "You will come up for graduation, won't you?" Juno asked. Flattered that he should care, Mrs. Dudley nodded and said that she was making every effort to attend. Kevin stood up and embraced his mother, exclaiming how great that would be.

"We'll take of you!" Juno decreed with enthusiasm. Louise gave him another embrace.

"You boys are such a delight. I'm so sorry you're leaving."

"We are, too," they both blurted out together and then laughed.

When they loaded their suitcases in Juno's car, Sarah came through her fence and stood with Louise as the boys said their good-byes. Kevin thanked Mrs. Kale for giving his mother companionship and suggested that she accompany her on the trip up to Williamstown. She said she might consider it. Then Kevin, to her delight, embraced her, too. The boys drove off and everybody waved to each other.

"My, what glorious specimens of youthfulness!" Sarah exclaimed as the car went down the driveway.

"Yes, I pray so," Louise replied, but there was something in her tone that gave Sarah a hint of Mrs. Dudley's concern.

Without wincing, Sarah said, "They're young. It'll all work out. You'll see."

Louise was afraid she had revealed her secret concerns about the young men and quickly said, "Oh, yes. They'll both have a brilliant future, I'm sure." Changing the subject, Louise asked, "Can you really go with me for their graduation?"

"Why sure! We'll only be gone two days; and I love to drive in that part of the country."

Louise nodded. She decided at that moment that she would go even though her husband was ill. She confessed that she felt that she was neglecting her duty, but she welcomed the relief from daily hospital visits.

"Then it's a plan!" Sarah smiled as she rearranged her bun of salt and pepper hair. "We'll have an adventure!"

Chapter 8

Driving into the Catskill Mountains, Juno and Kevin joked and laughed about the various plans they had for living together forever. Because of their uncertainty about the future, the two young men went from the possible to the ridiculous very quickly. They would live at the Carino cabin among the tall pines and spend their time fishing, swimming, and making love. Or they might escape to New York City where nobody would notice that they were lovers. There was also the possibility of taking up residence in Paris, where they could avoid family entanglements. Perhaps a trip up the Amazon would open up a new world for them where they could live in native simplicity.

"Maybe put a bone through our noses," Kevin suggested.

Juno laughed but said that he had no desire for a life in New Guinea. Suddenly they were silent.

After a few moments, Kevin asked in a sad tone, "What are we going to do, Juno? I can't live without you."

There was no immediate answer. Finally Juno said, "I think we're going to have to live it as it comes."

"Work the problems out as they arise."

"Yes. What else can we do?" Juno asked and then confessed a problem that he had not discussed with his friend. His parents were continually talking about marriage. They even had chosen a girl for him, and they were bringing her to the graduation ceremony.

Kevin looked at his friend in horror.

Juno noticed the grimace and continued, "I didn't tell you earlier because I didn't want to think about it."

"Who is she?'

"Well, she's Italian, of course, and her father owns a flour factory. You know how that would appeal to my parents. We're in pasta, you know."

"What can we do?" When he didn't answer, Kevin asked, "You don't want to marry her, do you?"

"God! No!" Juno quickly barked. "She's a beast. Well, she's not that ugly, but so demure in the Italian way."

"What do you mean?"

"She pretends to be shy and humble, when I know that her whole family's a bunch of aggressive bastards."

Kevin was immediately heartsick. He turned his head and looked out the side window. A tear came into his right eye. He felt crushed.

Juno sensed his friend's sudden change of attitude and said, "Kevin, I won't marry her, don't worry. I mentioned it merely because it's one of the things we were talking about. We said that there would be obstacles to our being together and that we'd have to work them out. Well, I wanted you to know that a problem already existed."

Kevin turned and put an arm on Juno's shoulder. "I couldn't live without you now. I almost killed myself the last time we broke up."

"Don't talk like that. We're together, and we'll work it out, you'll see."

Juno turned on the radio and found some light music. For some time the two friends drove silently up into the mountains. Both were thinking of the future and their immediate problems.

Finally Juno said, "Kevin, we have two days at the cabin before we go on to Williams. Let's really enjoy them and not think about what I've said."

Kevin nodded. "Yes, let's pretend that they are our future and that it will go on forever."

The idea stayed in their minds. When they stopped for some provisions, they joked about what they should eat; when they drove on to the cabin, they recalled amusing incidents at the college; and when they arrived at the retreat, they hurried into their hiking clothes and went off into the wild. Walking through the tall pines, Juno sometimes put his arm around Kevin and the latter sometimes put an arm around his friend's waist. They were entranced with the beauty of their surroundings. Shroon Lake appeared occasionally through the trees in the valley and birds flew overhead among the pines. Juno and Kevin seemed one with nature and suddenly they stopped and fell into a tight embrace. They kissed as if they had never experienced such bliss. They were one, body and soul.

As they walked along they suddenly came upon a bluff overlooking a beautiful valley. "This is Lover's Leap. Shall we try it?" Juno remarked.

"No," Kevin replied and embraced his friend. "I haven't quit loving you yet."

"You'd better not!"

"I couldn't," Kevin said, shaking his head as the two walked ahead along the path on the ridge.

That evening at the cabin, Juno grilled steaks while Kevin peeled potatoes. Soon they ate with gusto. Their long drive to the cabin and their hike through the woods had tired them. After they finished a piece of apple pie from the store, they lay down on the rug before a fire in the main hall. They were enclosed in a tight embrace when they heard someone on the porch. They had just succeeded in breaking apart when the door opened. Juno's parents had driven up as a surprise. It was, however, much more than that for the young lovers, both of whom had erections. It was an incredible disappointment. Not only had the newly arrived interrupted an evening of contentment; they had brought on a feeling of doom. With them was the demure, soft-spoken Miss Angelina Vegoni, the intended bride for Juno. The two young men jumped up quickly and, after quickly adjusting their trousers, greeted the newcomers.

The Carinos burst onto the scene. Mama Sophia, short, fat and busty, screamed joyously as she ran for a hug with her dear son. Papa Giovanni, also short and overweight, quickly joined them, and the trio circled merrily as each tried speaking louder than the others.

Finally Mama shouted, "And look who's with us!" She pointed to Angelina, who was standing serene and poised by the door. "Come here, darling, and say 'hello' to our Juno!"

Miss Vegoni smiled coyly but looked at the floor without moving.

"Now, don't you be nervous," Mama called out and walked over to the young girl. Taking her by the arm, Mrs. Carino led her over to Juno. "Now, you two say 'hello'!"

Juno greeted her kindly. She nodded and looked at Mama, who laughed and said, "Isn't she a sweetheart?"

Kevin, who had been standing by the fireplace during the whole carnival scene, kept stepping a little backward in hopes that his erection would be completely unnoticed. Suddenly big Mama saw Kevin and shouted, "Oh, here's Juno's friend."

"Yes, of course," Mr. Carino agreed and walked over to Kevin for a handshake. "We've heard so much about you. We are so happy that Juno has such a great friend."

"Yes, my dear boy," Mama agreed and gave Kevin a great hug and kiss on the cheek as she grabbed hold of him.

Juno introduced Angelina, and Kevin smiled and nodded. Before he could speak, however, Mama, still all smiles, loudly asked, "Why are you sitting on the floor, you two?"

Her son quickly answered, "We had just finished eating and were getting ready for a drink just as you came up,"

"Silly boys. You could catch cold down there, and you have your graduation coming."

"Aww," Papa interrupted. "They're young men. They don't catch colds like some sissy."

Everyone laughed. Even Angelina smiled.

The evening, which had started so magically and seemed so complete, was quickly turning into a family hullabaloo. Comments and discussions about their relatives, their pasta factory, their plans for Juno, and their delight with Angelina were endless. Kevin could not have been more concerned. He saw nothing of himself in the plans the family was making for their son, and he sensed their eagerness for the dreaded wedding between Juno and Angelina. There was never a chance for adding anything to the conversation. Occasionally, out of politeness, one of the Carinos would ask Kevin a question, but they usually answered it themselves. Juno looked at Kevin sometimes and when their eyes met, they both sensed the heartache of their situation. The evening was boring, and it seemed that their future was being taken from them.

After several glasses of wine, which Mr. Carino had imported from his native Tuscany, Mama suddenly yawned, but she quickly laughed and asked forgiveness. It was then that she announced that Kevin and Juno would have to share a bedroom since Angelina would be in the guestroom. "And don't you worry, boys," she added. "I shall keep my ears open. You're not going to disturb our dear little Angelina tonight." Everyone laughed. Even dear little Angelina coyly smiled as she looked down at the floor. Kevin and Juno looked at each other for a moment but concealed their delight.

When the two young men were in bed, Juno slipped over onto Kevin and whispered, "We don't dare do anything tonight." Then he kissed his friend and eased over on his side of the bed.

"I know," Kevin whispered and followed Juno so that he could kiss him in return. They clung together for some time, softly kissing. When they began having erections, they parted, wondering when they would ever be together again.

It was to be much sooner than they expected. The next morning at breakfast, big Mama revealed that one of Juno's graduation presents was a week on the family boat on Lake George in the Adirondacks. In her enthusiasm, she blurted out, "Angelina's going, and Kevin, you must come, too. It would be so much fun to have a beautiful boy like you with us."

Kevin smiled and Juno said, "Yes, Kevin, do come with us. It'll be a lot of fun."

"Is it such a big boat?"

"Oh, we'll stay at the Georgian Lodge. We keep the boat there."

Kevin smiled. "Well, it sounds wonderful."

"Then it's settled," Mr. Carino added. "Kevin must join us."

Kevin responded. "You'll meet my mother at the graduation. If she hasn't made plans for me, I'll be glad to go."

"We shall make her let you go," Mrs. Carino laughed.

After breakfast Angelina, Juno, and Kevin took off on a hike into the surrounding woods and hills. She, of course, stymied the conversation. For Juno and Kevin, the wonders of nature and the beautiful scenes around them, which had so enthralled them the previous day, were no longer so exciting. If one of them remarked about a lovely view, Angelina would only say yes or nod. Sometimes she would smile when Kevin attempted some witticism, but for the most part, she was no company at all.

When the threesome reached Lovers' Leap, Angelina would not gaze down into the crevice. When Juno's eyes met Kevin's, he made a motion with his arm as if he would gladly push her off. Kevin turned his head and hid his smile. He was delighted that Juno did not care for their companion and felt more secure in his relationship with his friend. They would have a future together, he was sure.

That afternoon, after Mrs. Carino's lunch of Italian specialties, they all departed for Williamstown and the next day's graduation ceremony. Fortunately for Kevin and Juno, Angelina rode with the Carinos in their large Mercedes. It gave the boys a chance for intimate conversation.

"How could you live with her?" Kevin asked as they drove away from the cabin.

"Don't worry. I can't, and I won't."

"Does she ever say anything other than yes or no?"

"I can't say that I remember anything else. I just hope she says no when they try pushing her into the marriage they're planning."

"Does that flour mill mean so much to your father that he would make you marry her?"

"It's not just the mill. It's the Italian business. Her family is also from Tuscany and they're old landowners. A marriage into that family would be considered quite an honor. So it's pride and money."

"But my Gawd! Surely they wouldn't make you marry someone you didn't care for."

"They don't see it that way. They can't understand why I shouldn't care for her. She's Italian, and she's rich."

"But your family's rich, too."

"Yes, but we'd be even richer. You'd have to understand the Italian mind to realize what I'm up against. Like I said, it's not just money, although that's very important, it's the honor and the Italian mind-set. I'm in a heck of a position, but I promise you, I'll never marry her."

Kevin threw his arm around Juno and slipped over by him. After kissing his cheek, he sat back in his seat. For the rest of the drive, the two young men again felt the joy of their togetherness. They knew that they could never be parted. They looked at each other and laughed, they told each other amusing tales, and they winked and coyly smiled at every opportunity. It was the most pleasant ride in Kevin's life, and he was thrilled.

That evening at the Williamstown Lodge, the Carinos joined the Dudleys for dinner. Sarah Kale had stayed in her room, saying that she was tired from the drive. The group began their evening with drinks in a log-beamed lounge. The Carinos did most of the talking, and Louise, Kevin, and Juno added comments, mainly when questioned. When it was time for dinner, Angelina, who did not drink alcoholic beverages, joined the two families. In the dining room, Mrs. Carino took over as hostess and seated Angelina and Juno on one side of the table and Kevin and his mother on the other. The two young men glanced at each other, and their eyes said it all. They understood that Big Mama was also involved in encouraging a wedding between Juno and Angelina.

During the course of the dinner, Mr. Carino revealed that Kevin had been invited for a week with the Carinos on Lake George. "It will be such fun watching these young people have fun," Mama blurted out. "I can hardly wait."

And the evening droned on.

The next morning, on a bright and beautiful spring day, the graduation ceremony was held in the Assembly Hall. Kevin received his degree in art history and Juno in business administration. The Carino and Dudley families, both proud of their children, talked together after the presentations and then parted. Kevin, having his mother's approval for the week on the boat, drove off with Juno as they followed the Carinos' Mercedes on the way to Lake George. Louise and Sarah drove south to Stamford.

"I hope they don't make that nice boy marry that dud," Sarah commented as they conversed on the drive through the Taconic Mountains.

"Kevin told me that they want the marriage because her family has a flour factory."

Sarah laughed. "Money! Money! Money! That's really what it's all about, isn't it?"

"One would think so at times. Look at my Roger. I can't help but think that the Clarks' millions are on his mind. And look at my Phillip? Money has driven him into drugs."

"At least Paul doesn't seem inclined to think only of money."

"No, for him it's only sex."

"Well, he is a very handsome man. If I were young, I'm afraid I'd fall for his enticements."

Louise slowed the car down and looked at Sarah. "No you wouldn't. He treats women so badly. He brought home an angel, and I thought she might reform him, but it didn't work out. He's just on the prowl all the time."

"Like a big tomcat," Sarah laughed. "Well, when I was young I was attracted to that type. Who wants a powder puff in bed?" She laughed again.

"Sarah, you continue to amaze me. I have to admit again that you are certainly not the person I thought you were for so many years."

"Well, we never really got to know each other. You were so busy with your family, and I was busy with a dozen committees; besides, we've changed with time. When Socrates said, 'Know thyself,' he forgot that we're a different person every five years. Thank goodness I finally dropped all of that save-the-world stuff. I'm much happier with my animals."

After being silent a few moments, Louise said, "Sarah, you do seem very well read and you know life so well. May I ask your age? I'm sixty."

"I'm eight-three."

"No!" Louise said in astonishment.

"Yes, my dear, but, thanks to my animals, I'm healthy as a horse."

Louise laughed. "Now I suppose you're planning on getting a horse next door?"

Sarah laughed and shook her head. "No, I've got enough to take care of."

"So do I," Louise commented and thought of George.

"Your husband is having a lot of problems, isn't he?"

Louise nodded. "I hate to bore you with it, but honestly, sometimes I just don't think I can stand it. Right now he's started a terrible habit. He dreams that he's in the bathroom and makes a terrible mess in the bed. So he requires nursing all the time."

"You poor dear! You must be very worried about him."

"Well, I'm still glad we went. I was so thrilled to see Kevin and Juno so happy."

"They're awfully cute young men."

"That's what worries me."

Sarah was silent for a few moments. "You think they're gay?"

Louise shook her head. "Sarah, please. Let's not talk about it now. I'd better concentrate on my driving. I don't want to cry."

"There's nothing to cry about! Seems it's in every species. Just recently read an article about female macaques. Heavens, the things they do beats any porn movie."

"Sarah, you do amaze me at times."

After a few moments of silence, Sarah said softly, "Don't make the mistake I did."

"What do you mean?"

"Remember, I told you that I drove my son away."

"But your son is married and has a child."

"That doesn't mean anything. I drove him into that marriage, and he is not a happy person."

"Oh, Sarah, you mean he was that way and married anyway?"

"You might put it that way. I think it was to please me that he did it, and I lost him because of it."

"Why?"

"As I told you before, he ran off to Montana. To stop my pleas, he married. But they are miserable together. I can tell. It will end in a divorce, I'm sure."

"Oh, dear, what should I do about Kevin?"

"Well, I would suggest that you do nothing. It's not the end of the world, you know. And you could lose him. Believe me, that's when it hurts. I just wish I had left my son alone and let him live his own life."

Mrs. Dudley thought of Kevin and Juno. Finally she said, "Well, I didn't object to his going on the trip with the Carinos."

"That's good, and I just hope they have a great holiday. That's a beautiful area at Lake George."

"I'm sure it will be wonderful," Louise responded, and her silent thoughts lingered on the two young men.

The Carinos arranged for rooms overlooking Lake George. Juno and Kevin arrived first at the luxury resort and checked in. They had adjoining rooms and were delighted with the exquisite view from their windows and the modern decor. Each room was furnished with the finest accoutrements. When Juno saw the Jacuzzi in his bathroom, he yelled for Kevin to come over. Kevin laughed when he saw it and said, "Guess we'll spend some time in there."

"You'd better believe it," Juno answered and grabbed his friend. They wrestled as Kevin tried pulling himself out of Juno's grasp. Both young men were teasing, and they were soon in a tight embrace. Their lips came together and held a long time. When they parted, they thought they saw someone on the balcony of the room.

"We'd better be more careful," Kevin commented.

"It was probably just one of the help. I'm sure they're used to everything here."

"Well, I hope he didn't see us."

"He won't tell," Juno said and closed the curtain. When he returned, they again embraced. "Our biggest problem will be avoiding that dumb Angelina. She bores me to tears."

"Don't you dare marry her!" Kevin smiled.

"That'll be the day!" Juno exclaimed and hugged him again. As they kissed, the phone rang.

The Carinos had arrived, and they had news. Juno's sister was joining them for a few days. He listened as his father and mother outlined the plans they had made for their stay. There would be boating, hiking, and relaxing. It would be a true family get-together.

"Yes, that's wonderful," Juno responded when necessary and agreed to meet the family for dinner. When he hung up the phone, he turned to Kevin and said, "Oh, shit! My sister's coming."

"What's wrong with that?"

"You'll see. She's a nosy bitch. She's probably coming to help Angelina nail me to a wall."

"She wants you to marry her?"

Juno nodded. "I just hope she doesn't bring her brats."

Kevin laughed. "It seems I'm in the middle of a real family outing."

Juno suggested they try the Jacuzzi, and they immediately undressed. Soon they were submerged in warm, foamy water, embracing and caressing each other.

That evening the family gathered in the gracious dining room for dinner. Juno's sister, Violetta Longhini, a fairly plump lady with long, curly, black hair, was talking with Angelina when Juno and Kevin entered. She immediately called out in her high soprano voice, "Ah, bambino!"

Leaving Angelina, Violetta rushed over and threw her arms around her brother, kissing him on the cheeks and talking. She ignored Kevin completely until Juno finally said, "Will you be quiet for a second. I want you to meet my friend Kevin."

Violetta looked over at Kevin and nodded with a faint smile but then continued talking, mixing Italian phrases in with her English. Kevin had the distinct feeling that she was suspicious of her younger brother and was slighting his friend on purpose. He assumed that there had been earlier incidents in which Violetta had caught on. She seemed the prying type, and Juno had already mentioned that she was nosy. Kevin disliked her immediately.

When Big Mama and Daddy entered with Violetta's three children, two girls and a boy, all in grade school, there was another uproar as the children fought each other for places at the preset table. They paid no attention to Kevin or Juno but pushed each other aside as they tried for various chairs. Mama, of course, was bawling them out, but her smile showed that she was only admiring them. Violetta paid no attention to her children but did ask Juno to sit by Angelina. The only chair left for Kevin was at the other end of the table by Big Mama.

A fine Italian dinner was served with an excellent red wine. The antipasto was well seasoned and when someone commented that it tasted like Mama had made it at home, she confessed with a broad smile that she had talked with the chef in the kitchen. They all laughed. Kevin enjoyed the enthusiasm and humor, but he noticed that Violetta avoided him in conversation and continually talked about Angelina and Juno. Partly enjoyable and partly boring, the dinner finally ended. Then Violetta suggested that they all take a walk along the beach. Again there was a hoopla, and the children ran for their sweaters. When they all gathered again on the patio, Mama and Papa sat on the veranda and watched their tribe walk off into the cool evening.

Violetta suddenly showed a great interest in Kevin. She took him by the arm and asked whether she could walk with him. He knew why, of course, but agreed immediately.

When they set off, she teasingly said, "Now, Juno, you and Angelina behave while I talk with Kevin."

She laughed and led Kevin away from the other couple. Juno had no choice and escorted Angelina away, arm in arm. Meanwhile the children were running ahead, yelling, jumping, and shouting comments about the sand, the moon, and the boats.

Suddenly one of the brats fell and skinned his knee. Violetta examined it and shouted for help. Juno and Kevin ran and took the kid from her grasp. The wound was minor, but Violetta demanded that they return for medical aid. The young men agreed and carried the patient back to the motel. The evening, which had been drawn out by Violetta's schemes, was brought to a close by her role as Florence Nightingale. Everyone retired for the night.

Back in their room, Juno and Kevin discussed the unpleasant evening activities. Violetta's arrival had diminished their enthusiasm for the vacation. They lay down on the bed and fell into each other's arms. After a few moments, Kevin said, "I wish we could lie like this forever."

"That's a long time!"

"It's how long I want to be with you."

Juno rolled over and kissed Kevin. They were silent until the latter asked, "What are we going to do?"

"About what?" Juno whispered.

"About us. We're finishing college and fate is taking us in different directions."

"What do you mean?"

"Your family will want you to go into their business, and I'll go either to grad school or accept the position the museum has offered."

"But if you're in grad school at Yale, as we had planned, we can still live together. That's not far from the factory."

"But I still haven't been accepted. If that doesn't go through, I'll have to take the museum position."

"Then we'll be together on weekends."

"I couldn't bear being away from you all week."

Juno kissed him again, and they embraced passionately and lovingly.

Suddenly they heard a strange noise. Juno jumped up and ran into the other room. A slip of paper was in front of the door. He picked it up and read, "Two thousand will keep me from telling on you." He took it back into the bedroom and handed it to Kevin.

"Who could it have been?"

Juno thought for a moment. "Well, it could be the person we thought we saw on the balcony yesterday." He paused. "It could even be Violetta."

"She'd do that?"

"Not for the money, but to scare us."

"Well, she succeeded."

Juno and Kevin looked at each other, lost in thought. Finally Kevin said, "Take me home. I'll say that my mother called and that my dad is worse."

Juno didn't respond, but walked over to the large window overlooking the lake. After a few moments, he said, "No, let's you and I go back to the cabin."

"What excuse can we give?"

"What you said. That your dad is very ill."

"What if your parents call you at my house?"

"They won't, and we can spend a couple of days before I take you home."

"That would be wonderful."

Juno ran and leaped on the bed. In seconds he had his arms around Kevin, and they were embracing. "Then that's what we'll do. We'll escape from whoever it is."

"What if the person tells, since we won't pay up?"

"I'll just deny it."

The two young men drew closer together and looked into each others' eyes. "I really love you," Kevin whispered, and Juno kissed him.

The next day, in spite of Violetta's protests and Mama and Papa's surprise, the young men prepared for their departure in Juno's sports car. The excuse about Kevin's father satisfied Juno's parents, but not his sister. She suggested that Kevin take a train or plane, but Juno would not hear of it. Then she reviled Juno for leaving Angelina when she had come on the trip for his sake. He ignored her comments and explained that he had more of an obligation to his friend, whom he had invited, than to Angelina, whom Violetta had included in the party. She was furious but finally gave up. She even began pretending that she was so sorry that Kevin's father was so ill and that it required his presence at home. When the young men drove off, Violetta stood with the family in the parking lot and waved and threw kisses. Under his breath, Juno whispered, "Didn't I tell you she was a bitch?"

Chapter 9

The next day, after arriving home from Williams College, Louise was preparing for her obligatory drive to the hospital when she heard the front door bell. She hurried downstairs and looked out one of the glass windows around the portal. To her surprise, Paul's former girlfriend Delores was standing outside. It was an inopportune time, but Louise opened the door and kindly greeted the visitor. Before she could explain her need for a hasty departure, however, the beautiful girl fell into her arms, sobbing pitifully.

Louise led her into the family room and sat her down on a couch. "My dear, what is the matter?"

Delores cried. Whenever she tried talking, she would look at the floor and cry again. It was obvious that she was ashamed and humiliated. Louise, in an effort to divert the girl's anxiety, explained the urgency of her own departure for the hospital. Delores apologized for bothering her and said that she would leave. Louise, distracted by the young lady's behavior, explained that she would call the hospital later and check on George. That said, she asked for an explanation from the distraught girl.

After some efforts, Delores finally calmed down and expressed her feelings. Louise heard so much self-debasement that she finally interrupted and asked, "Delores, what is the matter? I realize that you're greatly distressed, but you haven't told me why."

After taking a few deep breaths, Delores took out a handkerchief and blew her nose. Finally able to speak, she said, "I'm pregnant!" Then she began crying again.

Explanation was not needed. Louise had thought of the possibility and understood the implications immediately. Her son Paul had taken advantage of the young lady and then abandoned her.

Anger rose in Louise's breast, and her hands closed into fists as she gazed at the floor. Her world was already falling apart and now this! She wanted desperately to slap Paul's face. How could he sink so low? Well, she thought to herself, he's not going to get away with it. He's going to marry her! Looking up at Delores, Mrs. Dudley assured her son's victim that the family would take care of her. Then she asked, "Have you told Paul?"

Shaking her head, Delores said, "No. I've tried to see him several times, but he always makes excuses. Also, I'm so ashamed."

"That I understand. Well, you need not worry any longer. Once Paul knows, I'm sure he will do the proper thing. I know he cares for you very much."

Another bout of crying took place before Delores could say, "No, he doesn't. He avoids me. I don't know what to do."

Louise's rage again swelled up in her heart. She felt humiliation. Her fine son Paul, the idol of all women, was a heel, and she realized it. In her mind she assured herself that she would make him accept his obligation.

"Mrs. Dudley, was I right in coming to you?"

"Certainly! And you may stay here." Suddenly Louise remembered her husband and told Delores that, after she called the hospital, she would take her home if she wished.

Leaving the young lady, Louise walked into the library and called the hospital. They informed her that George was undergoing surgery. Internal bleeding had started, and her husband's condition was very serious. It was suggested that she notify her family. This suggestion only intensified her concern. Contacting her sons was no longer pleasant, but it must be done, even if it meant enduring their lies again.

When Louise called the Georgian Resort at Lake George, she was informed that her son had checked out. She then asked for Mr. Carino. When he answered the phone, Louise asked why Kevin had left. It was then that the Carinos found out that their son and his friend had lied. Louise caught on that something was amiss, but she could not discern what it might be. She had too much on her mind. When Mr. Carino said that he would find the boys and have Kevin call her, Louise thanked him and hung up the phone.

What have I done? she wondered for several minutes before continuing her calls.

Fortunately, Paul was at his desk when she called his law firm. Before she could tell him about his father or mention Delores, he blurted out his own news. He had planned on calling her and was delighted that she had called. His firm was planning a move to the World Trade Towers in lower Manhattan. He was very excited. "We'll be on the seventy-fifth floor of the East building. Just think of the view. It should be spectacular!"

Louise agreed.

Paul informed her that he would be at the hospital in the late afternoon. He could not leave immediately but would be there for sure by four o'clock.

Louise thanked him and started to mention Delores, but he again began talking about the move to the Trade Towers. He assured his mother that it would be a dream come true. Louise decided that she would just take Delores to the hospital with her and confront Paul when he arrived. She was thoroughly disgusted with him, but she recalled her own secret and thought that maybe her own genes had affected her children. Yet there was no time for dwelling on such a disturbing thought.

Roger was also in his office when Louise called. He was distressed at her news but explained that he could not possibly be at the hospital until the evening. He was involved in a very important meeting and part of it would be held during a dinner. There was no way he could excuse himself. Louise lied, saying that she understood and also that she wasn't sure just how serious George's condition was. If Roger came late, it would be fine. He thanked his mother and hung up the phone.

Roger then dialed Sharon. When she answered, he said, "Listen, I'll have to leave early this evening. Dad's in the hospital again and evidently in a serious condition."

"Listen, you bastard, you're not going to spoil my dinner party for that. He's going to be in and out of the hospital for years, so don't make a big to-do out of it."

Roger's voice showed his oncoming anger. "Well, I'll have to go. Don't you have brains enough to understand? Mother called. My father's ill."

"Don't raise your fucking voice at me. Haven't you caught on that your dear, sweet mother loves to interfere in our lives?"

Roger was silent. He was afraid of what he might say.

"Well," Sharon continued, "doesn't she? Listen, I was planning to fuck you through the floor after the party tonight."

"Well, after I go to the hospital, you can. Can't you calm that pussy of yours down for a few hours?"

"When the iron's hot, use it!"

"I'll use it, you cunt. I'll fuck you so hard you won't walk for a week."

"Wow," Sharon's voice expressed her delight. "Now you're talking. Come on over!"

Roger's tone was again angry. "Can't you get it through that pussy face of yours that I've got to go to the hospital."

"Oh, all right. See you later." Sharon hung up the phone with a loud crash.

Roger twisted his lips and grimaced. If Sharon had been with him he would have given her a sock in the face. The word "bitch" poured forth from his mouth over and over. He picked up a pillow from a chair and threw it across the room. His anger was stronger than he had ever felt in his relations with Sharon. She had no respect for his family. Her cunt was her driving force. He thought of his mother and wondered how he could bring Sharon into the Dudley family. She was bound to be a humiliation for the matron of the clan all their lives. Yet, after he had calmed down, he concluded that his marriage must take place. There was too much to gain from the relationship with Sharon's family. He would marry the slut and be rich and well connected. He had chosen such a life because it would give him the success he wanted. In his opinion, that was all that mattered. His mother might object to Sharon, but his success would bring great respect and prestige to the Dudley family. That aspect, he concluded, would console his mother.

When Roger arrived at Sharon's Fifth Avenue apartment, the door was open and his fiancée was standing in the hall giving instructions to a hired maid. The décolleté of Sharon's dress was cut in the middle to her waist. When she saw Roger, she abruptly ignored the hired help and walked quickly toward him. Each of her large, full breasts seemed eager for a breath of air and fought furiously as they tried exposing themselves. Roger opened his arms and Sharon fell against his body. "Well, this is more like it," her husky voice bellowed. "Now come in here and help me."

Roger leaned forward for a kiss, but Sharon backed away. "Don't mess up the makeup, silly. You'll get plenty of that later. Come with me, and tell this idiot girl what she should do as the guests arrive. I've got to see what the chef's up to now. Her name's Conchita, or something like that."

The embarrassed young Mexican maid stepped aside when Sharon walked by. Roger, wishing he could kick his beloved down the hall for being so rude, smiled kindly and walked over to the young girl. With his smattering of Spanish and her broken English, the two discussed the plan for the evening. When Sharon returned, she grabbed Roger and pulled him into her bedroom where she pushed him on her king-sized bed. Immediately she was on top of him and unzipping his pants.

"We can't now," he exclaimed, trying to sit up.

"Lie still. We're not going to. I just want a few sucks on that big cock of yours before I play Mrs. Rich-bitch."

"What about your makeup?"

"Shut up!"

Roger looked at the ceiling as he surrendered and fell back on the bed. Within seconds Sharon had pulled out his penis and was licking it. At that moment the door opened and there was Conchita, gazing with her mouth gaping.

"Get out, you idiot!" Sharon yelled.

The girl quickly closed the door.

After a few more licks, Sharon stood up and angrily mumbled, "Honestly, the help one gets these days! I really should hire robots."

Roger slipped off the bed and began putting his penis back into his pants.

"Why don't you leave it out for the guests to see," Sharon suggested with a smile as she picked up a brush from her vanity table. "The ladies would envy me all night."

Roger zipped up his britches. "I'm surprised you don't talk though your pussy instead of your dirty mouth."

"Oh," Sharon exclaimed in a haughty, naughty voice, walking toward him and swinging her hips back and forth. "Has your little sugarcums a dirty mouth? You poor thing! Well, bimbo, kiss that mouth right now, or you'll never get another blow job."

Roger grabbed her and kissed her on the mouth.

"Oh, you've messed up my lipstick, you ass."

"You did that on my cock!"

"Oh, shut up and go help that idiot girl receive our guests."

Roger curled his lip as if to mock her and walked out of the bedroom. In a short while the party was complete. Sharon had rounded up a group of socialites whose only interest was in making money. During cocktails Judge Finley, who was known as a legal charlatan, entertained the group by relating the particulars of a recent divorce case in which a wife had almost bitten off her husband's penis. Everyone was greatly amused, and several made puns that increased the hilarity. Sharon added to the merriment by grabbing her fiancé in the crotch and saying, "Roger, dear, just remember, if you ever try to leave me, I shall keep something for remembrance." All the guests laughed.

When the conversation became quite vulgar, Roger noticed that Conchita was casting her eyes downward when especially obscene words were used. He pitied her and wondered if anyone else in the group gave a thought to the young girl's feelings. Probably not, he concluded, and it made him think about the society he was marrying into. His mother would have been appalled at their behavior. Yet coarseness and crudity were acceptable, and he could not be old-fashioned.

Suddenly Mrs. Clarine Cox, an extremely wealthy Manhattan hostess who had never worked in her life, commented, "They really should build a high wall around the country to keep immigrants out."

"You having trouble with help, honey?" asked Mrs. Dumont Peters, known as Dewy because her eyes were always tearful from excessive makeup.

"They drive me crazy," Clarine answered, flipping the ashes from her cigarette into a Picasso-signed ashtray. "If I didn't have dear old Anna to run things for me, I'd go nuts."

"Well," chimed in Judge Finley, "that's not a bad idea, Clarine, but too costly, even though they're coming over the borders like ants."

"It seems to me that I'm paying enough taxes to build two walls!" Clarine rebutted, looking at the ceiling as if she were at her wit's end.

Roger noticed Conchita's embarrassment and asked, "Clarine, when did your ancestors come over?"

"Oh, that's different," she quickly replied, giving Roger a look of surprise.

Sharon sensed that Roger was planning a tirade in support of the immigrants, She gave him a stern look and abruptly interceded. "Conchita," she called out, "go ask the chef when dinner will be ready."

All the guests looked toward the young Mexican girl as if they had seen her for the first time.

There was a slight pause before Dewy said, "I found the cutest purse at Saks yesterday."

Roger was quite bored at times but joined in the conversation whenever he could make a witticism or compliment someone in an oblique manner. He was sure that he was playing the social game quite well. While he considered several of the guests to be ignoramuses, he laughed at their stories and jokes along with the others. The pettiness and mediocrity of those present showed Roger the sort of people Sharon attracted. They were, in his opinion, loathsome, but he still felt that he must play their game. He was confident that success was through such types and not through the great virtues of the Dudley family's faith and traditions.

After dinner the party returned to the salon, where Roger kept looking at the clock. Sharon noticed his anxiety and prolonged the conversation. When anyone suggested that it was time for their departure, the hostess found a topic that kept them seated. Finally Roger simply stood up and excused himself because of his father's illness.

Everyone was sympathetic except Sharon. She followed him to the front door and said, "You asshole. How dare you break up my party!"

Slipping into his raincoat, Roger whispered, "We'll go through that again later."

With a sneer on her face, Sharon replied as she opened the door, "If I'm here!"

Roger grinned sarcastically and said, "Be here, bitch!" Then he left for the hospital, fuming.

At the medical facility he was confronted with another dilemma. Outside his father's room, his mother and brother Paul were in a heated argument as they stood by a young lady who was seated nearby, crying into her handkerchief.

Roger suddenly remembered Delores and guessed the situation without being told. Mrs. Dudley was insisting that a marriage be arranged immediately, and Paul was desperately seeking another means of solving their predicament. Louise was appealing to her son's sense of honesty, nobility, and sincerity; Paul agreed with everything she uttered but found excuses for not fulfilling his obvious obligation. Certainly he cared for Delores, but he assured them that he was in love with someone else. Marriage would be honorable, but in his opinion it would not be a logical solution.

When he suggested an abortion, his mother stamped her feet and placed her arms around the weeping victim. "How could you even propose such a thing! You, a Dudley!"

Paul shook his head. "Oh, Mother, this is the twenty-first century, not the sixteenth." Mrs. Dudley turned from her son and began crying. He placed his arm around her, but she backed away. "But mother, don't you see that if we marry, we'll never be happy."

His comment only increased the misery of the two ladies. They cried even more intensely.

Roger realized that he would have to interrupt. He walked over by his mother and said, "Let's calm down. We should discuss this at home, not here." Louise nodded in approval and wiped tears from her eyes. Delores simply stared at the floor.

The scene was abruptly interrupted by two nurses who came very quickly down the hall and rushed into Mr. Dudley's room. They were soon followed by a doctor and two attendants pushing a roller bed. It was obvious that something serious had happened. Before the family could enter the room, an attendant stopped them so that Mr. Dudley could be transported to another section of the hospital. It was definitely an emergency because the medical staff seemed in a great rush, and no one would talk with the family. Naturally they followed the procession, but they were stopped at the door of an operating room.

"What can it mean?" Louise asked aloud, looking at no particular member of the family.

Her sons tried consoling her, but they admitted that the situation was evidently serious. A few moments later a doctor came out and explained that Mr. Dudley had apparently had a heart attack during his postoperative recovery period. There was definite cause for alarm, and he suggested that the family stay close by.

"Should I call my other sons?" Louise asked, her face showing fright. The doctor answered affirmatively.

Slowly and silently the family walked toward the waiting room. Delores asked whether she could leave, and Paul replied that he would take her home.

He bent his arm out for her acceptance. She looked up at him. When she saw his smile, she put her arm through his. Louise watched them walk away and felt as though her son had realized his responsibility.

Magazines were strewn around the coffee table in the waiting room. Louise picked up a *House Beautiful* and sat down for what she expected to be a long wait. In a few minutes, however, another doctor rushed into the operating room. Two nurses, pushing some kind of machine, quickly followed. Louise stood and moved near the door. She could hear nothing, but suddenly two doctors came out. They started past Louise, but one happened to look in her direction and stopped. He asked whether she was Mrs. Dudley. When she nodded, he inquired whether she had any of her family with her. Sensing that the worst had occurred, she opened her purse and took out a handkerchief. The doctor asked her to be seated. As she turned, she started falling forward, but the doctor caught her and seated her on a sofa. When he felt assured that she would not faint, he sat down beside her.

After wiping her tears away, Louise asked whether her husband had passed away,

"Yes," the surgeon replied and softly expressed his regret that resuscitation had failed after Mr. Dudley experienced a severe stroke during the operation.

Louise sat back on the sofa and cried. After a few moments, the doctor asked whether there was anyone he could call for her.

Louise shook her head and said hesitantly through her tears, "One of my sons is here. I shall just wait for him."

When he appeared confident that Mrs. Dudley was stable, the doctor said that he would have coffee sent to her. After again expressing his regret, he left.

Wiping her eyes, Louise looked around the room. For some reason she thought of an incident one morning during her youth when her mother told her that daydreams sometimes come true. The idea had made her very happy because the boy she liked at school had walked her home, and she was in love. The memory gave her a sense of joy, but the thought of her first love brought her back to her present predicament. Her husband of so many years was dead, and she was alone. She wondered what would have happened if she had grown up and married the boy who had attracted her so many years ago. The pleasantness of recalling the past suddenly passed away. She was now confronted with the reality of a funeral for the man she had once loved. If he had been faithful, which she had assumed through their marriage, her burden would not be very painful. Yet she now knew that he had not been, and the realization had frozen her heart. Somehow she did not care anymore, but still she knew that she must go through the formalities that society required. It seemed unfair, but what could she do? For the sake of her sons and the family reputation, a viewing would be a necessity. Yet it all seemed so pointless now. Again her thoughts raced into the past, seeking relief from happier days. Louise did not know how long she sat and reminisced before Roger arrived, but the time spent in her memories seemed brief.

Roger came in and took command of the situation. He drove Louise home and began making phone calls. First he notified the minister of the Episcopal Church that the family had attended for years. Then he called a family friend in their social club and asked about funeral parlors. He highly recommended the Walton Funeral Home because it was a most prestigious establishment. Roger called the funeral director and made the necessary arrangements. Then he returned to Louise in the family room and explained the arrangements he had made. She thanked him and sent him home. Now she was definitely alone. A glass of sherry and an empty house was all that was left of her thirty-eight years of marriage. She sat looking at the fireplace and thought of her husband.

"George was an adulterer. Does that mean he's in hell?" Suddenly she smirked. "How funny he would have thought that was! He couldn't have cared less. I'm the one in hell. I have to face all the regrets and kindnesses that will come from friends and acquaintances. How can I stand them? I'll just have to, for my sons' sakes, but what hypocrisy that will be." She sipped the sherry. "Who would have thought that my marriage would end this way? It wasn't at all as I thought it was. What a laugh." Her thought made her smile, and she retired and slept well.

Mr. George Dudley was ready for viewing the next afternoon from four to six. Louise wore a black hat with a veil that covered her face. Sarah, who had accepted an invitation to be with Louise, complimented her on her somber apparel.

Louise whispered, "I wanted to wear yellow polka-dots!"

Sarah laughed. Together the friends went to the funeral parlor at four o'clock, and Louise's sons began entering soon afterward. There was a surprising number of flowers around the casket, which Louise considered an extension of the hypocrisy in the whole affair. Yet she played the role of the widow and accepted the greetings of the large group of attendees.

The funeral the next day was not as tiresome. It even had moments of pleasure. While Phillip was absent because he was in prison, being seated with three of her sons was thrilling because it reminded her of happier days. She wondered whether they would ever give her such satisfaction again. How proud she was to be escorted by three such handsome men. Louise felt triumphant. The Dudleys were impressive. She had done her part in fulfilling the family traditions. It did not matter that her sons were not upholding the standards that she desired; on that day they were giants, and the gathered guests, in her opinion, could only observe her family with envy. Her own secret indiscretion seemed well hidden, so she could hold her head high among the congregation.

When the funeral dirge began, Louise quickly lost interest. The eulogy seemed a fabrication of assumptions that were not true. After a while, her mind concentrated on the present. Yes, she had four fine sons. Roger was marrying for money and position as if those things would bring him contentment; Phillip was dealing in drugs, which could only keep him in prison; Paul was marrying through obligation, which would not bring him satisfaction; and Kevin had that dreadful disease of the mind, which could only bring unhappiness. Yet there was now the added fear of the exposure of her ghastly secret. In her opinion, she was now as guilty as her sons in demeaning the family name. Tears filled her eyes. The guests assumed that she was grieving for her husband, but she was thinking of her own failure and the future of her children. When the service ended, Louise walked out with Roger, followed by her other sons. She was not as full of pride as she had been when she entered. The Dudleys were hiding their shame.

Friends and acquaintances who attended the graveside gathering at the cemetery remarked among themselves later that there had been no remorse evident among the family members. The widow stood solemn-faced and stared at the coffin. The sons seemed unaffected by the burial of their father.

When Sarah mentioned comments that she had heard, Louise nodded. "How could I cry when I knew that the man I loved deceived me? And my sons? Did they ever really care? I look back and realize that they always thought only of themselves. Their own interests were important, not what I or my husband wanted. There was no family comradeship or closeness. We were bound to each other, of course, but we were all individuals doing our own thing. If one had dropped out, it would not have mattered. One has, and you see, it hasn't mattered. We are too busy for remorse. How sad it is. And I thought we were the perfect family."

Chapter 10

Rarely was a marriage so gloomy. Nobody was enthusiastic, especially the bride and groom. Delores had refused the nuptials numerous times because she knew Paul did not love her. She would have preferred rearing the child alone. Louise, however, would not abandon her. She insisted that Paul marry, in spite of his protests. In desperation she threatened him with disinheritance, the one thing she knew her son feared. He realized that the Dudley trust, based on the wealth from the sale of his grandfather's machine factory, was now governed by his mother. He had always counted on his share for his future plans. If he didn't marry Delores, he would lose his dream. And his mother had offered a substantial sum from the trust if he carried out his obligation. There was no choice. His family honor, so often mentioned by his mother—and the money from the family trust—ruled his fate. He finally consented. Delores did not believe his change of mind, but her despair and Louise's pleading won her over. A quiet, simple ceremony was performed at the city courthouse. Delores and Paul were one.

It was quite a contrast when Sharon and Roger were married. Long Island society, especially in the Hamptons, was abuzz for weeks after the affair. The grand entrance hall of the Clarkes' huge, pretentious mansion had been turned into an orchid arboretum. A world-renowned horticulturist, working with a reputable florist, had created an atmosphere of make-believe. The unusual colors and forms of the various orchid species revealed that they had been flown in not only from Hawaii, but from all parts of the world, even as far away as the jungles of Sumatra. The wedding ceremony was held in the large niche at the bottom of the mansion's wide, white staircase. After exchanging diamond wedding rings and becoming man and wife, Sharon, whose exquisite lace dress must have kept the nuns of the famous French Lurgere Convent busy for weeks, ran up the stairs and threw her bouquet of white orchids, woven together by a long genuine pearl necklace, to her close friend Sarah, who was standing in the place that Sharon had instructed her.

It was assumed by many that the young ladies had even practiced the event, which took place before the guests were invited into the overly decorated dining room. Fortunately the weather was warm and pleasant, which allowed the French doors of the large room to be open. Otherwise the aroma of the thousands of red roses among the orchids might have been overwhelming. Sharon and Roger whisked through the wedding party and cut the massive wedding cake, which was covered with enough white confection-sugar angels and cupids to adorn St. Peter's. The champagne was Rothschild, of course, and Sharon's brother was soon drunk and falling on, or bumping into, one guest after another. While the wedding party drank and ate, the married couple slipped up a back staircase and changed into their travel clothes. A white Rolls Royce convertible was waiting to rush them to Kennedy Airport for their flight to a secret destination, which was later revealed as Sun City, South Africa. That had been Sharon's idea, of course, and Roger helplessly agreed. The wedded couple had not spent much time amid the incredibly fanciful and expensive world that Mr. Clarke had financed for his only daughter, but he was satisfied that he had shown society how a wedding should be managed. Society did not particularly agree, and negative comments about the affair circulated for some time.

A third wedding that June also strongly affected the Dudley family. Juno was married to Angelina, which gave the Carinos the flour factory they needed but almost gave Kevin a nervous breakdown. It seemed to him that the wedding of his beloved friend was the result of a ridiculous incident. It was one of those events in life that happens so innocently and causes much grief. When Mr. Carino answered Mrs. Dudley's telephone call about her ailing husband, he realized that he had caught his son in a lie; further thoughts on the subject aroused suspicions. He drove to the family cabin and discovered the young men in a bedroom engaged in wild sex. His disgust made him shout vulgarities and threats; he demanded that his son marry Angelina immediately. Juno submitted to his father's desires, and Kevin returned home completely humiliated and distraught. The wonderful life he had envisioned with his lover was not to be. He felt betrayed by circumstances beyond his control, and the future seemed empty and pointless. His life seemed over and, as many do in their youth, he considered suicide. His spirit, however, was partially revived by his acceptance into the graduate school at Yale. It meant that he would not be far from Juno and that a meeting would be possible. He was sure that his friend would come to him, so he left early for the campus and rented an apartment.

Again Louise was alone in her large, comfortable home, but not for long. To her utter amazement, Phillip, looking very tired and smelling of whiskey, returned one day with three suitcases. When he asked if he could stay, she agreed, but with great apprehension. Not only was she afraid of their dark secret, but his appearance and lack of explanation caused her concern. Having been through many painful and expensive ordeals with him, Louise inquired. He brushed off her questions with a plea for a later conversation. Since he could hardly stand on his feet, the mother helped her son up to his old room and let him collapse on the bed. He was quickly asleep, and the greatly worried Mrs. Dudley left him. There was no point in talking with him when he was drunk and probably on drugs. Yet how could they live together? They would eventually confront their sexual liaison and his drug addiction. That could only cause problems. What was she to do?

The next morning Louise invited Sarah in for a cup of coffee and expressed her anxieties about Phillip's return. The neighbor immediately asked whether Louise had inspected her son's suitcases for drugs.

Louise shook her head.

"Well, it would be too late now. Besides, if he's drinking, he might not have had money for drugs. I'd be very careful about your purse."

Louise was astounded that Sarah would suggest that Phillip would steal from her, but Sarah only smiled. "You can't imagine the stress a drug addict goes through if he needs a fix. They'll kill for it. It's a proven fact. Besides, if he's been on it more than five years, his brain is cooked, and there's nothing you can do."

Louise broke into tears. Sarah apologized, explaining that she only offered advice. Louise nodded in agreement and wiped her eyes. Then she asked Sarah what she would do in such a situation. "There are several things I'd do. First of all, be sure your checkbooks and valuables are in safe keeping. If he becomes desperate, and the whiskey implies that he might be, then he would be capable of anything for money. It would happen only because he absolutely needed it, but that's the dangerous aspect. Even you could not stand in his way."

"Oh, Sarah! What are you saying? You mean he might even harm me, his mother?"

Sarah nodded and continued. "And it would not be his fault. I know you've reared your sons in as fine a way as possible, but he would no longer be your son if he's truly desperate. He would be a thing needing attention. That is when you must be ready for the worst thing a mother could face. You must inform the federal authorities and let them take him to a rehabilitation center."

"Turn in my own son?"

Sarah nodded. "It's the only way to help him. You cannot fight such a thing yourself. You have to have professional aid. I knew one mother who refused and her son wasted his life and her money on drugs."

Sarah's insight into the behavior of a drug addict slowly became evident in the Dudley home. Phillip did not work and lounged about the house most of the time. The liquor cabinet was soon empty. When Louise did not refill it, he accused his mother of punishing him because he was not well. Arguments between mother and son became a daily routine.

"Don't you understand that I need a drink occasionally? I'll go crazy lolling around here without it, and I don't have the money to buy it. You gave your dear, handsome Paul money from the trust, why can't you give some to me? And what about Roger? He dipped into it, too. And Kevin is at Yale! Where do I fit into this pretty picture? Do I have to get married or go to school just to get a few bucks now instead of after you kick the bucket?"

Such banter always led Louise to tears, but Phillip was not moved. His accusations became cruel. "Your dear, handsome Paul knocked up that goodie-goodie, and you made him marry her. Is that what I'm supposed to do to get some money? And our great, successful Roger! He married Long Island's most available whore just to get money. You could have saved him from that. And dear little queer Kevin, off to school merely to be near his what's-his name? Why don't you help me? I'm your son, too? I need some money now!"

Louise's rebuttals never satisfied her son. "Yes, it's true that Paul sinned, and I've sort of rewarded him for it, but I couldn't refuse helping my first grandchild. And Roger and Sharon have done the respectable thing in getting married. And don't call Kevin that word. It must not have been true since Juno married, and Kevin went to school."

"Oh, don't be so stupidly naïve! Kevin moaned and groaned around here for days until he found out he could be near his precious boyfriend. And the only thing respectable about Sharon is that she hides her adulteries better than most. And Paul is hardly an angel just because he is married. I'll bet he's knocked up several since making his wedding vows!"

"Oh, Phillip!" Louise would exclaim in tears. "How could you talk to me so roughly and cruelly? What have I done to deserve such abuse?"

Phillip laughed and made a sneer. "What have you done? You've made your own son a motherfucker! Don't you remember?"

Louise gasped for breath and cried. She stood and walked to the fireplace. She couldn't face her attacker.

Phillip sneered and continued, "Well, don't cry for me. It's wasted sympathy. Besides, you're crying for your own shame, aren't you?" he laughed.

For a few minutes mother and son were quiet. Once Louise had control of herself, she sat down and said, "We've never discussed that incident. It should never have happened."

"But you enjoyed it. I know."

"Phillip, it was so wrong. It shouldn't have happened. You took advantage of me, your own mother."

A nasal sneer tore out of Phillip's throat. "I took advantage? Why wasn't it just the opposite?"

"Phillip!" Louise uttered, almost choking. "How could you insinuate that it was my fault? You held me so tightly and pulled me into the bed. I ... I ..."

"You stayed!"

"You raped me!"

"Oh, no, that wasn't rape. We did it, and you know it."

"Did you know what you were doing? That is the question. I was powerless. I ... I ..."

"You enjoyed it."

Louise looked at the floor and cried.

After a few moments Phillip whispered, his anger gone, "It's all right, Mother. We did it, and I'm glad. It was wonderful."

Shocked, Louise looked up at her son. What could she say? The experience had haunted her and, even though she knew that it could be considered abominable, she also knew that it had been enjoyable. She had never had such an orgasm, and it had been thrilling.

After another pause, Phillip, speaking in a kind, straightforward tone, fell back on the couch and expressed his anguish. "Look at me, Mother! Do I look like one of the handsome sons you are so proud of? Do the others have my wrinkles and balding head? Did I have the brains to bring back the A's you praised so highly in my brothers' report cards? Where did I go wrong? And why didn't I succeed? I wanted success. I wanted you to be proud of me. But there was nothing I could do to satisfy you. I used to cry in my room when I heard how you praised my brothers. I was nothing, and I knew it. I didn't fit into the family. I didn't do the things that society expected. I didn't have the talent or brains for climbing up the ladder. So, I turned to the bottle and then to drugs. I'm a king when I'm intoxicated or after a fix. Don't you understand how great it is to be what I always wanted to be? Don't you think I wanted you to be proud of me? When I'm drunk, it seems you are! And it's great. And so now everything is horrible. I don't have the money to make myself a hero or to be someone that you could be proud of. I'm just a hopeless drunk."

"Are you also still on drugs?"

"There you go, always accusing me!" Phillip jumped up and threw his cigarette into the fireplace. His rage was evident in his eyes when he turned toward his mother. "Yes, I'm still on drugs, and what are you going to do about it?"

Louise sat for a few minutes lost in thought. Her son's violent expression scared her, and she looked at the floor. She remembered some missing heirlooms that she was sure he had sold. She also remembered a phone call from the trust department of her bank. Phillip had inquired about his legal rights in obtaining money from the family holdings. There was no doubt that her son was being quite devious in desperately seeking money for his habit. It was then that she realized what she must do. The thought pained her dreadfully. How could she turn in her own son? Yet Sarah had been right. There was no other course. Her eyes drifted over to his shoes. He stood watching her without moving. Finally she raised her eyes and said, "I'll go get some bourbon. Sit down and relax."

On the way to the store, Louise dialed Sarah on her cell phone. When her neighbor answered, she informed her that it was time for the federal authorities. Sarah agreed, saying that she had observed the goings-on at the Dudley home and was amazed that Louise had withstood the abuse Phillip had given her. Sarah concluded by saying that she would make inquires about the matter.

That night Phillip drank heavily and fell asleep on the couch in the family room. Louise prepared for bed but decided that she should awaken her son so he could rest better in his room. She went downstairs in a light-blue silk housecoat. When Phillip did not move, she stood over him and nudged his shoulder. He opened his eyes and looked at his mother. Suddenly he grabbed her and pulled her down on him. Louise screamed, but he held her tightly, imploring her to be quiet. In seconds he had his arm inside her negligee and was caressing her breasts.

"Nooo," she moaned repeatedly, but he continued until he was able to slip down and lick her breasts.

Louise cried from fear and pleasure. Her husband had never given her such sensations. After some efforts at freeing herself, she finally realized that she either could not or did not want to free herself from his overwhelming strength. With a sigh of relief, she gave in to his desires. Phillip pulled his long erection out of his trousers and penetrated his mother. Oedipus and Jocasta, but more terrifying. This mother and son knew what they were doing, yet their rapacious desire overcame the historic prejudice.

The next morning Phillip came downstairs while Louise was having breakfast. He greeted her kindly, smiling. She could not look at him but returned his greeting. He was conscious of her feelings and said, "Mother, we've done nothing to be ashamed of. It was wonderful."

"Oh, Phillip," she replied, still looking away. "What have we done? I can't believe it."

"We loved as we cared. It's our business and no one else's."

"Oh, Phillip, it's so wrong. I can't bear to look at you."

He walked over to her and raised her head. Looking down at her, he said, "Mother, it's our affair. No one knows, and no one will."

"But we can't continue such a thing."

"That's up to us. If it continues, it's not bad; if it doesn't, it's just one of those things."

"How can you speak so lightly of it? We've done a monstrous thing."

Phillip sat beside her, forcing her to look at him. "Mother, that's not true. It was a beautiful thing. We love each other in more ways than one. You are my dearest mother, and I'm your disobedient son, but we're also soul mates. We came together because we both needed each other. That's what it's all about. We've helped each other as mother and son should."

"But not that way!"

"Who is to say? I don't care about ancient prejudices. We came together, and it was great. We've done nothing to be ashamed of because we both agreed, and it served us both."

"Oh, Phillip, your reasoning is beyond me. I feel as if I've let you down terribly."

"Heavens, Mother, you saved me. You didn't let me down. I needed you badly, and I think you needed me. We took love to a higher plane. It was an even exchange, and we've nothing to be ashamed about."

Louise shook her head. She could not talk about the subject. She was sorry that she had told Sarah to contact the federal authorities. She felt that she was as guilty as he was. Also, she feared what he might do when they came. After preparing Phillip's breakfast, she left, planning to work in the garden.

All morning Louise worried about the incident and whether it could happen again. She concluded that her son's drug addiction was playing a role in his behavior, but she also accepted the fact that she had enjoyed the sex. She realized that her husband had never brought her to orgasm. Yet Phillip was her son, and that point made her shudder. "It must stop," she concluded.

Later that morning a scene took place that stayed in Louise's mind the rest of her life. Four men arrived and escorted a shouting, crying Phillip out of the house. The abuse he yelled at Louise was heartbreaking, but she tearfully bore his insults to save him from himself. Unfortunately he shouted, "Motherfucker!" at her several times, and she was sure that Sarah had heard. The prospect that her neighbor knew about the indiscretion increased Louise's anxiety.

After informing her sons about turning Phillip in to the authorities, Mrs. Dudley's grief was lessened by Roger's arrival. He was dressed very neatly and looked very professional. He had been handling the lawsuit that Mr. Dudley's secretary had brought against the Dudley estate and he had good news. The accuser had never been pregnant. She assumed that she was, but it was merely a matter of a late period. There would be no lawsuit. The Dudley Trust would not be endangered. Louise breathed a sigh of relief and then told her son about the ghastly incident that had occurred that morning. Roger comforted her with some more good news. Sharon was pregnant. Louise laughed with joy. It was a nervous reaction from the stress of the morning. She hugged Roger and suggested they have a glass of sherry.

Roger led her into the family room and said, "Yes, the Dudleys are going to have another Dudley!"

Louise kissed her son. He had certainly revived her spirits.

Suddenly there was a knock at one of the French doors that led into the garden. Sarah was waving and saying something they couldn't understand. She seemed so anxious, Roger quickly opened the door.

"Turn on your TV," Sarah gasped. "The news! It's just dreadful."

"What?" Louise asked as Roger took the remote from the coffee table and pushed the starter.

Before Sarah could answer, the screen on the TV filled with a horrendous picture of fires in the Twin Towers of the World Trade Center in lower Manhattan. The three watched in silence, gasping occasionally as victims fell from the buildings and scared faces ran by the TV cameras. It was too horrific for immediate comprehension. Yet it was too realistic for a Hollywood pasteup. The word *terrorist* was not used at first. There was too much confusion and the element of disbelief.

After some time, however, Louise suddenly said, "Oh my God, Delores was going to visit Paul in his office today. Oh, surely they're not in that!"

Sarah and Roger looked at each other, then at the screen. One of the towers was crumbing. If Paul and Delores were in the building, they were dying at that moment.

Louise fell back on the couch, almost in a faint. Roger put a glass of sherry to her lips, and Sarah held Louise's head forward. She sipped some sherry and began crying. Her nerves could hardly stand more strain. Phillip's departure had destroyed the illusion of a happy, contented family. Now Paul and his wife were probably dead. Louise cried so uncontrollably that Sarah took her into her arms. When the second tower began falling, Louise turned and cried on Sarah's shoulder. It was a day no one would ever forget, but it was not over.

By late afternoon family members had either called or had rushed to the Dudley hearth. It was a typical reaction all over the country. People suddenly needed each other. Kevin rang from his apartment at Yale and asked his mother whether he should come to her. Roger took the phone and told his brother that he had everything under control. He then called Sharon and informed her of what was happening in Manhattan. She immediately left to join her husband. Sarah stayed with the Dudleys. Everyone was transfixed before the television.

In a short time the large round coffee table in the center of the couches was covered with highball glasses and empty beer bottles. Snacks and sandwiches were in abundance. Eating and drinking, the family watched the inconceivable and improvable scene. Comments and shouts erupted from time to time. The greatest shock of the day occurred when Paul, covered with dust, walked into the room.

"Paul!" the group screamed at once.

Louise jumped up from the couch and grabbed her son, sobbing on his filthy shoulder. When he pulled her away, her face was smeared with grime and sediment. He looked wretched. Everyone began asking questions, but Paul could hardly answer. He sat down and cried. Louise patted his shoulder and caressed him, but he could not cease crying. Finally he leaned back on the couch and uttered what the family feared.

"Delores was in my office when the building collapsed."

Questions came from everyone.

"Why?"

"How do you know?"

"Did you see her?"

"Why wasn't she with you?"

"How did you escape?"

"Are you sure she's in that?"

"What happened?"

After a gulp of a highball, Paul looked at the group through his dust-covered eyelids and slowly began talking. "Delores came to my office in the morning because we were planning a luncheon up on top." He stopped and stared at the floor a few seconds and then started again. "We had reservations. She had never been up on top."

Everyone was transfixed on the spectacle before them. Paul was a nervous wreck and could hardly speak. Yet no one interrupted.

Continuing, Paul slowly murmured, "I had to take some papers to a floor below us and asked her to rest for a moment because she was very pregnant." He quieted and gasped for air.

Sharon broke the silence. "Where was she?"

Paul's head lowered. Weakly he said, "At my desk by the window."

Again there was silence. Finally Paul uttered, "When I entered the department downstairs, there was a sudden jolt that seemed strange. Everyone stood up from their desks. Suddenly a man ran in and yelled that there had been an explosion upstairs."

Roger asked, "How many floors above you did the plane hit?"

Paul shook his head and looked down at the floor.

"Couldn't you run upstairs to Delores?" Sharon asked.

Paul shook his head. "No one knew what had happened, but there was chaos in an instant. Dust was filling the air in the hall. People started running. I ran, too. Someone opened an elevator, but I ran by it and was caught in the crowd at the stairs."

The family and Sarah sat quietly for a few moments. There was something missing in the story that had been related. Something was not clear. Slowly the group began asking themselves the obvious question: Why had he not gone back for Delores?

No one needed to ask. Paul suddenly slipped off the couch on his knees before them. "I don't know why I didn't go back!" The look of anguish on his face conveyed his fear and confusion. He realized that he had deserted his pregnant wife when she had needed him the most. His dastardly cowardice had marked him forever.

Louise sat forward and put her hand on her forehead. "Oh my God! Do you mean you could have gone back for her?"

Paul could only cry. It was obvious that he could have or should have, but he hadn't.

Louise sat back and moaned. "Oh, that poor girl!"

Paul put his head down to the coffee table and cried relentlessly. "My God, what have I done? Of course I should have gone back for her, but I didn't. I tell myself that I wanted to find out what had happened, but it wasn't that. I was just scared to death and didn't want to die. You can't imagine the horror of that scene. People were screaming and running in every direction. The stairs were like a riverbed, only it was full of bodies. I was swept away in a current out of Hades."

Roger asked, "But didn't you think of Delores?"

Paul nodded. "Of course I thought of her, but I couldn't go up the stairs. I told you that people were charging like buffaloes on the run."

"You could have fought your way along the side rail," Roger interjected, now ashamed of his brother.

"Awww," Paul piteously groaned and looked up at his brother as if he wanted some reassurance of human understanding, but Roger gave him none and walked away from his suffering sibling. He and Sharon departed.

Through his tears, Paul exclaimed, "Oh, God, what am I to do?" Then he leaned on the coffee table and continued crying remorsefully.

While Roger had showed his disgust, the others, now watching the despondent man, were more compassionate. They understood his human fragility, but their sympathy did not help him in his distress. What could they say?

Louise finally moved over to her son and put her arms around him. He lifted his head from the coffee table and cried on her shoulder.

"I left her sitting at my desk. I told her I'd be right back. I …" Paul broke into sobs. When he had finally controlled himself somewhat, he continued. "I imagine she went to the window when she saw people falling." Again he cried in anguish. "I keep wondering what happened. Did the ceiling come down on her? Did she go through the floor with all the stuff from the ceiling? Did she run into the hall with others? Was she trapped in a staircase? Did she …" Paul couldn't continue. Again his head fell to the coffee table, and he moaned. It was a pathetic scene. Finally Sarah suggested that she leave, but Louise waved for her to stay.

Sarah and Louise helped Paul stand and walked him up the stairs to his bedroom. He fell on the bed and continued crying. Louise tried reasoning with him, but he kept his head buried in his pillow. After a while he became quiet, and Sarah put a finger to her lips and pointed at the door, and the two ladies left.

In the family room, Louise poured two glasses of sherry. They sat looking at each other for a few moments. Finally Sarah said, "Louise, I wish there was something I could say that would ease your mind, but you know how outspoken I am. I fear your son will be tormented by this tragedy the rest of his life."

Louise nodded. A terrible tragedy had occurred. Both ladies comprehended the situation. Had Paul gone back for his wife, he, too, would have died. Would that have been a better fate for him? What could he now do that could possibly erase the disaster from his mind? How could he live with his cowardice revealed? Where was the balm for the wounded soul?

"Maybe it will restore his faith!" Louise commented.

"Did he practice his faith?"

Louise shook her head.

"Then he could find little comfort there," Sarah remarked.

"Oh, Sarah," Louise said, her eyes filling with tears. "Surely that is the only way for him."

"I'm not sure." After a few moments of reflection, Sarah continued. "I'm afraid he is going to have to find his own way out of his predicament. I can only wish him well."

Her face wrinkled in anguish, Louise almost cried out, "Oh my God, what a day! I tried helping Phillip, and he hates me for it. And now I can't help Paul. What can I do for them?"

There were no answers.

After a few moments of quiet, Louise turned on the television. The screen was filled with the enormous dust cloud that had resulted from the collapse of the Twin Towers. She quickly turned it off. Sarah said, "I hope you don't have to face another funeral now."

Louise turned and looked at her companion. A realization of the problems ahead came to her. If Delores had not perished completely in the ruins, there would be a body to bury. Funeral arrangements would have to be made. She shook her head. The thought was menacing. What more could this tragedy bring on the family? "You are right. We've got to think in terms of the present. Paul must contact Delores's family! There are so many things that will need our attention. Oh my, what will it all mean?"

Again the ladies were quiet. Louise went to a commode chest and poured herself a glass of sherry. She held it up toward Sarah as if asking her whether she wanted some. Sarah shook her head but suddenly asked, "Louise, I regret that I might add to your anguish, but I heard Phillip today when they were taking him away. He was terribly abusive."

Louise looked down. It was obvious that Sarah was puzzled by Phillip's horrendous remarks. However, the suspicion was now there, and Louise decided that she might as well discuss the problem with Sarah. After all, her neighbor had been very helpful and dependable. Besides, she felt that talking would help her relax. So, Louise lifted her head and looked at Sarah. "Could you ever even imagine that such a thing could happen?"

"Then it is true?"

Louise nodded her head. Sarah remained silent. It was evident that her thoughts were far away. Finally she said, "There is incest in the animal kingdom. We are merely a species, you know. So, it can happen. However, I must admit that it is quite a surprise."

Louise, forlorn, but relaxed at last, slowly told about her relations with her son as truthfully as she could remember. She described her feelings of disgust and rapture in detail. It had been wrong, but it had been exciting. For some time the situation had kept her in a quagmire of indecision. Finally she had concluded that her son's actions had been drug-induced, so she reported him to the feds. After saying that, Louise became quiet and sat back on the couch. She felt something approaching exhilaration because she had destroyed the fear of discovery. She felt free again.

"You did the right thing for your son," Sarah commented, "but as to the other matter, I don't know what I could recommend. I can only assure you that I will tell no one, and I want you to believe me."

"I do, Sarah. I wouldn't have told you if I didn't trust you. In fact, I am glad that I did confess it. I believe you can help me."

"I'm not sure about that. It seems to me that it's going to be your decision all the way. It's something incredible, but not improbable. As I said, it's in other species. I've just not run into it before."

Louise smiled. "I didn't tell you thinking that you had answers for me. I think I confessed because I've learned that it's easy to talk with you, so I think you can be of help."

Sarah thanked Louise and said that she was available any time for conversation.

After Sarah left, Louise remained on the couch, lost in thought. Her son might hate her for a while, but she was sure that she had done the correct thing. Even Sarah agreed. Yet the problem between mother and son had not been resolved. Louise could only wonder at its meaning and what direction it would take. Then there was Paul. He would now need her help. Both sons were in terrible trouble, and she felt that the weight of their predicaments had fallen on her. "Dear God, give me the strength for them!"

Chapter 11

After the death of his wife in the 9/11 catastrophe, Paul Dudley, whose handsomeness and personality had brought him social and professional success, began thinking seriously about his life. He was greatly troubled by the events that had brought changes in his established normal routine. Until this moment he had never been greatly concerned about political and social events in the daily news. His life had its own path, and he followed it with pleasure. He had never decided on particular goals; everything had simply fallen into place. Then suddenly his world had been disrupted. It was not the world of catastrophes and governmental squabbles that he had followed on TV news or in media magazines, but his private world. He was the center of a controversy that would not fit into the pattern of his life. It was a problem that his looks and personality could not diminish, it was a revelation that bared his soul, and it was a dilemma that he would have to solve. His easy stance in life was threatened, and it frightened him.

Word soon came that Delores's body had escaped the inferno of the Twin Towers collapse. While it was badly burned, her torso and teeth were identifiable. Roger, who had stepped forward to help his brother, went with Paul to the coroner's office for the legal proceedings. Driving there, Roger avoided discussing the grim task ahead and talked about global warming and how he was investing in windmills. Paul, usually interested in anything connected with making money, only listened. His dread of what was before him kept his mind occupied. His apprehension was justified. At the office the brothers were met by Delores's parents. It was a very awkward situation. They wanted a funeral in their church, but Paul remembered how distasteful the religious service had been in that branch of the Protestant church, and he refused by lying that he had already made arrangements in his own church. He then eased the distress he saw on the family members' faces by saying that they could have their own minister perform the ceremony if they wished. They immediately smiled and agreed. Paul would later regret his kindness.

The Dudleys desired a simple, quiet ceremony by invitation only. Delores's family agreed, but their understanding of "by invitation" allowed them to welcome all the members of their church. This aspect became readily evident during the time that Delores's closed casket was on view at the prestigious Walton Funeral Home. Small groups of people would break into song as they walked through the guest line; some even danced. Louise and Sarah quite often looked at each other askance and shook their heads. Paul remained seated and never looked up. Sharon and Roger pinched each other to keep from laughing. She said afterward, "I hope those people won't act like barbarians at the funeral." They did, however. The next day during the ceremony in the great Episcopal church, sounds of joy and clapping resounded into the street. The Dudleys sat in amazement but mainly amused. Only Paul bent forward and kept his head down. What seemed like an interminable sermon to the Dudleys was just a warm-up for the members of the other church. At the cemetery their joyousness and celebration were even more rambunctious.

Whether or not they were responsible for the terribly embarrassing incident that occurred, no one ever knew, but just as the minister was about to throw some dirt on the coffin, Paul cried out, "No!" He jumped up from his seat and ran over to the casket, which was suspended over the grave. "No!" he yelled and knelt down. "No! I can't let you go! I tried to save you, darling. I truly tried." Tears burst from his eyes. He was simply not in control of himself. His outburst had also caused everyone to be very quiet.

Finally Roger and Sharon went and helped him stand up. Leaning on them, first one and then the other, he slowly walked away, still sobbing and muttering incoherent phrases.

Afterward he could not believe that he had so completely lost control. It had brought shame into his life, a feeling he had not experienced, even though he was guilty of adultery, fornication, and illegal activities in his business dealings. His years of church attendance had shown him what society considered sinful, but that was for the masses. He was above such pettiness and did what he wished. Such a conception had given him a full and happy life. Now he questioned all of it, and it bothered him greatly.

After the unusual and unanticipated scene he created at his wife's funeral, many were afraid he was having a nervous breakdown. No one could comprehend that he was simply responding to a situation that did not fit into his scheme of things. Since he was ashamed of his behavior, he abandoned his family and went into seclusion. Not too noticeably, because that would imply that he was a coward. No, he usually let his mother know where he was and made up excellent excuses when he was invited for family affairs. Since his law firm was being relocated in another building, he had time on his hands, so he decided on a Caribbean cruise.

Once on board the *Island Princess,* he found his room, changed clothes, and went to the nearest bar. The drink of the day was a strawberry and rum concoction. He ordered a scotch with soda and asked whether the barman had a newspaper. He didn't but said that the ship library might have one. Paul looked around to see whether there was anyone he might talk to, but there were very few people in the bar because the passengers were still boarding. He walked out on the Level C deck. Standing at the banister, he gazed at the blue sea and azure sky.

Never changes, he said to himself and turned toward the stern of the ship.

His eyes met a rather plump, middle-aged lady standing about four feet from him. She smiled, and he said, "Great day for sailing."

"Yes," she answered, slurring the word in a quaint tone.

"Sailing alone?"

"No, my niece is with me. She's a great traveler."

"Oh, it's great to have company while traveling."

"You're alone?"

Paul nodded.

Suddenly a voluptuous blonde approached the lady, who introduced her as her niece, Ann. Gazing at the sun-tanned, blue-eyed girl, Paul took an immediate interest. He introduced himself, and they made idle conversation for a few minutes. Mrs. Shari Miller was a widow and loved cruises. Ann was a social worker in Montreal, where both ladies lived. Every time the two young people's eyes met, they seemed to speak to each other. After a while Paul was sure he had a lay and asked whether the ladies could join him for a cocktail before dinner that evening. They happily accepted the invitation.

When Paul returned to his cabin, a young steward was delivering his suitcases. After he placed them by the closet, he turned and asked Paul whether there was anything else he could do for him. Paul noticed that the young man looked down at his zipper and smiled. Always eager for sex, Paul put his hand down on his crotch and said, "You want it?"

The steward nodded and closed the cabin door. Paul laughed and lay on the bed. "All right, take it out, you faggot."

In seconds, the steward was on his knees, and he eagerly opened the fly before him. "Are you clean?" Paul asked.

The guy nodded and pulled Paul's penis out of his pants. "Wow," he exclaimed and immediately mouthed the extending prick.

Paul looked down at the steward and said, "Careful with the teeth, you bastard. There, that's better. Now suck, you scum."

It did not take long for Paul's fulfillment, and when he shot into the steward's mouth, he said, "Bet you've not had cream like that before, you little shit!"

The steward stood up and wiped his mouth. "May I come back?" he asked.

Paul laughed. "You liked it, didn't you, you scum? No, you may not come back. I'd rather have some hot pussy, so get the hell out of here and keep your mouth shut."

The steward backed away. He was hurt, but his obsession was stronger than his pride. "I'll come back any time."

"Get out!" Paul shouted, and the young man left.

What an asshole, Paul thought, as he turned on the TV for the daily news. As he undressed and prepared for a shower, a media anchor announced that the North Atlantic Treaty Organization was pressuring the Yugoslav government to end military operations against ethnic Albanians in Kosovo. Since the subject did not interest him, Paul walked into the bathroom, where he stood before a mirror. *Great body,* he thought and held up his large penis. *Great dick!* he concluded and said to himself, *Okay, Ann, it's your turn next!*

At the poolside bar in the front of the large liner, Paul found his two new friends sitting at a white, wrought iron table. He joined them and waved at a waiter. The threesome decided on the ship's drink of the day. Shari, joyous as ever, suggested a toast, and Paul immediately dipped into his reserve of cleverness and said, "Let's lift our hearts and glasses, too. The first's for love, the second's for you!"

Shari laughed wholeheartedly and spontaneously blurted out her approval, adding, "I think our cruise is off to a good start."

Paul agreed and winked at Ann.

After Paul sensed that his companions were not interested in international politics, the conversation stayed on the usual light side—nothing consequential. They talked about earlier cruises, how travel had changed, and which tours might be of interest during the coming days. Paul kept up his flattery and flirting, and both ladies enjoyed it tremendously. Shari was delighted with his conduct because it reminded her of former experiences. The cocktail hour was a great success for all concerned, and they agreed that they should dine together as often as possible.

After dinner Paul asked Ann whether she would like a walk around the deck. Shari excused herself, even though she was not included in his invitation. The young couple walked away and was soon arm in arm, enjoying a light breeze on a starlit evening. Ann snuggled close when Paul put his arm around her. Halfway around the ship he knew that she was easy prey. He escorted her up some stairs to his room.

At the door she suddenly realized what she was doing and said, "Oh, do you think we should go in?"

"Why not? It's just for a chance to kiss those beautiful lips of yours."

Ann smiled and walked into the cabin. In seconds Paul had her enclosed in his arms and was kissing her. Soon his tongue was in her mouth. He then moved toward the bed, where he put a hand into her dress and freed one of her breasts. In seconds he was kissing and licking it. Ann sighed but started to protest. Paul quickly had her on the bed and was sucking both breasts. She was soon ecstatic. In no time he had her dress pulled up, and his fingers were inside her. Again she moaned with rapture. Her submissiveness was all Paul needed. Unzipping his pants, he plunged his penis into her vagina.

After his successful conquest of another virgin, Paul retired early and drifted off into slumber quite content with himself. Suddenly he realized that he was falling. He grabbed for something, but it did not hold him. He threw both arms up, but he could not catch a steel beam. Further efforts at saving himself were futile. He was falling faster and faster. There was no help. He cried out but continued to fall. Death was imminent. He screamed but awoke holding on to a railing in the headboard. He gasped for air and fell back on his pillow. Breathing heavily, he thought of Delores and winced.

God! How awful, he thought, picturing her fall during the 9/11 catastrophe. He shuddered. As his thoughts cleared, he asked, *Why did I ever want that woman?*

The remembrance that he had made a mistake in marrying Delores soothed his conscience. His egotism blamed her for her demise. She had brought it on herself. He soon succumbed to sleep.

The next morning Paul did not want breakfast with Ann, even though he had promised when he escorted her back to her cabin. She was afraid that he might be ill, but when she left the dining hall and saw him playing shuffleboard with a brunette, she was terribly hurt. In tears she hastened to the deck where Shari was sunning. The latter knew immediately that something was wrong when she saw Ann with a handkerchief at her nose. In seconds Ann blurted out her confession. She had given herself to a lying scoundrel, and he had deceived her. Shari placed an arm around the distraught young lady and tried words of comfort, but Ann was mortified. Shari let her cry until she was calm enough for a walk to their cabin. There, Ann licked her wounds like any stray cat and thought up various means of revenge. Shari agreed with her but knew that her devious plans were only talk. Nothing could really be done. Ann was simply a victim of a vulgar hustler.

Paul, in the meantime, was after more important quarry. The brunette with whom he had been playing was the daughter of the captain of the liner. By chance Paul had overheard a conversation between two waiters pertaining to a beautiful brunette who was seated at the captain's table. In no time he had managed an introduction and then invited Loraine Sutton for a game of shuffleboard. He quickly realized that his next conquest would not be easy. The captain's daughter was used to Romeos on board and immediately told Paul that he could "drop the compliment crap" and watch his game. Paul laughed, but she gave him a glance that implied that she was serious. Such a defense did not deter Paul. He was a skilled rogue and enjoyed a challenge. By the end of the game, he had talked her into having dinner with him that evening.

She let him know, however, that she was not being fooled by his graciousness. When they parted, she said, "Don't think I don't see through your act, handsome. I simply haven't anything better to do. I might as well play you along." Paul laughed as they parted.

Lorraine had practically been reared at sea. Her father had started in the yacht business and was very successful. When he felt that his situation was upscale and comfortable, he began the career he had always wanted. He became a sea captain. Lorraine had attended private schools in Europe, but home had always been a large, well-accommodated ship. Such a background explained her athletic abilities. Her exquisite form showed that she swam often. Paul was intrigued by her because of her defiance. It seemed as if she were always wearing a gauntlet, which she could use for an attack at any time. He had never met anyone like her and found himself quite taken with her.

One day when Paul and Lorraine were walking around the central deck of the ship, they passed Ann and Shari, who were sunning on lounge chairs. Paul nodded, and Shari greeted him by bending her head in a kindly fashion. She was still in hopes that something would develop between her niece and the handsome man. Ann just turned away. Lorraine pulled Paul's arm, and they walked away. When they passed the corridor leading to his cabin, he suggested they stop in for a chat. Lorraine smiled and said, "Listen, you gigolo! When I want to fuck, I'll let you know. Got the message?" Paul smiled and bowed as they walked on.

Having lived on many seas, Lorraine was not interested in trips ashore, especially on the Caribbean. Her theory was that all the islands in that sea were too similar. She preferred the Greek islands, where every "bobble" in the sea had a fascinating history. Consequently, the couple spent much time aboard when the ship was in a port. Their togetherness soon developed into an intimate relationship, with Lorraine in command. Paul could see that she would dominate him if they should decide on something serious, yet he rationalized that it might not be a bad thing. Lorraine was an heiress, and she was "quite a catch." He could use such a wife. Therefore, one day when they were looking at the sea from an upper deck, he started his "I'm alone" act, but she pulled the curtain on him.

"Stop the sniveling. You're about as alone as a taxi in New York city."

"Will you please quit wearing that coat of mail that you're always in?"

Lorraine laughed. "Well, I see I called your bluff again."

"You're nothing but a spoiled brat."

"Well, it's obvious that you deserve everything I pass out. In fact, I find you easier to put in your place than anyone I've known."

Paul hunched his shoulders. "What can I say that could break through your armor?"

"Nothing. I'm in charge and don't forget it."

"All right, I surrender. The battle's over. Marry me."

Lorraine looked at Paul with a strange smile on her face. "You'd marry me and give up your precious freedom? Don't make me laugh."

"I would."

'Then what's your ulterior motive?"

Paul's grimace showed his disgust. His lips curled, and his cheeks stretched in a silly smile. She was pinning him down, and he could not think of any rebuttal. She knew he was scheming.

"Oh, no motive?" she asked and laughed. "Who's kidding whom?" When he did not answer, she paused and turned away from him, smiling. Finally she replied, "Well, let me think about it. There has to be a motive. No one does anything without one. I'll figure it out. I do find you amusing, however, and," she hesitated for a moment before continuing, "who knows, I might agree."

"You'd make me very happy," Paul said seriously, but he had not convinced Loraine.

"Yeah, I'll bet!" she laughed, then put off any response to his proposal. "Paul, dear, let's not talk about such important things. I'd like to have a quiet, peaceful evening. Let's go up on the top deck and dance in the moonlight."

They arrived at the top of the ship in time for a waltz. Both were excellent dancers, and they whirled around the large floor with ease. After the dance they drank champagne. Feeling light-headed, they decided on a walk around the deck of the vessel. The moon was bright in the dark sky, and the ocean air was filled with romantic music. They stopped in various corners and danced alone, usually ending with a kiss. When they returned to the dance floor, they were both experiencing a sense of lightness and joy. It was a perfect, moonlit evening, and they were exemplary examples of youth and happiness.

After several dances, Paul suggested they return to the level of their cabins and walk along a dimly lit deck. Loraine agreed, and they were soon standing in front of Paul's door. "Oh, so that was the ulterior motive," she commented and laughed. "No, I'm not so high that I'll succumb tonight," she teased. "Besides, I told you that I'll let you know when I want a fuck, so don't forget it."

Aggravated, Paul asked, "Must you be so crude?"

"You love it and deserve it. Don't try to kid me. I know you, Paul, and I like you, but we'll play it my way."

"What about my way or my feelings?"

"You can take it. Now take me to my cabin and kiss me good night."

Paul escorted Loraine to her room and kissed her at the door. Holding her tightly, he asked, "How can you leave me after such a wonderful evening?"

"Maybe it's my period. You'll never know!" She laughed and slipped into her room, whispering, "See you at breakfast."

Paul, feeling as if he had made some headway in his relations with Loraine, went to his room and wrote his mother that he was planning on bringing a marvelous girl home with him for the Thanksgiving holidays and that he was hoping they would be married. The note made him feel even better, and he decided on a nightcap. He went to the bar on the deck above his cabin and sat down at the counter. After ordering a whiskey and soda, he looked around. The perverted waiter he had relations with when he came on board was waiting on tables. Once, as he passed, Paul turned and softly said, "Hey, come to my room."

The young man nodded quickly and went on with his duties.

Paul finished his drink and went to his cabin. He turned on the TV and undressed. In a short time there was a knock on the door. It opened, and the steward stepped inside. Few words were spoken. The obsessed young man quickly rushed to the bed where Paul was spread out like a turkey waiting to be stuffed. His erection was ready for action. The young man climbed up on the bed and gladly began his ritual.

Paul was breathing quite heavily as he approached his orgasm, but suddenly the door opened, and Loraine stepped in. Sensing that something was happening on the bed, she switched on the lights. Catching a glimpse of the oral sex in progress on the bed, Loraine said with loathing, "You bastard!" and quickly ran out of the room.

Disgusted at being caught, Paul shouted at the young man, "Get out, you asshole!"

Slipping off the bed, the steward asked, "Don't you want me to finish? You were almost there."

Not finding the words he wanted for an expression of his hatred, Paul merely stuttered, "Jest git ... get out!"

At the door the steward said, "You're gay, too!"

Paul cursed him.

The next morning, Paul passed the captain's table at breakfast without looking at Loraine, who was drinking coffee. He was sure that there was no way he could appease her anger, so he had decided on avoiding her. Anyway, what could he say?

After he sat down and had ordered his breakfast and a newspaper, quite a surprise awaited him.

Loraine came over with her cup of coffee and sat down opposite him. In a pleasant tone, showing no animosity, she said, "Well, you sure botched up our romance, didn't you, you pervert?"

Paul threw a spoon down on the table. "Listen, you! I'll not be called that."

Loraine laughed. "Oh, don't take it so seriously. It's actually rather funny."

"What's funny about it?"

"Well, you've been working hard to make me, and then when I finally decided that you should have me, you were preoccupied. Don't you think that's hilarious?"

"No, I don't. And I'm sick and tired of your bossing me around. Let's just drop it where it is."

Loraine laughed. "Oh, no! I'm not through with you yet. Remember, we'll play our game my way."

Paul looked at her in disbelief. He couldn't understand her intentions. She had been repulsed by what she saw, and yet she was planning to continue their affair. It didn't make sense.

"You think I haven't seen oral sex before? You idiot, I'd have done that for you."

Paul was even more astounded. Before him sat a truly original type! She was upset only because she wanted to do the blow job, not for any moral or social reason. It seemed preposterous. Finally he smiled slyly. "All right, you get the job next time."

Loraine laughed. "Well, now you're making sense. If you'd had any patience, you'd have found me at your door last night."

"But you said that you were going to bed. You gave no indication that you would come to me."

Loraine twisted her lips. "If you knew anything about women you'd have known I was coming." She looked aside and exclaimed in an ironic tone, "What a womanizer!"

Shaking his head, he smiled. "Who could ever understand you!"

Finishing her coffee, Loraine stood and said as she walked away, "Better luck next time!"

Paul sat pondering. What did she mean by that!

An announcement of a Bali Party was in the cruise ship's morning bulletin. It would be on the top deck that evening, and the passengers were encouraged to wear suitable attire. Many spent most of the day wondering what to wear. Should the attire be beach clothes, flashy color ensembles, or what? Paul, while sitting at the bar in the middle of the afternoon, heard one lady describe her concept of what would be proper. She would wear the straw skirt and hat she had bought in Hawaii. Her companion thought her choice was excellent and mourned the fact that she had not brought her own Hawaiian outfit. Paul knew he'd wear his white suit and rainbow-colored tie, but he did not know whether he should invite Loraine. After much thought, he sent her a note by a steward and waited for the results.

Loraine did not answer Paul's note, but when he saw her that evening, swirling around ever so graciously on the dance floor in a very light chemise, she waved to him and smiled, throwing her head back as if she were laughing. He waved back, but she did not see it. Her partner, a handsome ship officer, swept her away with the music. Paul walked around the dance floor for another glance at her but suddenly found himself in front of Mrs. Mercer and her niece, Ann. He turned toward them and lifted his glass. Shari responded, "Good evening. Won't you join us?"

Glad to have the invitation because of his awkward position, Paul sat down on the end of the lounge chair where Ann was sitting and greeted her. She was not very receptive, but Shari began a conversation about the beautiful evening and how wonderful it was sitting under the stars and bright moon. Paul could only agree and decided on a rather daring move. He asked Ann whether she would dance. Shari spoke up before Ann could refuse, "Of course she would. Who wouldn't want to dance under such a sky?"

Ann looked at her aunt with displeasure, but she stood up and took Paul's arm. He escorted her onto the dance floor, and they quickly went into movement. After a few turns, they approached Loraine and her partner. The two couples passed by each other without recognition. Ann finally talked. "So, she stood you up?"

Paul laughed. "No, my dear, I didn't ask her.'"

"Am I supposed to believe that?" Ann smirked without looking at her partner.

"Well, believe it or not, it's true." The frankness and sincerity of his tone touched Ann and made her more curious. After they finished the dance, Paul escorted Ann back to her seat.

Shari greeted them and added, "You two looked terrific together on the dance floor."

"Thank you," Ann said.

Her tone revealed that she had made up with Paul, so Shari immediately continued. "Let me get us all a drink," she suggested and waved to a waiter before Paul could refuse. Shari told him to sit down. He had not planned a visit with them, but he obeyed as she began telling about a humorous incident that had occurred during dinner. Seems a lady asked for the sommelier, and the waiter brought her some milk. Shari laughed loudly.

Paul smiled, but he had not understood the word, and Ann had noticed. She informed him that the lady had asked for the wine steward in French. Paul smiled and nodded his head as if he had known the word, but it was obvious that he hadn't.

"We Canadians who live close to Quebec speak some French," Ann continued, glad to have a subject she could talk about.

Paul changed the subject. "Would you like another dance?"

"Go on, Ann," Shari insisted. "I love to watch you two."

Ann agreed, and soon the couple was floating around the dance floor. Feeling that Paul was again pursuing her, Ann relaxed and became very friendly. He noticed her change and started pinching her waist and kissing her ears when he had a chance. They were soon being watched by others, including Loraine. When the music stopped, Paul went with Ann to the bar, and they had a drink together. Shari came and said that she was tired and would retire.

When Ann said that she would go with her, Shari showed her resolve. "No, you stay and have a good time. I'm going alone. See you both in the morning!" She waved and walked away.

Paul smiled at Ann. "That aunt of yours is something else! Shall we rumba? The music is calling."

"I can't rumba!"

"Well, let's walk around the deck. The moonlight's intoxicating."

Ann nodded. "Yes, it's beautiful, but don't lead me to your cabin."

Paul laughed and teased. "Would I do that?"

Ann slipped off the bar stool. "You know you would. So, let's walk on this deck."

Paul held out his arm, and they walked past the dance floor. Loraine was dancing, but Paul paid her no attention.

At the back of the ship, the lights were very low. Paul and Ann stopped and looked out over the dark ocean and watched the waves receding from the bow of the vessel. He put his arm around her and held her close. She snuggled up to him and put her head on his chest. They stood silently for a while and then he slowly started walking her around the deck again toward an elevator.

At Paul's cabin door, Ann hesitated before entering. When he kissed her softly on the lips, she relented and allowed him to carry her across the threshold. While only the day before she had sworn eternal hatred of the man who was quickly undressing her, she soon went limp in his arms as he placed her on his bed. During the night he entered her three times. In the morning Paul agreed on a luncheon meeting, and Ann slipped out of the cabin.

The shipboard lunch the next day was a barbecue on the top deck near the swimming pool. Ann, dressed in a bright orange and red chemise, went by her aunt's cabin and told her about the wonderful evening with Paul. Shari was delighted. She was sure her plan was working. Seeing that her niece was colorfully dressed, Shari put on a fancy dress of blue and white checks. Together the two ladies went to an elevator. Shari stepped off first and immediately saw Paul seated with Loraine at a nearby table. The aunt turned in order to hide them from her niece, but it was too late. Ann saw her Romeo and took hold of the wall.

"Oh!" she exclaimed, "How could he?"

Shari put her arm around Ann and escorted her to a table some distance from the others. When they sat down, they could see that Paul and Loraine were laughing and looking straight at them. Ann was deeply humiliated. She stood up and started walking back toward the couple. Shari called for her, but she continued. Once at the table, she tried slapping Paul, but he caught her hand.

Loraine jumped up and asked, "What's going on?"

Ann was clearly overcome with emotion and too distraught for answers; she began crying. By that time Shari had caught up with her niece and put her arm around her. Leading her away, she gave Paul a look of scorn, which Loraine found amusing and said to her companion.

"So, you broke another heart, you asshole!"

"I didn't mean to," Paul rebutted.

"Course not. Then why did you?"

"Now listen, I came up here to meet her, and you were sitting here. I thought I'd sit down for a minute with you until she came. I didn't see them until they passed us. It's not my fault they misunderstood our sitting together, is it?"

"Then why didn't you go and explain? That poor girl is crying her eyes out. Evidently you were her first."

"I wasn't ..."

Loraine's laugh interrupted his comment. "Oh, you really are an ass. The way you treat women is repulsive and to think I thought of marrying you. Well, I won't and I won't go to your home for the holidays."

"Aw, come on, Loraine. It's not my fault that girl was an easy lay, is it?"

Amused, Loraine asked, "Why didn't you have that faggot suck you off again?"

"You know, you're really repulsive at times. You'd rather I do that than lay a piece of flesh, right?"

"Well, at least that way you wouldn't hurt a young girl so badly!"

"You're impossible to understand."

"Oh, you'll get the message. You see, I've met your type many times on these ships, and I like to tease the hell out of them. But don't worry. You can have a piece of my flesh, as you called it, but when I'm ready and not before."

Paul shook his head and grimaced. "Did it ever occur to you that now that I know what kind of a bitch you are, I might not want you?"

Loraine laughed and replied smartly, "No, that hasn't occurred. You see, I know your type. You put on an air of being interested in world affairs, but you actually think only of yourself and your own self-gratification. You really are quite pathetic, and you'll end up alone and miserable."

Paul sat back in his chair, raked a hand through his thick dark hair, and looked at Loraine for a few moments. "You certainly have a negative opinion of me, don't you?"

"Oh, not completely. I like you well enough for a good lay."

Paul leaned forward and whispered in a sarcastic tone. "I wouldn't fuck you if you were the last woman on earth."

Loraine laughed again. "Fine! Now let's go have a game of shuffleboard."

"You expect me to play with you after the way you've insulted me?"

"I didn't say anything you didn't know, so don't be silly. Let's enjoy the morning breezes up on deck."

She stood, picked up her purse, and held out her arm for him. He took it and escorted her away.

As the couple walked along the deck, Loraine made light conversation. Suddenly he noticed that they were in front of his cabin door. She had led him there.

"Well, aren't you going to invite me in?"

Paul looked at her in disbelief. Was it possible that she was serious, or was it another attempt to make a fool of him? He opened the door, and she stepped in quickly, throwing her purse on a chair. When he closed the door, her arms went around his neck, and she kissed him.

He broke away quickly. "What is this, another game you like to play?"

"Don't be silly. Here, unzip my blouse in the back." She turned around.

Paul pulled her back around and said, "I'm not going to do it."

Loraine again put her arms around him and whispered, "Darling, you've passed my test. I've told you off, and you've accepted it. Now, if you've been serious with me, let's get on with that marriage bit you were dealing."

A look of incredulity appeared on Paul's face, but he turned her around and unzipped her blouse. Loraine was quickly undressed and in the bed. Paul sat on a side and took off his shoes. He looked at her beautiful breasts and winked.

She said, "Come on, big boy, let's get to it."

As Paul slipped onto the bed, Loraine grabbed his penis and began playing with it. She bent down and sucked and then sat up and kissed him. He was soon fully erect and entered her slowly. They spent the morning in bed.

Toward noon Loraine dressed and left without saying a word. Paul closed his eyes and rested, but his thoughts were about her. What an unusual woman! He concluded that he wanted their marriage more than ever and felt confident that she now wanted him. He remembered Delores. What a difference there was between the two women. Loraine had none of the uptight religiosity of his deceased wife, and she wasn't from an impoverished background. No, Loraine was quite a catch. Paul even felt content that he was free to marry her. He believed that it was a shame that Delores had perished so cruelly, but he felt that it had actually been better for them both. Any thought of his dead child never entered his mind. His conceit was still his raison d'être.

Late the next morning, Paul finally arose and dressed. He dressed in beach apparel and went up to the top deck, where he could have lunch in the pool bar area. To his utter astonishment, the first table he saw when he came off the elevator was occupied by Ann, Shari, and Loraine. They saw him, waved, and laughed wholeheartedly. Their behavior so surprised him that he walked in another direction and found a table on the other side of the pool. When he sat down, he was almost trembling inside. He could still hear them laughing. What did those bitches mean? Should he have gone to their table? Were they making fun of him? If there was one thing he could not stand, it was being laughed at. It was as if they had seen through the mask that had hidden his true self for years. The incident had made him aware of the concept of himself that he had nurtured. It had given him protection from reality. He had not needed the religion he had been reared in. He was his own man and saw life as it really was. Yet they were laughing at him and were judging him severely. It was all too bizarre. Greatly disturbed, Paul went to the elevators at the end of the ship and found refuge alone in his cabin.

For most of the day, Paul remained in his room. He exercised in front of a mirror and found that his body still looked great. He washed his hair and confirmed his belief that he was handsome. He ordered his lunch and ate in his cabin, and when the steward came for the lunch tray, Paul allowed him to satisfy his obsession. During all the activities of the day, Paul was thinking of his own life and what Loraine had said to him. He concluded that he himself was not at fault. He was still handsome and wealthy. She was the one to be judged. She was a monster who preyed on men, using her sex as a means for revenge. Why she needed revenge and for what reason, he could not discern, but in his opinion, it was evident that she was not normal. He decided that avoiding her would be wise. When he dressed for dinner, he formulated a plan that would keep him away from the women who had denigrated him.

In the main dining room, Paul asked to be seated alone. He was following a waiter toward the back of the large hall when he suddenly heard laughter. He looked and saw Shari, Ann, and Loraine laughing and waving from a table near the windows. Disgusted, he returned to his cabin and packed his suitcases. He knew the ship stopped at Barbados the next morning, so he made arrangements to leave the cruise. While he was waiting on deck for his departure, however, Loraine approached him. Her lips were twisted as if she were teasing, and her smile was sly. "So, you're a coward, too," she said when she was close.

Paul wanted desperately to hit her, but he restrained himself. "Must get back for a business deal," he lied.

"Yeah!" Loraine commented, nodding with down-twisted lips. "What about the deal here?"

"What do you mean?"

"Why don't you admit you're running away because you can't take it."

"Can't take what?"

"The fact that three ladies saw through your act."

Paul laughed. It seemed his only defense. "I got what I wanted, didn't I? Maybe you bitches aren't so smart after all."

"Aw, cram it!" Loraine blurted out. "Guess you'll never see just what a heel you are."

"And you, you bitch, will never see just how frustrated you are."

Loraine turned for another comment, but the gate had opened and Paul was starting down the gangplank. She went to the side of the ship, but he was too far along. *Bastard!* she said to herself.

Paul turned around and looked back up at the ship. He saw Loraine, but walked on, thinking, *Dizzy cunt!*

Chapter 12

For weeks, Louise tried visiting Phillip in the federal sanitarium, but he refused any communication. Finally, in the fourth week, he agreed to see her. Mrs. Dudley was surprised when he came toward her in the meeting hall with a smile on his face. He appeared genuinely happy and took her hands into his when he sat down.

"Mother, or shall I call you Louise from now on? I have a wonderful plan."

"My darling boy," she exclaimed and rubbed a hand over his head. "I am thrilled to see you feeling so well. You have forgiven me, haven't you?"

"Of course, Mother, you did the right thing."

Tears came into Louise's eyes. She took a handkerchief from her purse.

"No need for tears, Mother. From now on we're going to be happy."

Louise looked at her son with an air of confusion on her face. What was he trying to say? What was his plan?

Phillip lowered his voice. "My darling, we have made a wonderful discovery. We love each other as a mother and son have never loved. Don't frown. It's a marvelous revelation. We need each other. I know that you can be my salvation, just as you were my creator."

Still looking mystified, Louise asked, "What are you saying, Phillip? I don't quite understand."

"Oh, it's all so simple. We have made this amazing discovery. You and I can save each other from the abysmal lives we've been living. You know that you were unhappy with Father. He never satisfied you in bed."

"Phillip!" Louise exclaimed, looking around for any listeners.

"Yes, Mother, it's true, and you know it. You were never happy with Father. Now you've found happiness with me."

Louise bit her lip lightly. "Oh, Phillip, what are you saying?"

"I'm saying the truth. We were made for each other. I can satisfy you, and you can save me."

Louise looked around again before continuing. "What do you mean I can save you?"

"With you I know that I can beat the drug habit. You give meaning to my life. I can be a new person."

Louise bit her lip again. "Do I really comprehend what you are saying? You want us to live together. You want us to continue what has happened?"

"Of course, Mother. It's so natural and so right."

"Oh, Phillip! If you only knew how concerned I've been! If you could only realize how ..."

He interrupted. "Don't say any more. Of course I realize how unusual it all is. We'd be fools or mountain rednecks not to understand how complex the situation is. Yet we are intelligent and educated people. We can appreciate what we have discovered. It's a salvation for both of us. We can be happy together."

"How? Even if I thought for a second that there was a possibility for such an arrangement, I wouldn't be able to do it. Your brothers would be horrified, and society would condemn us. How could we live like that? Besides, I couldn't do it."

Phillip put his knees together and took one of his mother's hands. Looking into her eyes, he whispered, "There is a way for us to do it."

The assurance in his voice made Louise ask, "How?"

"We'll move to the Caribbean. It's another life down there. Nobody bothers about society's cares. We could be free to live as we please."

"How?"

"You've plenty of money, and I can work. We'd start over. It would be a beautiful new life. Oh, Mother, don't you see? We can help each other and find new meaning in everything. We won't just exist as we do now. We'll live!"

Louise sat back in her chair. She looked at her son and wondered what she should do. He was so happy and was pleading for her help. He was also offering her another existence, which did not displease her, and she knew it. Could it be possible? Finally she said, "My darling Phillip. You have certainly overwhelmed me. In some ways, you've brightened my day. To see you so happy means a great deal to me."

Again he took one of her hands. "To know that we could be even happier is worth fighting for."

Louise smiled. After a few moments, she said, "Phillip, you've convinced me that I must think the matter over very carefully. I can't believe that we can do what you're saying, but I must think about it."

"Of course, Louise! You must think about it more seriously than you have about anything in your life. Your future happiness and mine depend on you. Save me, my love, and I shall make you my queen."

Tears again filled Louise's eyes, and she wiped them with her handkerchief. After a short pause, she decided that she should go. There was much to think about, and she could not hurriedly turn down her pleading son. They parted after a warm embrace.

Driving home Louise realized that, in her conversation with Phillip, she had not once mentioned the "wrong" aspect of his plan: their immorality. Yet it was now clear to her that she was contemplating the impossible. She found herself nodding as the revelation sank into her consciousness. She suddenly felt as liberated as a prisoner from a dungeon. She had actually accepted her son's proposal. Whether wrong or right, she had a new sense of happiness. She, a mother, would save her son; he, her son, would save his mother. She smiled. It was too bizarre and too meaningful. An urgent desire for discussion with Sarah came upon her, and she drove home at a faster speed than she had ever driven before.

Sarah was working in her garden when Louise walked out on her patio. Again she did not notice the beauty of the flowers in the row of concrete urns. She called over to her neighbor, and Sarah waved back. When Louise called out an invitation for a rest on the patio, her neighbor agreed and said she would be over as soon as she finished putting the alfalfa in the llama's trough.

Louise was on the patio with a tray of fresh coffee and cookies when Sarah came through the garden gate. Trivial exchanges of conversation led to the important subject. Louise, in great detail, outlined the premises of the plan her son had proposed. Sarah sat stoically without interrupting. When Louise finally sat back in her white straw lounge chair, Sarah commented, "Your son Phillip has more sense than I thought he had."

"What do you mean?" Louise asked, brushing back her hair.

"Well, if you do carry out his plan, moving to the Caribbean is probably the best part of it all. There's plenty of society down there that will accept any sort of arrangement. Besides, they need not know that the two of you are so closely related."

"Sarah," Louise said, smiling, "you are a dear. Not once have you criticized. I'm so thankful."

"Oh, don't think that I approve fully at this juncture. It's not for me to pass any moral judgments. Frankly, I can't imagine it, but it's so new that I've not had time for reflection."

"Do you think it can work?"

Sarah knocked some alfalfa straws off her blue jeans and paused. Finally she said, "I'd hate to see you move."

Louise laughed. "I'd miss you, too, but you could come and visit."

Sarah smiled. "I suppose."

The two ladies looked at each other in wonder. Louise wanted her neighbor's approval, and Sarah was uncertain about what she should say. Only questions came to mind. "Have you told Phillip that you agree?"

"No, but he was very understanding. He told me that he knew it would be a radical move on my part and that I should have plenty of time for forethought."

Sarah's eyes narrowed. "Yet it seems to me that you've accepted the plan. You want it carried out."

After a brief silence, Louise nodded. "Yes, Sarah, I do. It's impossible for me to believe that I do, but I do."

"What is his reasoning for such an original plan?"

As Louise answered, she looked aside. "He believes that I can save him from himself, mainly drugs, and he thinks that he can renew my life in the process."

"Sex?"

Louise nodded.

Sarah thought for a few moments. "He might be right. From what you've told me about your relations with your husband, it's time you did have fulfillment. Also, you are a positive influence on your son, and if you saved him, as he puts it, it would certainly bind you two most successfully. The plan is not a bad one."

"Oh, Sarah, thank you."

"Now, don't misunderstand. I'm not saying that I like it, but I must say that it has a mentality of its own. It's just too new, too creative, for easy acceptance. Yet, if it works, it would certainly have been worth it. I think that's the way I feel."

Louise smiled. "Sarah, you're a wonderful friend. You have such insights. You understand, and I am most grateful."

Sarah stood up. "Well, I have to admit, the plan is much better than the book I'm now reading."

Louise laughed as she walked with her neighbor to the white board gate between their gardens.

Sarah asked, "How much longer does Phillip have in the sanitarium?"

"It will depend on the doctors, but probably a few months."

"That's good. It will give you time to think things out for sure. I'd suggest that you keep very busy during this period. It will help you keep things in balance."

"Thank you, Sarah, you've been a great help."

Sarah hunched her shoulders and waved as she walked away.

Time provides healing, but memory lives on. For months Louise found comfort in conversations with Sarah. She followed her neighbor's advice and kept herself as busy as possible. She would normally have reached out to her church, which had meant so much to her all her life, but she could not reconcile her thoughts and plans with the teachings she had believed in, Thinking of her situation, she was at times depressed and at times exhilarated. She sensed that she was undergoing a radical change but could not picture the consequences of the life she was leading. She felt best in discussions with Sarah, whose understanding and practicality helped make sense of the complexities in the bizarre plan.

The Dudley sons were still an integral part of Louise's life, but she avoided being a nuisance, not wanting to rely on them for comfort. Besides, she could hardly discuss Phillip's plan with his brothers. Roger and Sharon invited her often, but she usually refused because she knew their invitations were made only out of a feeling of obligation. Paul called sometimes, but it soon became obvious that he evaded meetings with all members of his family. His disreputable behavior at Delores's funeral had only made the situation worse. His moaning and crying out that her death was his fault even though he had tried to save her had caused considerable consternation among the mourners. The family assumed that his shame was so great that he could not face them. They did not know at the time that he had taken a Caribbean cruise and continued his wanton ways before he started working in the new offices of his company. Kevin drove off to Yale in a new yellow convertible, which he delighted in driving. He quickly immersed himself in research and was soon enjoying his graduate studies. Yet there was still time for Juno who, unbeknownst to Louise, drove over every now and then to continue their relationship.

Once a week Louise visited Phillip, and they grew closer with each visit. Phillip understood that his mother was accepting his plan, but he never forced a positive answer from her. He could sense that she was in agreement and that they would work out many details after his release. For the time being they merely enjoyed each other's presence.

As time passed, Louise felt more and more at ease. Her family seemed stable, and she no longer needed sleeping pills. Then, to her astonishment, during one of Kevin's vacations at home, she found another paper he had written, which caused her considerable concern. This time, she confronted Kevin, the culprit.

Sipping a late-afternoon sherry on the terrace, Louise and Kevin relaxed before an early dinner. "Kevin, I have to confess that I read some of the paper you left beside your bed."

"I don't care," he replied, shrugging his shoulders.

"But I do," Louise asserted. "It's so irreligious!"

"Mother, you've missed the whole point of the essay. It's entitled "The Trial of the Gods.""

"I know that."

"But you don't see the point. It is a condemnation of the shortcomings that the so-called Gods have given mankind."

Louise winced. "I just don't want you to lose your faith."

"Why, have you?"

Louise was caught off guard. He had sensed something that she was afraid to face in her own mind. Trying to avoid an answer, she continued, "But you've mocked Christ."

"Not just Christ! He's not the only one. Krishna, Buddha, Mohammed, Moses—all of them are in jail and awaiting trial."

"It's so absurd."

"No, you don't understand. They've all failed us."

"Don't repeat that again! How could you say such a thing? You were reared to respect your religion."

Kevin shook his head. He paused for a moment, trying to think of a rebuttal. Finally he said, "But it's not trivial. It's treating a serious subject in a humorous manner. The Great Ones are preparing dinner. Jesus would naturally be the one to pour the wine. Mohammed, of course, would have his seventy-three virgin maidens serving the food. Moses breaks the bread like he did the tablets of the idolaters. And Krishna ...""

"Oh, that's enough. I read about that meal that the gods were preparing."

"Then you should read about the trial. The Gods are being held accountable because they let mankind down!"

Louise twisted her lips and asked, "How?"

"All of their teachings and actions do not explain the vital questions that face a human being."

"What questions?"

"Well, for instance, what's it all about?"

"What's what about?"

"Life! Life as we know it. We don't know what it's about. We have no set principles that are for sure. Nothing is truly positive, except change, according to the Greeks."

Louise could not argue with such a response. She merely shook her head and winced again. She thought of her own situation and felt that she could not argue principles. Did she have any herself?

"Mother, nothing in the philosophy of the Gods explains poverty, hatred, and illness, just to name a few. Besides, I'm fed up with God's inadequacies."

"What do you mean?" Louise asked, her face showing her confusion.

"Oh, take the city of Jerusalem, for instance! What kind of a supreme being would put a cornerstone of three of the world's greatest religions in one place? It could only lead to trouble. Why not send Christ to India and Mohammed to China? Just think of how much tension in the world that would have done away with!"

It was too much for Louise. She had already felt uneasy with the explanations for human existence that Sarah had related. Now her son was just as sacrilegious. "So, you no longer believe?"

"No, you're wrong. I have great respect for our religion. Without the great religions, mankind would have no crutches. We need to have them. Dostoevsky has shown that there is only contentment in the metaphysical."

Louise shook her head. Sarah had mentioned Dostoevsky recently and Louise knew that there was no point in continuing. Finally, she smiled and then asked Kevin what he would like for dinner.

Kevin left for school and found Juno waiting at his apartment when he arrived. They embraced, but the host sensed something amiss. The kiss that the guest gave him was perfunctory. Kevin asked, "What's up?"

Juno sat down, smiled and said, "Some things have happened that put a different light on everything." Kevin's eyes winced as if he did not understand. "My father found out that I've been coming to see you."

"How?"

"The bastard had me followed."

"No!" Kevin exclaimed, then added, "Can't he ever leave you alone?"

"He's concerned now because Angelina is pregnant."

"Oh, no!" Kevin uttered as he sat down on the sofa with his friend.

"Yeah, the bitch is going to have a baby. Just what I need!"

Kevin did not utter a word. The situation was very complex, and it could greatly affect their relationship. What kind of solution could there be? He could not lose Juno, but the circumstances were tearing them apart.

Juno reached over and pulled Kevin closer to him. They looked into each other's eyes. They both understood and fell into each other's arms. After a few embraces, Juno stood up and began undressing.

"Oh, no, not now," Kevin said, looking away.

"Why not?"

"I'm just too weary. This means the end, doesn't it?"

"Not if we're clever."

Kevin winced. "Juno, don't you realize, you're going to be a father. Surely that changes things between us."

"Why? Many married men carry on affairs outside their marriage."

"But where does that leave me? Am I supposed to wait continually for a few stolen minutes with you? What kind of life is that?"

Juno didn't answer, but finished undressing and lay down on Kevin's bed. "Come here, you. I want you and need you."

Kevin began slowly taking off his clothes. He was sorrowful. It seemed a pointless effort. They would satisfy themselves, and that would be it. The old romance was gone. He had merely become Juno's outlet for sexual relief. It seemed unfair, as if he were being violated. Nevertheless, he disrobed and slipped under the sheet with his lover. They forgot their momentary misery and enfolded in a passionate embrace. They clung together as if such closeness would dissipate their fear of what could be happening in their lives. Reality intruded only after they had enjoyed the love that Plato praised so highly. Yet the famous Greek philosopher had not expressed anything about the anguish that can follow. The poet Rupert Brooke did: "Not the tears that fill the years—after—after!"

Kevin did shed tears. Sometimes it would happen as he walked through the leaves falling around him on a windy autumn day. Other times when a depression overcame him after they had agreed on a separation. Kevin became engrossed in his studies and suddenly found himself enjoying the company of a particularly robust and good-looking, dark-haired librarian who occasionally helped him with his research. One day, after a rather involved search for pictures of Bakst's famous theatrical scenery, Dave Broussard, the librarian, asked Kevin whether he would be interested in having a drink with him. Surprised but pleased, Kevin agreed, wondering whether Dave might be gay. They met that evening at the Corner Inn, a noted student hangout. After settling in a back booth and ordering a beer, they looked at each other and smiled. Who would start the conversation?

Dave was tall and very athletic. His fine physique indicated his devotion to exercise, so Kevin commented, "You don't look like the usual librarian."

"Why?"

"They rarely have a build like you do."

Dave smiled, showing some irregular teeth that were rarely visible when he spoke. "Yeah, I like to exercise. Do you?"

Kevin nodded. "However, I've been rather lax of late."

"Depressed?"

Kevin nodded again.

Dave brushed back his thick, brown hair. "Everyone goes through it. You will, too."

"I suppose," Kevin agreed. "But tell me what you do if you're depressed."

"I meet someone new," Dave casually responded and sat back to observe the reaction.

Kevin looked into Dave's eyes. He wondered whether his suspicion was true—that Dave was gay and was interested in him. Dave's remark, however, provoked a sense of caution in Kevin. If Dave was promiscuous, it might mean that he only wanted a one-night stand. That kind of activity did not appeal to Kevin. He realized that he was seeking a replacement for Juno. Consequently a feeling of apprehension overtook him, and he decided that he had better refuse any physical contact with Dave until he knew him better.

Changing the subject, Kevin asked Dave where he had studied library science.

Dave smiled knowingly, and again pushed back the long, dark hair that fell across his forehead. Then he revealed some biographical information. He had been in the military service in the first Iraq war and had then studied at Columbia University. He enjoyed doing research and found Kevin's work very intriguing. He finished by asking, "And what led you into the world of art?"

"I like to write, and art has always appealed to me."

"You never thought of the stage? You're a cute guy."

"A bit, but I'm so short, and the world's so tall."

Dave laughed.

"Well, look at you: tall, dark, and handsome!"

Dave suddenly leaned forward. "Let's go over to my place, and I'll show you my library."

Kevin hesitated. The invitation could have been sincere, but it also sounded like an obvious approach. Dave had been so helpful and kind, however, that a refusal would have been rude. Kevin nodded, and Dave picked up the check for their beer. After a short walk in the cool, autumn evening, Dave stopped in front of a brick apartment building. "This is it."

The moment that had caused Kevin concern had arrived. He said, "You know, it's sort of late. Maybe I'd better come another time."

Dave laughed and put his arm around his companion. "Aw, we won't talk long. Besides, it's only nine o'clock."

In spite of his wariness, Kevin nodded and let the librarian lead him into his first-floor apartment. Once Dave had turned on the lights, the visitor saw what he expected: books everywhere. "You must do a lot of reading."

"When I'm not exercising, I'm reading. I like my life."

"You're lucky."

"You don't? That's strange. You seem like a young man with his head just high enough in the clouds to be quite content with himself."

Kevin laughed. "Funny the impression one can make on another person, isn't it?"

"Yeah!" Dave replied and placed his arm around Kevin. He led him to a book shelf and began talking about particular volumes. The conversation drifted from parapsychology to Velasquez's artistic style, the Bodegone. During their discussion Kevin realized that his host was occasionally holding him quite tightly, yet the physical closeness was very pleasant. While Kevin was commenting about Catherine the Great's purchase of the famous Crozat collection in Paris, he looked at Dave, who leaned over and kissed him. The student of art quickly turned his head away and looked up hesitantly at the librarian, then in an instant he raised himself and kissed in return. The two men clung together for some time. Finally Dave began leading Kevin toward a bedroom. Kevin demurred, but Dave's strong arms easily overcame any hesitation. Once in the bedroom, the couple lay on the bed and embraced for some time. Being greatly aroused, they undressed and became as one.

At two in the morning, Kevin slipped from under the arm of his sleeping friend. As he dressed, his eyes admired the statuesque body. The librarian awoke and asked why he was leaving. Kevin crawled back on the bed and suggested that they meet at the Corner Inn later in the morning. Dave nodded and rolled over into the position in which he had been sleeping. Kevin said he would be there at eight, finished dressing, and quietly left for his apartment. Walking through the cool, early-morning air, he felt rejuvenated. It seemed strange that he could have so easily accepted the love of another man. Was it possible that Dave would now substitute for Juno? Was the relationship that he thought would last all his life really over? He smiled. At that moment the hurt that Juno had inflicted on him did not seem important. He had just made love with a fellow intellectual, and it had been wonderful. They were made for each other. How much more satisfying life would be with someone who could converse about art and music! Kevin found himself walking faster and actually skipping at times. He was happy.

The next morning at eight o'clock Kevin was sitting in a booth at the Corner Inn having coffee. His thoughts were about Dave, and he knew that at any minute the tall, swarthy librarian would walk in and join him. There was something exciting about waiting for a new love. It would be their first meeting after their night of sex, and Kevin wondered how the experience had affected his friend. What kind of a mood would he be in? Had he enjoyed the experience as much as Kevin had? Was this truly the beginning of an astonishing relationship? His mind was in a whirl for some time. Then suddenly Kevin realized that it was twenty past eight. Was it possible that Dave wouldn't come? He stared at the advertisements on the wall. If he didn't come, what would it mean? That he didn't like Kevin? That he had only wanted a one-night stand? The thought saddened him, and he began looking with anguish at his watch and at the door. At nine o'clock Kevin left the restaurant, greatly saddened.

At the library Kevin could not concentrate on his research. Dave was absent from his desk and did not appear that morning. Kevin decided that he would visit Dave's apartment. Once there, he found the door open. He knocked and Dave came from the bedroom wearing a gray sweatshirt. His hair looked windblown, and he was holding a towel as if he were preparing for a shower. "Hi, Kevin, what are you doing here?"

"We were going to meet at the Corner Inn this morning."

"Yeah, but I couldn't come. I usually run in the mornings."

Kevin's face showed his astonishment. "Couldn't you have run by the Corner and told me that you weren't coming?"

"I never run in that direction. I go to the park."

"Couldn't you have made an exception since you knew I'd be there waiting for you?"

Dave smirked. "Why are you acting as if I broke one of the Ten Commandants? I knew that, after a while, you'd realize that I wasn't coming."

"But that's not the point."

"What is the point?"

Kevin looked at the ceiling, and his lips twisted. An obvious explanation would have to be stated. "It's a matter of manners. Surely you see that!"

"Oh, how bourgeois!"

"Hardly! Manners show respect, and evidently you don't care a bit for me."

"I should think that after last night you ..."

At that moment a blond, curly-haired young man dressed in a blue sweat suit walked out of the bedroom. Dave made an awkward introduction of his running mate and Kevin, greatly disturbed, quickly excused himself. He instantly concluded that Dave was very promiscuous and that his own experience was what he had feared: a one-night stand. He practically ran to his room and fell on his bed.

If only Juno would come! Kevin thought but soon concluded that he, too, had broken the bond between them. Juno had married, and he had bedded another man. Kevin was terribly confused. Nothing seemed of value, and he felt desolate.

Kevin avoided the library for three days, but some information he needed for his research was available only in the archives. As he was sitting in the Historical Research Hall, he suddenly heard a voice behind him. He knew it was Dave and turned toward him. The librarian, wearing a multicolored tie and white shirt, was smiling and said, "You've been avoiding me."

Kevin looked at the floor. "I assumed you were occupied."

Dave smiled again. "I just run for exercise with Bill. I know what you're thinking, but there's nothing between us."

Kevin looked at the ceiling. He did not believe Dave nor did he know what he should say.

Dave sat beside him and whispered, "Listen, you don't own me. We had a good time the other night, and we can have more. It's up to you; but just don't try to put me in chains."

Turning toward Dave, Kevin replied. "I wasn't, and I won't. I just ..." Kevin hesitated. His confusion was obvious.

"If you want me again, come to my apartment at nine o'clock." Dave patted Kevin on the shoulder and walked away.

Kevin's first thought was of a blunt refusal. He would not go. If Dave did not see how ill-mannered he had been, then there was no point in continuing the affair. That is all it was anyway, just an affair. It was not a relationship that had meaning; it was just sex. No, he would not go. He would rather shoot himself than lower himself to Dave's level. The guy evidently cared only for himself. His actions proved it. He had not even given an apology for his behavior. No, he would not go see him.

All that day Kevin's thoughts returned again and again to the librarian. For some time his conviction was firm: he would not see Dave again. Yet by midafternoon Dave's positive qualities gained control of his thinking. The librarian had been very helpful and had initiated the affair. Perhaps he was a bit ill-mannered, but in a self-serving world, did it matter? Wasn't self-satisfaction the credo of his generation? If he really liked Dave, perhaps he should tolerate some of his idiosyncrasies. He would go at nine o'clock, but just for a chat, and would try for a better understanding of the guy. Then perhaps a meaningful relationship could develop. Yes, that was the plan, but the fulfillment was, as so often in life, another matter.

When Kevin arrived at Dave's apartment, there was no answer. He went outside and entered the back section of the building. There was no light in the apartment. Dave was definitely not at home, but how could he not be? He had invited Kevin. It was truly discourteous behavior. Sadly the visitor returned home, disgusted with himself and with Dave. After an hour of not concentrating on his research, however, Kevin took a walk. He knew where he was going and headed directly for Dave's apartment. When he went into the back section, lights were burning. Dave was at home. Kevin ran to the front and up the stairs to the door. Again it was ajar, and he stepped in as he knocked.

Dave came out of the small kitchen and said, "Oh, you've come!"

"You said you'd be here at nine."

"Yeah, but I got caught up in some things."

"But isn't that another example of your …"

Before Kevin could finish his accusation, Dave took him into his arms and embraced him, pressing their bodies close together. When they separated, Kevin tried speaking, but Dave simply picked him up. "What are you doing?" Kevin asked.

"What you want," Dave answered and carried his friend into the bedroom.

"No," Kevin protested, but when Dave placed him on the bed, he allowed the librarian to cover his body with his great athletic frame. In no time they were undressing and involved in various sexual activities. Kevin had never had scatological experiences and scooted abruptly away when Dave began such activity. The aggressor was amused and pulled Kevin back, rolling him onto his stomach so he could lick all over the back of his torso. To his amazement, Kevin found the sensation very satisfying, but it still seemed unnatural. *What next?* he wondered as he gave in to the desires of his companion.

Before leaving the apartment, Kevin asked Dave whether they could meet for breakfast the next morning, and Dave agreed. He did not appear at the Corner, however, and Kevin was again quite upset. *What kind of upbringing did Dave have?* he wondered. *How could he be so indifferent to the feelings of others and yet be such a conscientious librarian?*

Kevin also remembered their bedroom activities and could hardly believe that he had participated in such behavior. Still, he knew that he was enamored of Dave and would gladly meet with him again.

Meetings did occur, and Kevin no longer pined over his lost love with Juno. Yet Dave also continued his apparent absolute lack of concern for Kevin's ideas of proper conduct. If he was late for a rendezvous, he was just late. If he did not call when he had promised, he just did not call. There was always a simple explanation and another pronouncement about his not being chained or restricted. Kevin gradually accepted his mood swings, but he found them distasteful. He did not care for his lover's free spirit, but he tolerated it for the pleasure of their sexual activities. Kevin knew that he was in love with a person who could not return his feelings. The realization caused him to write a poem, which he left on Dave's pillow.

One can't hold back a falling star,
It has its own volition.
One's love can only stand afar
And wish for its fruition.
The star sails on alone through life

It seeks but cannot find.
The love, still true, remains afar
As if it did not mind.

Kevin waited for a response from Dave, but it did not come. Desiring some kind of recognition, Kevin went to the librarian's office and asked whether Dave had found the slip of paper he had left on his pillow.

Dave responded, "Yeah, I liked your poem. It reminded me of one by Truman Capote."

"Is that all?" Kevin asked, disappointed.

"What do you want, a critique?"

"No, I just thought you'd understand me better."

Dave smiled. "I do understand you. You're in love. I like you, too, but let's not play Romeo and Juliet over it. Let's just enjoy it while we have it. Okay?"

Kevin nodded. After he left, his mind was whirling. He concluded that since Dave had mentioned his own amorous feelings, there was the possibility of making the affair a long-term relationship—the sort of life that Kevin desired. Yes, it could be possible. He would just wait until Dave himself realized the possibility. Until then, Kevin would be everything that Dave could want. His conclusion gave him a sense of joy and accomplishment. He was in love, and he was loved. Is there anything else worth having?

A chance arrived for the fulfillment of Kevin's desire for a long-term relationship with Dave. Mrs. Dudley called and asked when her son would be returning for Thanksgiving weekend. She was making plans for several special parties and wanted to know if she could count on his being there. Kevin sensed that his mother wanted at least one son home for the holidays, so he assured her that he would be home. Suddenly realizing a good opportunity, he added that he might bring a friend with him. Mrs. Dudley was pleased at the prospect because her son seemed happier than he had been previously. Both mother and son, for different reasons, were delighted with the possibility of a guest for the weekend. Kevin wondered, however, how Dave would act in the Dudley environment. So the student decided that he would invite the librarian home for a short trial visit before the holidays. It would give them plenty of free time together, and Kevin was sure that Dave would be impressed by his family home and background. The weekend could be the beginning of their life together. When Dave accepted the invitation, Kevin was positive that his plan was feasible and would bring fruition.

When Kevin first proposed the weekend at his home, Dave had hesitated. He looked at Kevin and smiled, but it was a gesture that implied doubt. Kevin quickly went into great detail about possible activities they could engage in during such a visit. He exaggerated, but Dave was touched by his eagerness.

"You really want me to go home with you, don't you?"

Kevin nodded.

"Well, let me think about it. When do you have to know for sure?"

"We can go this next weekend, if you're free."

"So quickly?"

"Mother would be delighted."

Dave smiled again, but it reflected a different mood. Kevin sensed that his friend would accept, so he said, "Yes, we'll have the run of the house together. Mother's always going to some club or church activity. We can do anything we want."

Dave laughed and winked. "I know what we'll do, don't you?"

Kevin smiled and nodded in agreement. "Then it's settled, right? You'll go?"

David nodded and brushed his hair from his forehead. Kevin moved close and they embraced.

A beautiful, New England fall day had set in when Kevin and Dave started their sojourn to the Dudley family home in Stamford. Both young men felt revitalized by the fresh, cool air. As they drove along, Kevin related interesting episodes from the famous Dudley clan's past. Dave began calling his companion a "high brow" and somewhat derided any pride connected to one's ancestors.

"But you said they were interesting," Kevin commented in rebuttal.

"Yes, they're interesting, but you shouldn't let them dominate your life."

"They don't. Have I ever mentioned them before?"

"No, but you act like you're a judge of proper behavior, like some aristocrat."

Kevin surmised that a change of subject would be best and asked where Dave had grown up. The librarian began a tirade about his family and talked about them unkindly. He seemed amused by calling them a poor pack of ignoramuses. Kevin was surprised at the blatant negative comments Dave made about his kin, but decided that he was exaggerating for a definite contrast to the Dudleys. When he suggested that Dave was not being candid, the librarian assured his friend that his family was rural farmers and that they were not educated.

"But you're so knowledgeable," Kevin replied.

"I got the GI bill from the army and entered the university. I didn't have parents to spoil me like you did."

"Oh, am I spoiled?"

"You'd better believe it. Bet you've never had a day without money in your pocket."

"Is that my fault?"

"No, damn it! It just shows the difference between us."

A silence set in. Kevin wondered if he had made a mistake in inviting Dave. If he made such crude statements at the Dudley home, it would be embarrassing. Kevin was sure he would not, but a sense of foreboding accompanied his assurance.

When Kevin's yellow convertible drove into the circular drive of the Dudley home, Dave exclaimed, "Just as I thought. You had the silver spoon in your mouth, didn't you, kid?"

Kevin did not answer. He merely drove to the front of the house, stopped, and slipped out of the car. "Well, here we are, Dave. I hope you'll be glad you came with me."

Entering the Dudley manor entailed the usual flourish of greetings and tours around the house. Having a guest brought out Mrs. Dudley's usual exuberance. As they walked through the rooms, she related news that caused both Kevin and Dave some consternation, but for different reasons. Mrs. Dudley revealed what she considered joyous news. By a streak of luck, all of her sons would be home for Thanksgiving after all. She had thought that she would have only one son for the holiday, but it had turned out otherwise. She then turned to Dave and said, "And you are invited, too, Dave. I think Kevin should have a friend here, too."

Kevin was apprehensive and Dave displeased. They looked at each other, and their eyes revealed their anxiety. Kevin was afraid of family squabbles, and Dave did not desire a weekend of social conversation, which was something he loathed. Yet they sat down on a couch in the family room and listened patiently as Mrs. Dudley explained the reason for the family homecoming: Phillip had been granted a parole for good behavior.

"Oh, no!" Kevin gasped. "When?"

"This afternoon! Isn't that wonderful?"

"Oh, no!"

"Now, Kevin, don't give Dave the wrong impression," Louise looked at the guest. "All my sons really do feel close to each other." Then she continued. "Besides the good news about Phillip, my son Paul is bringing a new lady friend. Also, Sharon and Roger are usually at her parents' home for the holidays, but her father is in the hospital, so they are joining us, for a change. All my sons will be home. I'm just thrilled."

Kevin made a strange sound and squirmed. Louise looked at him rather askance, but her continued enthusiasm showed her delight. She finished relating her news by saying, "Oh, I know you'd like all of them, Dave. And

Kevin, you should be glad that Paul has found contentment at last. I'm looking forward to meeting his friend, and you should be, too."

When Mrs. Dudley went for ice, the companions looked at each other. Their eyes said it all. Dave said, "I won't come for that!"

"You don't have to."

"Let's leave now."

Kevin looked at his friend in dismay. Finally he said, "We have to stay. It would be too rude to leave."

"So what?"

"She knows we came for the weekend. I can't do that to her."

Dave brushed back his hair and grimaced. There was no way out, and he knew it. Curling his lips, he said in a sarcastic tone, "So we'll get to meet your brother Phillip! Isn't that great?"

Louise returned with the ice and made an announcement. "It's wonderful because, as I said, all my boys will be here, but I am also going to make an announcement that might startle them."

"What is it?" Kevin asked.

Louise smiled, "You'll see, and don't even try to guess. I won't tell you now."

Kevin looked at Dave and hunched his shoulders. "It probably has something to do with Phillip. He's always in trouble."

Louise shook her head. "Now, be fair. Phillip is not the only one of my sons who has had problems. Wouldn't you agree?"

Kevin replied, "Well, Roger's in a mess, and Paul's certainly a bounder."

Louise was amused that Kevin did not consider himself a problem. "Yes, you're the perfect one," she teased.

Kevin laughed.

"You should be glad that your brothers are handling their problems well. I was delighted that Paul found someone after his tragic loss."

Stifling a laugh, Kevin said, "Yes, I can just see Paul suffering." Turning to Dave, Kevin added, "He's probably chased every skirt on that ship. He's the handsome one and can have any woman he wants."

Mrs. Dudley pretended that she did not hear Kevin's remark and excused herself under the pretense of preparing their dinner. When she left, Dave informed Kevin that he wanted to run a while before they ate. Not listening to his host's comment that they would be eating shortly, Dave went upstairs, quickly changed into his sport outfit, and left the house.

Dinner was soon ready, and the hostess and host were compelled to wait a considerable time. Louise did not object because it gave her a chance for conversation with her son about his studies. Kevin, however, was displeased with his friend's behavior and candidly confessed that he felt that Dave was indeed a very rude person. In Kevin's opinion, however, his friend's conduct was the result of the uncultured home in which he had been reared. After he told his mother about Dave's background, Louise asked, "Then what do you two have in common?"

Kevin smiled and looked away. He almost said the word "sex," but controlled himself for his mother's sake.

After some time Dave rang the front doorbell. Kevin opened it and commented that the run had delayed their dinner.

"So what?" Dave replied and went upstairs for a shower.

Again there was a delay. It was almost more than Kevin could stand, and he was glad that Dave had not accepted the invitation for the Thanksgiving weekend. Louise, however, was amused at Dave's behavior. She was sure that his friendship with her son would not have a long duration.

That night when the family retired, Louise heard rather loud talk coming from Kevin's room. She went into the hall and listened. Often the language was not understandable. It was obvious that Kevin was criticizing his friend's manners, but occasionally there was a word that seemed out of context. The next morning, before Dave joined the family at the breakfast table, she admitted that she had heard voices and had assumed that they were quarreling. She implied that she did not want to interfere in their relationship but would like to ask a question or two about some words she overheard. When she said "rim," Kevin snickered and looked down at his cereal.

"Why is that funny?" Louise asked.

Kevin put his napkin over his mouth. "It just is, Mother, and I can't tell you what it means." Again he sniffed and smiled.

"Why not?"

"It's too distasteful."

Louise looked at her son with a quizzical look. "I take it that it implies the rim of something?"

Kevin choked and ran out of the room laughing. He quickly returned quite composed. "Mother, please, not now."

"I don't see why not. I'm quite curious. I remember the sentence I heard. 'I'd bite my tongue off before I'd rim you!'"

Kevin laughed again and wiped his eyes with his napkin. "Mother, you've said it all. That's what it means."

Louise thought for a second and stated, "I take it that it pertains to kissing."

Kevin nodded and laughed. When he saw his mother looking at him as if waiting for an answer, he finally said, "It's a matter of kissing the rim of the derriere."

Louise looked at the ceiling. A pained look developed on her face. "Kevin, surely you don't do that sort of thing."

Exasperated, he replied, "If you didn't want to know, why did you ask?"

"Oh!" Louise exclaimed as she stood and walked out onto the patio. The thought of such degeneracy bothered her, but she quickly composed herself and returned, realizing that her son would say the same about her own conduct with Phillip.

Returning to the kitchen, she suggested that Kevin and Dave go for a swim at the club and join her for lunch there.

Kevin went upstairs and awakened Dave by jumping on the bed and putting his arms around him. Dave woke up and pushed his friend away. "God, man, let me wake up."

Kevin refused and started kissing his guest all over his torso. Dave finally laughed and pushed Kevin over on the bed and slipped on top of him. "So, you little imp, you didn't get enough?"

Quickly Kevin moved from under Dave and stood by the bed. "We're going swimming after breakfast. Okay?"

"Yeah, why not!"

Kevin was glad that his friend accepted the plan, but at the club Dave continued his venomous remarks about the Dudleys' upscale life and the spoiled upbringing it had given Kevin, who was tired of the sarcasm and was even more pleased that Dave had not accepted the Thanksgiving weekend invitation.

That afternoon Phillip was brought home in a police car. At the door Mrs. Dudley signed a release document and followed her son into the entrance hall. Suddenly she found herself in Phillip's arms. He embraced his mother tightly and kissed her on the lips. She froze but did not break away. Unbeknownst to them, Dave had come up the hall and had observed the homecoming. He quickly returned to the family room and awaited the others.

Louise led Phillip into the room and made introductions. Kevin entered and greeted his brother kindly, which made Louise feel at ease. The group conversed for a few minutes before Mrs. Dudley left for the kitchen and Phillip to his room. No sooner had they departed than Dave said with an ironic smile and a teasing tone, "They sort of like each other, don't they?"

Kevin, noticing the obvious suggestion in his friend's words, frowned. "What on earth do you mean?"

Dave laughed, "Well, they sort of go for each other, don't they?"

Displeased, Kevin asked again, "What do you mean?"

"Well, it just so happened that I saw the homecoming. They went together a little more passionate than I would think befitting a mother and son."

Kevin's face wrinkled, showing his displeasure. "Are you crazy? Are you suggesting that there's something between my mother and brother? How disgusting you are!"

Dave's shoulder hunched, and he replied in a nonplussed tone, "Well, it seemed rather peculiar to me."

"Really, Dave, how could you suggest such a thing?"

Pursing his lips, Dave said, "Well, you didn't see them kiss."

Upset, Kevin responded, "Mother kisses us all the time. How could you see anything so revolting in it?"

Dave smiled and sat down on a sofa. "Well, let's drop it. I was merely giving you my observation."

"Keep it to yourself," Kevin sneered and left the room.

That evening, after some rather stilted and trivial conversation at the dinner table, Kevin and Dave made excuses and returned to Yale. Louise was perplexed about their departure, but Phillip was glad. It would give him and his mother time for making their plans.

Chapter 13

After the federal authorities finally agreed on the Thanksgiving holidays as the time for releasing Phillip to his mother's charge, Louise and her son began very serious conversations. They had talked rather lightly about their life on an island in the Caribbean, but since Phillip was now free, a definite decision was necessary. It was easily made. What had been amusing suddenly became reality; what had been far-reaching was now before them; what had been a loose bond of affection was now an admittance of love. Whether their love was sanctionable was never given thought. They had come together; they were mother and son, and they were son and mother. It did not matter. Each found fulfillment in the other. When Phillip held Louise's hands, she saw the child she had nursed and held to her breasts. That love still gleamed in her eyes and heart. When he held her hands, he felt the strength of her love and knew that he could overcome his demons through her. Between them there was an inexplicable potency that was beyond human reason. Their feelings for each other were not demeaning or degrading; they were uplifting and refined. With such strength, they were capable of confronting the problems that were undoubtedly ahead, but they knew they were right and could win. It was decided that they would announce their decision to the family at the annual Thanksgiving dinner.

On a warm, fall afternoon Louise walked out on her patio and gazed at the beauty of the yellow and red leaves falling from the trees. She wondered whether she would miss the change of seasons on the islands. What a different life she would have! Was she really up to the challenge? Suddenly she saw her neighbor leading her llama around her garden. She called over and invited her for some tea. Soon they were exchanging news as they enjoyed the warm weather.

After a while Sarah said, "I think you've invited me over for more than a chat, am I right?"

Louise laughed. "How well you know me! Yes, I have reached the denouement of the melodrama that I've been boring you with for some time."

"It was never boring. Imaginative, perhaps, but never boring!"

They both laughed.

As Louise revealed her plan to Sarah, the neighbor only nodded and smiled. "Well, I didn't think it would come to this, and I shall miss you terribly. However, I do believe the happiest people follow their heart rather than their mind. Look at Tolstoy and Dostoevsky. The former searched for meaning all his life and was miserable; the latter knew happiness in his heart, his faith. I'd like to think that you're doing the right thing, but of course I am apprehensive."

Louise placed her cup of tea on a white, wrought iron table. "I'd like to know why."

Sarah thought for a moment. "Well, there are so many aspects to consider. I'm wondering first of all about your other sons. What will they think or say when you reveal this most bizarre plot of your melodrama, as you put it."

Louise nodded. "I've thought a lot about that, but I have an answer for each of them. I've concluded that we are not the upright, religious family that I thought we were. All of my sons have strayed from the faith they were reared in. Oh, they might not think so, but I've plenty of material to convince them otherwise. If anything, I've come to the conclusion that we represent a rather dysfunctional family. We claim to stand for one thing and then do another. We've never been truthful with ourselves." She paused. "But now I have! I realize that I do care for my son in ways that perhaps can be misunderstood, but that's not my fault. And if saving him demands this way, then thank God that I can do it."

Sarah shook her head. "Who would have thought that the upright and proper Mrs. Dudley could become so honest and insightful! I tell you, Louise, I do believe that you can carry this plan off and that maybe you should."

"You still have doubts?"

Again Sarah smiled at her. "It's a rough road ahead for you, my dear, but I'll be on your side."

"Thanks, Sarah. I knew I could depend on you. You've already helped me so much, and I know that I'll be calling on you for advice in the future. Right now, I'm very pleased with your attitude."

"When do you plan telling the family?"

"I've decided to announce it at our annual Thanksgiving dinner. Fortunately, all four sons will be here. Yes, our happy family will have quite a session that day!"

Sarah had a few moments of quiet reflection. Then she said, "I've never quite agreed with Tolstoy about families."

"What do you mean?"

Sarah took a gulp of black coffee. "In the beginning of *Anna Karenina* he maintains that all happy families are happy in the same way, and all unhappy families are unhappy in their own way."

Louise's face showed that she was confused and did not quite understand.

"I think happy families can be just as diverse. They could be well adjusted and happy because of money, faith, or other things. They don't really have a single common thread, do they? His generalization is too smooth, too broad. It doesn't cover the essence or point out the single basic element."

Louise interjected, "Is a family ever happy? That is, is there a time when all the members of a family are really happy? I can't find it in my past."

"Well, it's not the happy families that I'm really interested in. It's the unhappy families that I question. I believe that there is maybe a primal urge toward disaster, which makes families unhappy the same way. Tolstoy should have reversed his generalization."

"What do you mean, a primal urge?"

"An instinct, maybe, or a cell pattern in their DNA. Something makes families disintegrate. It could perhaps be a sociological problem. I don't know, but I look at my own family and realize that we were happy until the truth came out. My son was gay, and I forced him into a marriage. That's the sociological aspect, but what made him that way has a deeper cause."

Louise was quiet and looked out over the garden. "Yes, I think you're right. My sons were content or even happy when we gave them everything they wanted. Yet that wasn't enough, was it? Why did Phillip become an alcoholic? Why did Roger marry for money? What made Paul so licentious? Why is Kevin gay, as you say?"

Sarah smiled. "We'll never know the answer. I just feel that Tolstoy generalized too broadly. Both happy and unhappy families can be happy and unhappy in the same way."

Louise laughed. "Sarah, I can't quite follow your logic because you're always ahead of me. However, I can name one happy family that might not be too happy very soon!"

Sarah laughed with her neighbor and said, "I have never been so curious! I'll be waiting for a minute-by-minute report."

"The action might require that," Louise responded. "I'm curious, too, about how it will all end."

"By the way, I remembered a television program that I saw some time ago about incest. They called it 'genetic sexual attraction.' Seems that one's DNA has something that can cause one to transcend ordinary feelings and create a very special relationship. Whether this applies to your situation, I couldn't say, but it's interesting."

Louise paused, but before she could comment, Phillip joined the ladies on the patio. Louise stood up and asked him to sit with Sarah while she took something out of the freezer for dinner .

Phillip agreed and lay down on a patio lounge. "I believe Mother has told you our plan."

"Yes, and I must say that it amazes me."

"Really! Why?"

Sarah smiled and adjusted her weight in her chair. "Well, you'll have to admit that it's not a common pact of circumstances!"

Phillip also smiled. "Yes, I do admit it, but I believe you understand or Mother wouldn't have told you."

Sarah nodded. "Yes, we share a lot."

After lighting up a cigarette, Phillip inhaled and exhaled. "You see, Sarah, for the first time in my life I feel as if I really belong to the family."

Sarah's face showed her surprise.

"Yes, it's true. You see, my brothers were always what Mother and Dad wanted—that is, successful types. Roger was brilliant in school, Paul was so handsome it made his way in everything easy, and Kevin is just too cute a kid for anyone to dislike. I was none of the above! I was a poor student, I was ugly, and I had few friends. My path to drugs was straight. I had no other way to go. I was left out, and I felt it in the family. Mother was kind to me, but her disappointment was evident all the time. I couldn't take it."

"You're not telling me anything I didn't know," Sarah interrupted. "I've watched you for years and always thought you were left out. However, I didn't think you were ugly. You're a big guy and not bad-looking, but of course you're not a Paul. Also, from what you've just said, I think I comprehend better the reason for your wanting the love you are now sharing with Louise. You have finally found a place in her heart that pleases you. Yes, I understood you better than you realized. I also understand how a mother can unconsciously misdirect her son. You got bad vibes from several directions. I did the same with my son."

"Yes, your Danny Boy told me many things. In fact, he and I did things that you don't even know about."

Sarah's jaw dropped. "Like what?"

"Oh, we did things in that shed back there that boys often do."

"Sexual?"

Phillip nodded and laughed.

Sarah only shook her head. "If only I had known."

"Well, he lived through it, and I guess he's happy now."

Sarah did not respond. Her hurt was too deep, and she did not feel like discussing it at that time. "I'd say that you seem the happy one now."

"Yes, I am. I know that what Mother and I are doing is right. For the first time I am sure that I can fight drugs and win. Mother is sacrificing much for me, and therefore I could never let her down. Before I felt left out, but now I know that I am in. That is, that she loves me as much as my brothers and that my failures did not matter. She is a wonderful woman, and I love her desperately."

Sarah smiled. "In more ways than one, I understand."

Phillip laughed. "Yes, we sleep together, and it's wonderful. I'm quite well endowed, you know, and can please a woman quite easily. It's the one thing I'm better at than my brothers."

"Now really, Phillip! Isn't that rather blatant? However, I assume you're correct."

Louise returned. There was silence for a few seconds. Then Louise stated, "Well, the great weekend is starting, and I believe I'm almost ready. Heaven help me!"

"I think you can handle it," Sarah commented and took her leave.

The remark pleased Louise, and she continued thinking about the next few days. All her sons would be home for her incredible announcement. How would they take her plan? It could cause bitterness and discord in the family. Could such an arrangement possibly be accepted? She wondered about the reactions of her sons. Kevin's attitude toward Phillip was regrettable, but she remembered that he had teased Kevin about his inclinations, and the affront had caused much hatred in Kevin. He could be the one son who would greatly oppose the plan. Paul would not care, so long as he received his share of the Dudley Trust. Roger and Sharon could hardly object since they had lived in sin before their marriage. All the sons were prevaricators, but Kevin's opinion seemed more important than the others. He was her youngest, and she had babied him excessively. All her sons had been spoiled, but Kevin, being the lastborn, had been greatly pampered. She wanted the approval of all her sons, and maybe because he seemed the most vulnerable, she wanted Kevin's the most of all.

During the days before the Thanksgiving weekend, Louise and Phillip were busy with the family lawyer, their trust auditor, and a realtor. They also completed much shopping for the traditional Thanksgiving dinner. However, their plan for revealing their intentions with the whole family after the traditional feast was thwarted by Kevin's unexpected early arrival. Louise and Phillip had already retired to the master bedroom when, after midnight, they heard a noise in the hall. Both were awakened, and Phillip jumped out of bed and hurried toward the door. When he opened it, Kevin was passing by in the hall. He stopped and turned toward Phillip who turned on a light. Kevin froze in the doorway and Louise grabbed her negligee.

A painful expression immediately covered Kevin's face. Out of his throat tore a cry of anguish. "Oh, nooo!" He quickly turned and ran up the hall.

"Oh my God!" Louise gasped and ran after her son. She waved at Phillip, indicating that he should not follow her.

When she entered Kevin's room and turned on a light by the door, she found a scene that distressed her greatly. Her son was sobbing remorsefully on his bed. She hesitated. The hurt in her heart was almost unbearable. She could not decide whether she should touch Kevin or leave him alone. Slowly she approached the bed.

In a soft voice, she pleaded, "Kevin, my darling, please let me talk with you."

Sobbing, Kevin turned his tear-stained face toward her, and he blustered, "Leave me alone!"

Louise stood transfixed. She had never experienced such mental torment. Her shame had harmed her beloved Kevin, and she was mortified. Her only escape was in the tears that began falling from her eyes. She crumpled into a seated position on the front of the bed frame. Both mother and son cried for some time. Finally Kevin crawled off the bed and took his mother in his arms. Louise stood, and the two, still crying, embraced closely. They had nothing to hold on to but themselves.

After what seemed an eternity, mother and son separated and sat down on the bed. Still crying, Louise uttered, "Kevin, you have to understand. I can't live without your love."

Kevin, who seemed to be grasping for words, replied, "Mother, I ... can't ... believe it."

Again they embraced. Holding her son's hands, the mother tried to provide understanding. Never before had a mother expressed such things to a son. . She revealed her shame but also her frightful fear that the salvation of one son might cause the loss of another. Louise loved her family and was distraught about the circumstances that had brought about their dilemma. Yet she was resolute in carrying out the plan with Phillip and prayed that Kevin and her sons would understand and help her in the torment she was enduring and in the joy of her newfound life.

After much discussion, Kevin, still in shock about his mother's revelation, ceased crying and retired. The burden of comprehension had tired him greatly, and he tumbled onto his bed greatly relieved that he could momentarily escape from the realization that of what had been verified. The whole affair seemed monstrous, but it was his dearest mother, and he eagerly sought comprehension. His ponderous thoughts weighed him down, and he soon drifted into a deep sleep.

Next morning Louise and Phillip were at breakfast when Kevin, looking very tired, entered the kitchen and said in a soft but kind tone, "Hello, everybody!"

The pleasing quality of his voice immediately created a mood in which the family members felt comfortable. Conversation started about the weather and then turned to the usual comments about their night's sleep. Somehow they had all slept better than they had expected. Louise began preparing pancakes with maple syrup as they talked. Slowly the dreaded topic that had caused such anguish the last evening came into their discussion. Kevin could not look at his mother or brother as they both tried explaining their precarious situation. Yet when he spoke he glanced at them. He just simply could not face them while hearing unimaginable details. The three were very cordial and expressed great affection during their sophisticated reasoning and polemics. By the end of their breakfast, Kevin could understand why Phillip believed that the relationship with his mother could save him, but he was not convinced that it could be true. Kevin had no faith in his brother's conversion and was fearful for his mother's well-being. In addition, Kevin, who had never thought of his mother as having physical needs, was perplexed by the insinuation that Phillip and his mother had sexual contact. It was too bizarre and, in his opinion, degrading. At times he almost shuddered when the subject was referred to. Kevin remained calm, however, even though his eyes filled with tears several times. Still, he did not cry. No conclusions or agreements were made during their conversation, and they parted peacefully. Kevin felt uneasy when Louise embraced him as he was leaving the room, yet each of the family members was thankful that there had not been any unpleasantness or recriminations.

After Kevin left, Louise and Phillip looked at each other. They were both quite satisfied with the way Kevin had listened and discussed the situation with them. It was obvious that he was greatly disturbed, but his calmness encouraged them. They were sure that he would eventually understand and accept their plan, strange as it then seemed.

While Kevin gave his mother and brother the impression that he could possibly accept their intentions, it was another matter when Paul returned and learned about the situation. Handsome Paul's arrival was full of the bragging that characterized the way he usually related his latest conquests. When asked why the lovely girl he had invited had not come, he laughed and said that the invitation had been a ploy. She had been with him when he wrote the note, but he had not been serious. It was a lie, of course, but Paul's explanation was somewhat believable. He related his exploits and adventures during the cruise one after the other. There was no mention of his activities with the perverted waiter or the cruelty in his seductions. It was all presented as if he had just been a happy-go-lucky fellow on a delightful cruise. It was also noticeable that he never once mentioned the tragic demise of his wife and son. He had evidently thought only of himself while on his vacation.

During his fanciful version of his trip, Paul noticed that Kevin seemed morose as the family sat listening in the family room to his tirade about life on the Caribbean. Interrupting himself, Paul asked Kevin, "What's with you, sunshine? You're not your usual beaming self."

Kevin looked away without answering, and Paul looked at his mother for an answer.

Mrs. Dudley avoided commenting and announced that it was time for her shopping trip for groceries. She suggested that Paul freshen up, and the family would hear more about his trip during lunch. After she departed with Phillip, Paul asked Kevin, "What's going on around here? Seems like something's amiss?"

In a snide tone, Kevin said, "You won't believe what's going on around here."

Paul's demeanor changed, and in a serious tone he asked, "What do you mean?"

Kevin looked at the floor. How could one explain or even relate the event that was taking place in the Dudley family? After a slight pause, he began with, "You'd better sit down."

Exasperated, Paul snarled, "Will you get to the point?"

Kevin briefly told his brother a few vital aspects of the situation in the family.

Paul suddenly laughed. "Mother, immoral? What in the hell are you trying to say?"

Kevin went into details, but Paul continued deriding his explanations. "Mother, a degenerate? Who's kidding who?" Yet Kevin continued, and Paul finally scoffed, "You little bastard, you're making that up!"

Kevin swore it was true.

Paul smiled ironically. He could not decide whether laughter or anger was apropos. He could not accept what his brother had just related and said in disgust, "You little faggot! What are you after, my cock?"

Kevin grimaced as he ran out of the room.

When Louise and Phillip returned, they found that a different mood prevailed in the house. Paul met them in the entrance hall and yelled, "What in the hell are you two thinking of?"

The couple stopped abruptly and stared at Paul. With a disgusted grimace on his face, he made a fast downward wave and walked up the hall toward the family room. Mother and brother quickly placed their packages on the floor and followed him. Once inside, Paul asked in a loud, irate tone, "Is that garbage that Kevin is telling me true?"

Phillip replied in an indignant tone, "Watch what you're saying, or I'll beat the hell out of you." He started toward Paul, but Louise stepped in front of him.

The brothers made several furious comments until Louise quieted them. She asked them to be seated and then calmly turned to Paul and tried explaining the situation. The look on his face only showed more and more disgust. Finally he could take no more and said, "You, immoral? Oh, don't make me laugh."

Phillip again warned Paul about undue comments, and Louise quieted them a second time. Then she took the offensive. "Paul, you have no right to be using that word with me! Are you so moral that you can judge?"

With anguish still in his facial expression, Paul blurted out, "But Mother, it's so wrong and disgusting!"

Phillip intervened in a loud voice. "Disgusting? You should use that word! What about the way you acted on 9/11? You didn't even have the moral fiber or nerve to help your wife. You let her die while you saved your skin!"

It was the first time that anyone in the family had openly accused Paul of cowardice in reference to his behavior during the notorious terrorist incident. The comment overwhelmed him, and he crumpled on the couch in tears, saying "Oh my God, what is happening here?"

Louise tried putting an arm around his shoulders, but he quickly stood and ran out of the room. Phillip and Louise looked at each other in dismay, but they also felt relief. They sensed that Paul would calm down.

After Paul rested and had time for contemplation, he concentrated on his own situation. There was the matter of the Dudley Trust. Mrs. Dudley was the soul benefactor of the large inheritance, and Paul wanted his share if Louise and Phillip were actually going through with their plan. For his own protection, he called his brother Roger and told him about the situation at the Dudley manor. At first Roger thought Paul was kidding because of the improbability of such an occurrence, but, after listening for a while, Roger could tell by his brother's tone that he was serious. The revelation required Roger's immediate attention, and he said that he would come over that evening.

When he told Sharon, she laughed. "What? Mrs. 'Perfect' is naughty? Oh, no, that's impossible."

Yet it was true.

That evening the four sons of the Dudley family met with their mother in the family room. At first the gathering was very unpleasant. Each son, apart from Phillip, expressed his disbelief that such a relationship could be possible, and each condemned their mother and brother for creating such a liaison. The accusations, containing such words as *immorality, abhorrence,* and *degeneration* finally brought on a rebuttal from Louise. She stood and had her say.

"My sons, it is now my turn, and I want you to listen carefully. While you might not understand what has happened between Phillip and me, I want you to know that you have no right to criticize. If you can't understand how Phillip and I are both trying to help each other, then I regret it greatly. But I'll say it again. You do not have any right to criticize. Look at yourselves! How do you think I feel about you? Let's examine ourselves. First, you, Roger! You who married for money and thereby brought a slut into our home. Then you, Paul! You have disgraced us with your cowardice and promiscuity. And you, my sweet Kevin! You would dare use the word *immorality.* What about your activities with Juno? All of us have strayed from the principles of our faith. It's as if we never really paid attention during all those years of attending church. I don't understand what has happened to us. Is it the times we live in? Has the world changed? Are right and wrong no longer defined as we once believed? Look at us! We are all doing what we want no matter how it affects anyone else. My sons, I love you all, but you must understand that what Phillip and I are planning does not decrease my feelings for you one iota."

Louise finished, took a handkerchief from her pocket, and wiped the tears from her eyes.

There was silence for a few moments. Finally Phillip spoke. He informed his brothers about the provisions being arranged with the family trust. Louise had decided that the estate would be divided at the present time rather than at her demise. Each son would receive income from the trust. It would be substantial enough for each of them to be independent. When Phillip finished his presentation, there were many questions pertaining to the financial arrangements, but the previous criticisms were not repeated. It was as if the explosion of emotional comments had freed the family members of their underlying tension, and they could be more pragmatic about the situation. Louise felt greatly relieved and passed out sherry for all. The family seemed united again.

The next morning Louise and Phillip worked in the kitchen preparing the annual Thanksgiving dinner. She had originally planned on telling the family about her plans with Phillip after their Thanksgiving feast, but she was now relieved that the members were already informed, and she hoped that the family could relax and enjoy the occasion.

When Sharon and Roger arrived, the daughter-in-law had a smug smile on her face. Her brother, Jerry, was practically smirking. Louise paid no attention and welcomed them. Sarah also came and, as a personage outside the family, her presence created a sense of cordiality. Drinks before the fireplace in the family room were served, and the compromising situation facing the Dudleys was avoided for some time. Commonplace chatter and worldly news were finally interrupted when Jerry, speaking in his affected voice and waving a hand, made an effort to be amusing. "Tell me, Phillip, what do you now call Mrs. Dudley? Mother or Louise?"

Everyone was taken aback by the forwardness of the question, but Jerry continued. "Perhaps Mother Louise would be apropos. No, I guess that's too religious, and that would hardly fit the occasion." His remark and subsequent laughter infuriated Paul who stood up, closed his fist, and started moving toward him.

Roger caught his brother. "Not here, Paul."

Looking at Jerry, Paul snarled, "You faggot! Keep your mouth shut!"

Leaning back on the couch, Jerry said, "I was only trying to liven up the conversation."

"Well, keep your rotten thoughts to yourself. You're a sick man, anyway."

On the defensive, Jerry replied, "Look who's talking!"

Louise and Phillip both rose and helped Roger block Paul from attacking the guest. Sharon reached over the couch and put her hand over Jerry's mouth. "You've said enough, idiot!"

The family calmed down, but since the liaison between mother and son had been mentioned, the conversation turned to the family dilemma. Louise and Phillip had not yet told her children about the plan of moving to the Caribbean, so it was a pleasant surprise when Roger presented a constructive suggestion about such a move. It was obvious that he had given the matter much thought and had sought a means of helping his mother. He proposed that his mother and brother try living in the Caribbean for a while before making any drastic changes in their lifestyle. Sharon added, "Oh, you'll love it down there!" Others agreed with Roger's proposal, but they were not as sure as Sharon that New Englanders would be so fascinated with life in the Caribbean. Paul, having just returned, was adamant that his mother and brother were making a mistake, but Sharon thought it was a grand idea. Sarah, as an outsider, listened with pleasure as the family members discussed the plans for a move to the tropics. She was glad that they were not quarreling in a mean-spirited way. The conversation was positive in nature and showed some acceptance of the unique plan. When Sarah left after the Thanksgiving feast, which was pleasant and enjoyable, she whispered to Louise, "They've conceded. I'm very happy for you."

Chapter 14

Louise and Phillip were invigorated by the bright sunshine throughout the Caribbean. Manet, the great French artist who began the Impressionist movement, was influenced by lighting effects he observed while in the Caribbean. Gauguin also noticed that special light when he visited in 1883, and he felt that it affected his art. The Dudleys were also impressed by it as they traveled from one island to another in search of a place where they felt they could live comfortably. For two weeks they were carefree and fun-loving. In a salon on St. Thomas Louise had her hair dyed blonde in an effort to look younger and Phillip had his hair cut into a crew cut. They both purchased beach wear and bottles of sun tan oil. Exploring various islands seemed like an adventurous fantasy. Finally they chose St. Thomas because of its natural beauty and because they quickly found an apartment overlooking a beautiful cove that stretched out into the sea. It was for them a paradise.

A regular routine quickly developed. They slept late and had breakfast on their patio, which gave them a view of the distant sea. They took walks here and there, discovering new paths and interesting sights. Somehow they did not think of themselves as mother and son. They were just a couple and were greeted that way by the friendly people. No one knew them, and they did not ask for attention. They both developed suntans and adopted the casual dress preferred in the tropics: shorts, a top, and tennis shoes. Their income assured them a leisurely life, and for some time they enjoyed it fully. Yes, they were sure they had made the right decision.

As the Christmas holidays approached, Louise began thinking more of her other sons. She had heard from Roger and Paul but not from Kevin and that gave her some consternation. However, the newness of everything still held the couple in awe. Sunsets of brilliant colors heightened their evenings in their small garden, blue skies of incredible lightness greeted them each morning on the patio, and time passed quickly in their various activities. When Louise did mention Kevin's silence, Phillip would console her by mentioning the boy's studies and his friend Dave. Still, Louise suspected that something was wrong. Roger had informed them about matters pertaining to the family trust; Paul had communicated because he needed permission for an advance of his stipend; but Kevin had not answered any of Louise's letters or calls. It was worrisome, but she began keeping her apprehensions from Phillip because he seemed so relaxed and happy. Finally Louise invited her sons for the holidays. Roger and Paul sent regrets, but there was no word from Kevin. Christmas would not be the pleasant event so often enjoyed by the Dudleys in their home.

Phillip found a small, artificial Christmas tree in a shop and decorated it with roses that he made from red crepe paper. He agreed that his production was over "rosed," but its novelty added to their enjoyment. Louise ordered a smoked turkey from the States as the centerpiece of their Christmas dinner. With little effort, they soon had aspects of the holiday season and drank eggnog on Christmas eve in traditional family fashion. Louise had a short cry by herself during their festivities, but Phillip's enthusiasm made it a pleasant holiday. Sarah's phone call and greetings also added contentment.

Neighbors in the cove invited the Dudleys for a New Year's Eve party. Both Louise and Phillip felt rather uncomfortable about accepting the invitation, but they did because, as fledglings in the area, it was time to leave their nest. In preparation for the occasion, Louise had her dyed blonde hair touched up and sat in the sun for hours in hopes that a deep tan would help hide small wrinkles. When she dressed for the party, Phillip declared that she looked younger than he did. Louise was amused, but she accepted the compliment with great pleasure. Their age difference was one of her worries, and she was sure that it could reveal their secret relationship. Phillip drank several shots of bourbon before they left, and his habit of taking a nip occasionally was another of Louise's concerns. Yet he seemed in control of himself, and she made no issue of it.

They were greeted at the Coats's with open arms and quickly introduced around as the Dudleys, Louise and Phillip. The guests were mainly neighbors in the cove, and during the evening they were quite hospitable. Louise was invited into a bridge club by several ladies and Phillip, after a few drinks, was scheduled for golfing outings. In conversations, the Dudleys were given much information about various aspects of life on the island. They learned the best places for shopping, which beaches were the best, and what they should avoid. In a short time both Louise and Phillip had relaxed and enjoyed the party. During the hugs and kisses that took place after a grandfather clock stuck twelve, however, Phillip made a faux pas that startled Louise. In his enthusiasm he threw his arm around her and said loudly, "Well, Mom, Happy

New Year!" There was something in the tone of the newcomer's voice that caused a few people to stare for a moment, but no one took it seriously.

Louise whispered, "Phillip, I think you've had enough bourbon!"

"Awww, relax," he replied. Not pleased, he left her and started hugging another lady near them. Louise walked to the side of the room but was also soon engaged in a hug and dance by a neighbor. When they were near the patio door, her escort walked her out into the moonlight. After trying to kiss her, which she avoided by turning her head, he whispered, "We could make wonderful music together." The remark was followed by a hug that pressed Louise tightly against the man's bulging erection. She quickly broke away and returned to the party. After several more encounters, she reached Phillip, but he was enjoying himself and would not leave. She could only retreat to another corner.

Louise attributed the problems that began developing in the Dudley household to the New Year's Eve party. Phillip's new acquaintances began taking much of his time. He played golf, joined a cigar club, and developed a great interest in boats. At first Louise was pleased that Phillip's life seemed so full of pleasure and contentment. She joined him occasionally for a party on a friend's yacht, but the gentlemen always talked sports and smoked cigars. Their wives played cards and drank tropical concoctions. While Phillip was content, Louise felt they were losing their closeness. She could not understand exactly what caused her discontentment, but she sensed that they were drifting apart. Phillip did not need her as much, and she began worrying.

At such times in the past Louise had talked with Sarah, so she was delighted when Sarah accepted an invitation for a visit in St. Thomas. During the week before the neighbor's arrival, the Dudleys planned various activities. Louise suddenly realized that Phillip was arranging excursions and outings for her and Sarah only. When she asked why he was not involved with them, he responded, "Oh, I'll be busy with the guys, fishing and golfing." The upcoming visit had given Phillip more free time. Louise was afraid that Phillip had slipped back into his old habits, but she did not want a confrontation.

Sarah left a snowstorm in Connecticut and flew into St. Thomas, arriving on a bright, sunny day. The Dudleys met her plane and, after greetings, took the visitor for a ride to Drake's Seat for a spectacular view of the sea and mountainous coves. Sarah was very impressed. Then Phillip took the two ladies to a charming seaside restaurant in Magens Bay for lunch.

When he drove away, Louise said as she escorted Sarah to a poolside table, "If I only knew where he was really going."

"Oh?" Sarah asked. "Is there trouble in paradise?"

Louise nodded. "Sarah, I'm so glad you came. I need your shoulder again."

Sarah smiled, made comments about the weight she had gained, and then asked, "Now, what's going on?"

A waiter came and both ladies ordered a vegetarian sandwich with coffee. Then Louise began opening her heart. Everything had been so wonderful in the beginning, but ever since that New Year's Eve party when they met so many new people, Phillip had been away quite often on fishing and yachting trips. He was still quite caring and always had believable explanations for being away longer than expected or for having missed something they had planned. Still, Louise was in doubt about his activities. Sarah asked if they were still in love. Louise nodded again, but Sarah added, "And in the bedroom, too?"

Louise shook her head. She hesitated, finding it difficult to speak. Then she revealed that Phillip had not been interested lately. Again she nodded. "Yes, it makes me think that he's taking drugs again. That can lessen the need for sex, you know."

Sarah looked at the view in the distance. She was not sure of what she should say. Fortunately, at that moment the waiter brought their coffee. Sarah said, "This reminds me of our pleasant coffee times back home." Louise agreed and asked about conditions in Connecticut. The conversation changed to details about the weather and the upkeep of their homes. Louise was pleased at the report Sarah gave about the Dudley home, which was closed for the winter.

During the week that Sarah stayed in St. Thomas, a rather regular routine developed. After breakfast, during which Phillip would ask what the ladies were planning that day, he would depart for a game of golf or sailing on a yacht. After a couple of days, Louise commented, "Now you've seen what I've been trying to say. He is either avoiding me or is doing something that he's hiding from me."

Sarah suggested that they drive to the golf course, but Louise refused. She was sure Phillip would think that she was spying on him, and that could only cause conflicts. Sarah agreed but hoped that Louise would not fall into a depression because of her suspicions. She listened attentively as Louise related her fears and admitted that she felt depressed about the situation. Everything had been so fine, but now it seemed as if she were living alone on a deserted island.

Sarah again made a comparison from literature. "You know, Anna Karenina let her suspicions bring on a mental breakdown. She had ignored the social mores, and it eventually tore into her heart."

Louise smiled slyly. "I have gone even farther. I have ignored the laws of nature, and now I'm paying for it."

Sarah looked at her friend with concern. "Louise, you're taking on guilt that is not healthy. How can I possibly help you?"

The ladies looked at each other with sympathy and understanding. What could either of them say?

The established routine continued during Sarah's visit. Phillip made excuses and absented himself. Louise and Sarah walked, played cards, ate lunch at different restaurants, and passed the time until Phillip returned. On the last day of Sarah's visit, the hostess had a grand idea for a diversion. She remembered a butterfly farm in the port area and suggested a visit. Sarah was delighted because she greatly admired the order of *Lepidoptera*. Louise was surprised that her friend knew the Latin name for the insects and told her about her first visit at the farm. She remembered that butterflies have a very peculiar sex life and that there would be a lecture about it.

"I can hardly wait!"

Sarah laughed and said, "Seems that everything down here is peculiar!"

Louise smiled. She knew what her friend was thinking of and also felt it was humorous.

Off to the butterfly farm they went and had an enjoyable time watching the various colors fly around them. When the director called the visitors together, he explained the habits of the insects in a rather high-toned voice. "What Mother Nature had in mind by making the sexual life so complex, no one knows, but their antennae play a significant role in their mating." He then began using words that the ladies did not understand: dimorphism, pentulation, etc.

Afterward Sarah said, "Thank God I wasn't a butterfly."

Louise agreed and asked, "Did you understand what he was talking about?"

"No, but it did seem that the female was constantly releasing a perfume that attracted the males."

Louise laughed. "I didn't mind that, but when he talked about the female having two reproductive openings, he lost me."

Sarah smiled. "Well, I understood that one opening was for copulation and the other for laying eggs. In other words, in one hole and out the other."

Louise laughed again. "Sarah, you're talking like they do down here in the islands. I do believe people say anything that comes to mind. Quite often it's blasphemy."

Sarah commented, "Oh, those poor female butterflies!"

Both ladies enjoyed the adventure into butterfly land and returned home in a joyous frame of mind.

During the evening before Sarah's departure, the phone rang, and a voice told Louise that she could pick up her husband at a particular bar on the waterfront. Both ladies drove there and found Phillip in a drunken state. A pathetic scene ensued. Phillip cried and begged Louise's forgiveness. She tried comforting him while Sarah helped lead him out of the restaurant. In the open air he vomited and became quite sick. They seated him on a concrete curb while Louise went for the car. At the apartment, Phillip crawled along the sidewalk, crying and vomiting all the way. Inside he wobbled to the bedroom and fell onto the bed, where he quickly fell asleep. The next morning Louise took Sarah to the airport, and they had a tearful good-bye.

Connecticut had social services that helped Louise, but on an island devoted to pleasure, she felt a sense of loss. Whom should she call? After much thought, she decided that it would be better if they returned home, where Phillip could receive treatment. When she presented the idea to him, he was adamant that he did not need help. He had acted badly, of course, but it was a lesson for him, and it would not happen again. Louise was too familiar with such logic, so she waited for the next slipup.

For several days there was a normal routine. Breakfast on the patio; golf for Phillip; lunch at a club for Louise. In the evenings they prepared dinner together and lounged before the television. When they retired, they slept peacefully. Phillip's lack of interest in any romantic endeavors did not worry Louise; she was just pleased that they seemed at home together again.

One morning the phone rang while they were drinking coffee and admiring the high waves on the ocean at the end of the cove. Phillip slipped into the apartment and answered. He called out to Louise that Bob, a golf mate, was waiting at the golf course, and he would dress. It seemed quite normal, but when he didn't return by the late afternoon, Louise became concerned. She knew that Phillip would laugh at her anxiety when he returned, but she could not help herself. When the sunset disappeared, she became quite nervous. She found Bob's number in Phillip's private phone book, but she hesitated. Bob's wife was an acquaintance, not a friend. Yet her desperation made her call. There was no answer. Louise felt a sense of dread. Something was wrong! The day had started so peacefully, and now it was in turmoil.

At ten o'clock a policeman appeared at the door and requested that Mrs. Dudley accompany him to the police station for the purpose of identification. Phillip Dudley had been killed while escaping from a yacht during a drug raid. Louise cried. It had been such a blunt announcement. There had been no condolences or mannerly presentation. Louise found out later that a fellow officer had been killed in the fracas, and the police were in no mood for ceremony. Still crying, she collected her purse and keys and left with the officer. Realizing that Phillip had been deceiving her for some time and that her new world had been destroyed, Louise could not control herself. When they reached the police station, a woman officer came and put an arm around Louise as she stepped out of the patrol car. Fortunately, the female officer stayed with her during the identification process and afterward in a small lounge. When Louise finally gained control of herself, she thanked the woman kindly for her help. The chief of police informed Louise that she would be questioned the next day and had the officer escort her to a car that took her home.

At the door, Louise thought, *How does one enter a house that is no longer a home?* She thanked the female officer and closed the door behind her. Gazing through the patio door at the lights in the cove, she sat down and cried again. There was no future now, and she had no past. In saving her one son, she had lost the others. She was not even a mother now, just the widow of her son. It was too complex and worrisome. She fell back on a chaise lounge and continued crying. What could she do?

The drug bust had been one of the largest ever carried out near St. Thomas, and a famous rock star, Guy Damos, was involved. Consequently, it attracted reporters from international news agencies. By chance, the name of the assassinated dealer, Mr. Phillip Dudley, was published along with that of the noted singer. The next morning Roger, looking though the *New York Times* during a hurried breakfast, came upon the incident and could hardly believe his eyes. He immediately lifted the phone and called his mother.

Mrs. Dudley had slept little during the night. It seemed that her loss was of more than a son; it was of her life. When the phone rang the next morning, she assumed it was the police. What joy she felt when Roger greeted his mother kindly and asked what he could do. Crying again, Louise replied that she did not know what she herself should do.

Roger, recognizing his mother's distraught condition, quickly said, "Mother, I'll fly down as quickly as I can. Sharon will probably come with me, and we'll fly out this evening if possible."

Louise, through her tears, said, "Oh, thank God, Roger. I would be so appreciative."

After the call, Louise fell back on a lounge chair and cried. Suddenly she heard Strauss's *Artist's Life* liltingly flowing from the kitchen radio. The beautiful melodies, one after another, revived her. As she sat up, a dance she had attended at Vassar came to mind. How happy she had been that evening. Her husband George had proposed during that very music. How long ago it seemed. And how much unhappiness had been the result of that joy!

When Roger and Sharon arrived late that evening, he immediately took control of everything. He arranged for his brother's body to be transported to a crematorium in Connecticut; he helped Louise pack her belongings so that she could return home with them; and he called the airlines for their travel plans. Sharon wanted a brief holiday while they were in the Caribbean area, but Roger felt they should take his mother back at once. He believed that, under the circumstances, the apartment, the friends, and the sunshine would be unbearable for his mother. Sharon, in a rare moment of sympathy, agreed. The next day the Dudleys returned home.

Chapter 15

Snow had whitened Connecticut during the Dudleys' flight from the Caribbean. Louise looked at the gray sky and remembered how the bright light of the sun in the islands had been so welcoming and refreshing. Now she was entering a world of light and dark where only shadows and sadness reigned. The love that had taken her south was now only in her heart. Here in the north she would confront only the bias and ugliness of prejudice. For a while it had all been so beautiful. She had been young again, and she had been loved. Now it seemed that she was old and all alone.

Lights were on in the Dudley home when their car drove up the circular drive. Sarah had opened the house for them and was waiting at the door when they arrived. Before departing, she hugged Louise and made polite remarks to Roger and Sharon. Mrs. Dudley wanted her to stay, but Sarah explained that she had done her part for the homecoming and felt the family should be together for a while. Promising a visit the next day, she left.

Once the Dudleys were drinking cocktails before the large stone fireplace in the family room, Louise felt somewhat at ease. She was in her home again. Here she had once been content, and here she had reared her children. That world seemed so long ago. Tears filled her eyes, but she wiped them away without crying. There was no point. She had obliterated the past by moving with her son to the islands. Now she must create a new life under completely new circumstances. What should she do? What kind of life could she now create with her sons? Fortunately Roger had responded and had been extremely helpful, but what would Paul and Kevin do? Such thoughts crowded her mind until she fell asleep on the couch.

Sharon, showing more concern than Louise would have expected, awakened her mother-in-law for dinner. Louise was very thankful and allowed Sharon to help her rise from the couch. At the dinner table the young couple kept the conversation light and merry. Sharon told about her wild brother Jerry's latest intrigues and escapades, and Roger entertained them by making fun of several of his colleagues in his prestigious law firm. By the end of the meal Louise was completely relaxed and truly thankful for their efforts.

"My darlings, you've gone out of your way to make my homecoming so pleasant. You know how worried I am about what I should now do, but you've taken my mind away from it completely."

"Just let things happen," Sharon suggested.

"Yes," Roger agreed. "I know you're strong enough to find yourself again."

"I worry mainly about Paul and Kevin. They didn't accept my situation very kindly."

Sharon laughed. "Oh, don't worry about them. Paul will always be the same, and sweet little Kevin will come crawling back to his mommy."

"You think so?" Louise asked, hoping it was true.

"Of course," Sharon insisted. "Look at Jerry. That rascal is always at Mother's knee, begging to be forgiven." She laughed again.

Louise was not sure of Sharon's logic but thanked her and Roger for their support.

The couple proposed that they spend the night, but Louise insisted that they continue with their own lives. She, in her opinion, could not ask for more than what they had done. Once alone, Louise walked about the Dudley home. Through every hall and in every room it seemed as if she might come upon something or have some idea that would help her in her search for direction. The house did not respond; it only reminded her of the past, which she had discarded and to which she could never return.

The next morning Sarah came to the kitchen door while Louise was having coffee. Louise welcomed her. The friends embraced, and it was like old times. Never did coffee taste as good to Louise as when she poured out her thoughts and heart to her trusted friend. After some time Louise said, "If only a Chinese fortune cookie could tell me what to do!"

Sarah laughed. "You don't need a cookie. You just need to get busy. It's Sunday. Why don't you go to your church? You used to be so proud of walking in with your family. It might have meaning for you, and you've certainly got many old friends and acquaintances there."

"What if they don't want me there anymore?"

Sarah looked surprised. "What kind of a religion is it anyway? You haven't changed. If anything, they should be glad to welcome you back. Isn't there something about forgiveness in your faith?"

Louise thought for a second. "Yes, you're right. It should be like always, a sort of refuge. I can join the women's league again and maybe even the bridge club."

"See, that's a good start. You should find a lot of help there. Now let me get out of here so you can go. Thanks for the coffee!"

When Sarah left, Louise accepted her advice. Since it was Sunday, she dressed and went to church. However, her enthusiasm had not prepared her for her reception.

Entering the vestibule of the large, elegant Episcopal church, Louise immediately saw an old acquaintance, Mary Druthers, the president of the Ladies Social Club, of which Louise was a former member. Louise quickly went to Mary and stopped her as she was entering the minister's office. Mary turned quickly, but her smile left her face when she recognized Louise. Looking around as if to check who might be watching, Mary took Louise by the arm and led her aside. Without hesitation, she said, "Heavens, I am very surprised to see you here."

"Yes, I've been away," Louise responded, smiling.

"No, I mean after ..." Mary hesitated. "After! Well, you know what."

"What do you mean?"

"Oh, Louise, must you embarrass me? Of course you know what I mean." Then, after looking around again, she added, "Please excuse me now, I have some things that must be taken care of before the service." She began walking away before she finished her sentence.

Louise stood still, feeling numb. She could not believe that Mary, whom she had respected so highly for her work in the church and the social club, could possibly want to avoid her. Feeling weak, Louise braced herself against a wall. *What have I done that she should judge me so severely? Was it any of her business? Am I not the same person? Is this not the church of Jesus Christ who preached forgiveness? What kind of Christianity is being preached here? Not that I wanted sympathy or consolation, but I did expect some degree of human kindness. What should I do?*

At that moment Louise heard a voice beside her. She turned and saw two other women from the social club. They both greeted her, but quickly turned and entered the great hall. It was too much for Louise. She quickly left the church, ignoring another greeting that she heard on the outside steps. Her thoughts were only on escape. Now even her church seemed against her.

Consolation did not dwell at the Dudley hearth. When Louise arrived at home, she found Paul watching international news on the TV in the family room. He had returned unexpectedly because he had just left another romantic entanglement. He did not stand up when she entered, and his response to her greeting was sort of a grunt. It was obvious that he was in a very foul mood. His latest girlfriend had, in his opinion, accused him unjustly of not being faithful. Paul was incensed that she would not accept his explanation, even though it was a lie. He was sure that there was no way she could know the truth, and so he insisted that he was being honest. Her refusal caused their breakup, and, for the moment, Paul again hated all women.

Louise sat down by her son and leaned softly on his shoulder. Tears began running down her cheeks.

Paul, however, sneered and said as he turned toward her, "What happened? Truth hit you in the face?"

Louise stopped crying and slipped away from her son. Looking him in the eyes, she asked, "Whatever do you mean?"

"Well, Sarah told me that you went to church, and I guess they didn't particularly want someone like you there."

Louise frowned and looked downward. Finally she muttered, "You'd speak to your mother like that?"

Paul, handsome and debonair as ever, almost laughed. "Well, let's face the truth. You can't expect to dwell among the saints at church when you've broken all their moral laws!"

Louise bit at her lip. How could her son be so disrespectful? Had everything she had ever done for him been forgotten? Was all the humanity he had learned in church been in vain? She could only stare at him in disbelief.

Still smiling, Paul continued, "Don't take it so hard! Maybe you're lucky to be free of those ole busybodies. Now you can live as you please and not worry if this or that is right. Just live as you've been living."

Her eyes full of tears, Louise looked up and asked, "What do you mean?"

"Well, do whatever you wish. There are no restrictions once you break the code."

"What code?"

"Well, you could hardly say that you and Phillip were just mother and son!"

"And why not?"

"Well, you did create a new conception of motherhood, didn't you?"

Louise stood and glared at him. Weakly, she replied, "Paul, I never in my life expected one of my sons to hurt me as you just did. How could you?"

Still smiling, Paul answered, "Well, if the truth hurts that much, than you shouldn't bother with it."

"You still don't understand why I went with Phillip. I thought it would save him, but it didn't, and I failed."

Louise walked away and went upstairs. Paul's coarse laughter echoed in her ears. She rushed into her bedroom where she could cry. Her tears flowed for some time, but suddenly she remembered the line from Milton that she had memorized in English literature class. She recalled that one can make a hell of heaven in one's mind. She rose from the bed and stood before the large mirror over her dressing table. Looking at herself, she wondered who the woman was whose reflection stood before her.

What have I done to myself? What can I do? My actions have not only destroyed me, but also my family. Paul is suddenly a stranger, almost an enemy. How can I ever change his attitude toward me? How can I stand to be around his incriminating glances? And my dear Kevin! How will he react? If only there were somewhere I could go. Just disappear!

Louise stood silently. Her thoughts could not continue. Everything seemed in a blur. She looked in the mirror again, wondering what she should do. Then she walked closer and examined herself. Her figure was fine; her hair needed dye; but her face was youthful. She was not wrinkled, she had no paunch on her stomach, and her hands were not aged. Why was she even thinking such things? Did any of it matter? She had no future; she had only a past.

She left her bedroom and stopped at Paul's opened door. "Paul, dear, are you staying for dinner?"

He came to the door with a sly smile. "Yes, Mother, just like old times, isn't it?"

Ignoring his tone and avoiding his eyes, Louise said, "Fine. I'll go to the kitchen. It'll be a little while."

"Yes, Mother, dear," Paul replied with irony.

Louise heard his laugh as she continued down the hall. *This is my hell,* she concluded. *I created it, and now I must endure it. God help me!*

While preparing the dinner, Louise heard a tap on the kitchen door. To her delight, Sarah had stopped byAfter they had chatted a while, , Sarah said, "Louise, I've given you a lot of thought. I had hoped that your church would help you, but I see that they are bigots. What you need is something that has meaning. I think I can make a suggestion."

"Please do, Sarah."

"You know I love animals Why don't you and I do volunteer work at the animal rescue downtown!"

Louise looked at her friend and suddenly felt at ease. "Sarah, how kind of you!" She paused and thought about the suggestion for a few moments. "I do love animals, and they certainly return one's affection."

Sarah smiled. "You might even end up with a llama someday."

Louise laughed, and tears came to her eyes. "Sarah, you've made me feel so much better. There are things for me to do, aren't there?"

"Certainly! And there's no telling to what it all might lead us to."

"You are a true friend. I know you can help me."

Some potatoes boiled over on the stove. While Louise wiped up the spill, Sarah left, saying that they would continue their discussion later.

Louise thanked her and started humming a tune.

The next day Kevin returned from his studies at Yale. He was alone because he and Dave had quarreled. This time Kevin was determined that their affair be finished. His decision had depressed him, so when he saw Louise, he ran into her open arms. Both mother and son were delighted with being together again, and they hugged for several seconds.

"My dearest Kevin, I have missed you!"

"Oh, Mother, I've missed you, too."

After they had settled before the fireplace in the family room, they confronted the subjects they had avoided. Louise told her son about Phillip's demise and how utterly devastated she felt for failing him. Kevin did not feel that she was at fault, for she had done everything she could for him. Having said the word *everything,* Kevin thought of the physical relationship his mother had with his brother and snickered.

"What's funny?" Louise asked.

"I thought of 'everything'," Kevin replied and looked down, smiling.

Louise understood his implication and commented. "Kevin, my darling, I do hope my behavior did not hurt you too much. I know now how monstrous it must have seemed to many people, but I earnestly hoped that you were not too offended by it."

Kevin moved close to Louise. "Oh, Mother, I couldn't believe it at first, but I now rationalize it as follows: you have accepted my perversion, so I can accept what happened to you."

Louise's eyes filled with tears, and she turned away as she took a handkerchief from her pocket. After a few tears and some consolation from Kevin, she said, "Kevin, what are we to do now?"

"We'll go on as we always have."

"It's not that easy," Louise remarked and told her son about her experience at the church and then about the behavior of his brother Paul.

Kevin belittled the conduct of the religious zealots and made very disparaging comments about Paul. "He's a miserable type anyway," Kevin concluded. "His ego has made him far more perverse than you or me. He's used his handsomeness for the shadiest of motives, and I hate his type. If he had been on the Titanic, he would have dressed as a woman and jumped into a lifeboat. He's my brother, and I'll accept him for that, but as a decent human, he fails utterly."

Louise sighed. "If he is as you say, what a pathetic person he must be!"

"True, he is. But we're not! We've not hurt anybody outside of ourselves. We've done nothing to be blamed for. We can be happy, I'm sure of it."

"Oh, Kevin, what a wonderful boy you are."

"Really, Mother, it's true. I returned home very saddened because Dave and I had fought, but talking with you and understanding your hurt has made me realize that we have much more happiness ahead. We have each other and we have a great understanding.

While the world doesn't agree with us, we can be happy our way."

"What do you mean the world doesn't agree with us?"

"Our brand of metaphysics still believes in hope and happiness. The world wants only the rational and that is leading it to a mechanized, robotlike existence. It laughs at us in its misery because it knows no better."

Louise put a hand on Kevin's shoulder. How proud she was of him. He would help her through her torment. He had the strength she needed for support. Suddenly she felt very happy and said so. They both agreed on having a drink to toast their new relationship.

After some pleasant conversation over the bourbon and soda, Louise asked, "But what should I do now?"

"You should live, not as we did. What I mean to say is that we should not live under the confines of a hypocritical church. We have the best that religion has to offer. We have it in our hearts. We don't need those ridiculous sermons and biased observations. We can live our own lives because they're ours."

"Yes, God is not in the church, but in us."

"It's the becoming of a new world, Mother. Vico was right back in the eighteenth century when he said that mankind would reverse its development. We started as barbarians, became religious fanatics, and then created technical marvels in the modern age. It's reversing now. We've gone into religious wars again like in the Middle Ages, and barbarism is already showing itself in mankind's behavior. What it will lead to, no one knows. We do know that the old religions are fading, governments are disappearing, and a new society is developing. We don't know what it will be, but we need not be afraid. At least we have each other."

Louise stood and walked to the fireplace. "I'm very proud of you, Kevin, and I love you very much. We'll be all right because we have each other. I know I can depend on you, and I want you to depend on me. Somehow we'll be happy that way. I really feel it, and I'm happier now than I have been for days."

"I'm glad, Mother. And you know what you should do? Go back to school! Yes, study something you like. I think you'd make a great nurse. You are so sympathetic. Patients would love you."

A surprised look spread over Louise's face. "Why Kevin, you've been thinking of me. You want to help me; and you're right. I would enjoy going to school, and maybe being a nurse is what I should consider. However, Sarah has given me another idea. She and I are going to volunteer at the animal shelter. I don't know for how long or what we'll do, but I know it will help me now."

"That's a great plan, Mother."

"Sarah said I'd probably end up with a llama."

Both mother and son laughed.

Kevin stood and gave her a kiss; then he excused himself and yawned before going to his room.

Louise sat down, lost in thought. "Yes, it is up to me," she thought and remembered another poem from her classes at Vassar:

"My mind to me a kingdom is …"

She could not recall the remaining lines, however. Yet the phrase strengthened her resolve, and she finished her drink feeling quite content, realizing that she must design her own life and live it.